This novel is a work of fiction. Unless otherwise indicated, all the names, characters, businesses, places, events and incidents in this book are either the product of the author's imagination or used in a fictitious manner. Any resemblance to actual persons, living or dead, or actual events is purely coincidental.

ISBN: 9798842891368

ACKNOWLEDGMENTS

Special thanks as always to my beautiful wife and family.

I have to place on record a **huge** thank you to John Dunning (J.D.) who was my chief co-conspirator, adviser and proofreader throughout. His enthusiasm for the project was infectious.

Also, once again, thank you to Tanya Knapper for providing fresh insight and advice.

Big shout out to my Hub family and to the many fans of the Jake West Trilogy worldwide who encouraged me to write again. Hope you enjoy the change in genre. Thanks as always for your support.

Finally, a massive thank you to A.J. Hateley who stepped in again to produce the cover. What a talent.

FOR MY FAMILY

Chapter 1 – Present Day

There are days in your life when you just know something bad is right around the next corner, and it is coming for you. Days you will surely come to regret in the fullness of time. Today was shaping up to be one of those days. He should have said no. Refused and taken the probable fallout, regardless of the severity. But all he had was unanswered questions and a whole load of misgivings. As well as a feeling gnawing away at his insides of impending doom. It wasn't enough to risk it all. To possibly throw away everything. He had to be sure. He had to go. The alternative was unthinkable. Still, fear of the unknown can paralyse a soul and he almost succumbed.

The main thing he hated was not being in control. The thought that nameless faces in some dark, dank corner of wherever, had already decided on his movements and actions. In his absence. Without involving him in the decision-making process at all.

Moving him around like a pawn on a chessboard simply because they could, and had determined it would be that way. Controlling him like a brainless puppet, a mindless marionette dancing about at somebody else's whim, moved by an invisible hand, for he had absolutely no idea who was pulling the strings. Clearly, they considered him irrelevant, insignificant, a patsy who would do as ordered. Well, he had news for them; he was not that man. He was the one who usually called the shots. He loathed the fact that he knew nothing of their plans and that it had been intended that way. It just wasn't right. He was strong, used to being respected, revered even. To a man like him, this was torture.

He slowed his advance as he stepped onto Baker Street, anxious not to arrive too early, his mind working overtime and his stomach churning. He needed answers and he needed them now. What was happening here? And why him?

His hands were tied to a large extent, his options limited. It did not mean he had to walk meekly to the slaughter though, did it? He could still have his say. Let them know he had retained the larger portion of his backbone, despite all evidence to the contrary. That they were dealing with a free spirit who would only be pushed so far.

Yes, enough was enough, he decided. Today at the very least would see the beginning of his education.

The city centre café looked almost deserted as he approached, the dinnertime rush having vanished and the afternoon lull set in. Just two of the eight available tables in the terraced area were occupied now. An elderly lady was tenderly caressing her latte on one, seemingly lost in her thoughts and sat in the corner by choice no doubt, as she happily enjoyed the sun and savoured each careful sip of her drink, every precious moment she could of peaceful solitude.

The only other customer in sight was the man he was here to meet.

'Hello?' he began, without delay.

The stranger looked up at him as if he were dirt on his shoe. He was not perturbed though. Not yet anyway.

'Let's get straight to it then. What *is* this?' he said, deliberately adopting an assertive stance from the very beginning.

He had arrived exactly on time and dispensed with the usual pleasantries and introduction by choice. Whoever they were, *they* had set the tone for this meeting by their actions, not him. He was here under duress, so there was no point in pretending they were best friends.

'Sit down,' the man ordered, sternly.

'No,' he replied, unwilling to give an inch. 'Not until you have informed me why have I been summoned here. What's going on? Who *are* you?'

'Sit down, Mr. Townsend, please? Sit down and I will explain what I can. I promise.'

A change in approach already. That was unexpected. His face sank a little and his shoulders dropped. His initial dominance and control may have been imaginary but, if it existed at all, it was undone now by that reply, wrestled away from him with a single polite invitation and the re-enforcement of the principal fact he already knew; that information was key here. He had none. His unknown visitor would therefore dictate the pace and direction of travel. After all, without the answers he had come to collect, walking away was not an option, given the stakes.

Damn!

The way the meeting had been arranged, the brevity and nature of the unexpected talk he had endured, the most unlikely source... all served to emphasise that he really did not have much of a choice now. He was game for a fight but he was nobody's fool. You have to pick your battles. He had no option but to listen and obey, despite his severe frustrations and misgivings, at least until he discovered how much trouble he was in. Or what he had unknowingly signed up for.

'Okay, okay… But I do not like this one bit. And if I don't receive an explanation right now, I'm going to leave. Whether it is the end of my career or not. Understand?'

'I understand you. Fully.'

That was another promising reply. More than he had expected. Whoever this stranger was, he was good at reading the room. He pulled out the chair just as the waitress approached to take their order.

'Sure, why not? Cappuccino, please?' He cast a downward glance. 'You want anything?'

A solitary shake of the head in reply.

A man of few words. Good.

There would be no preamble with this guy. No beating about the bush, just as he wanted. He hoped it would be a recurring theme. Something told him that it would. He took a seat.

'So? I'm here, as ordered. You have my undivided attention, so talk.'

Only the faint buzz of the nearby traffic pierced the early afternoon tranquility and a short pause was all he required to size up his new acquaintance. There was nothing remarkable in his appearance at least. Mid-fifties, probably. Square face. Square jaw. Square glasses. Square haircut, come to that. Just plain square all round. That was the only way to describe him. No extraordinary features at all. The kind of guy who would easily be lost in a crowd. But then, he supposed that was the idea.

Two days ago, he was sitting in his office at work when the telephone rang. There followed an extremely baffling, mysterious and alarming, very short and very odd conversation. One he would give anything now to have missed. The unexpected caller was the lady who sat at the very top of his organisation. Not her secretary, or any of the thousands of minions she had working for her. No, it was the woman herself, which was unheard of. However, even more astonishing was the actual content of the call itself as, over the next minute or so, he was subjected to a stream of one-way, instructional dialogue.

'Ian? Are you listening?' she had begun, 'this is Sue Baxter. I'm going to be very quick. Don't talk. Don't say a word. Just listen to what I have to say. That's an order. We are all under orders here now. I know this is highly irregular but… Damn it, I'm just going to come out with it! After I hang up the phone to you, I am going to deny all knowledge of this talk. It *never* happened. If you say *anything*, it will be the last thing you ever do for me, or anyone I know. You will be finished, your life destroyed, and I will refute everything. Clear your diary for Thursday, Ian. You are going to meet with someone. A man. You have no choice in this matter, believe me. He will be at Malone's café at fourteen hundred hours, waiting for you. Sitting outside, weather permitting. He will be wearing a Union Jack lapel badge for identification purposes. You are going to meet with him and listen to what he has to say. And you are going to do *anything* he asks of you. That is all I am permitted to tell you.'

Then, even more disconcerting than the big boss lady actually contacting him personally and calling him by his first name, was the fact that she had just simply hung up the phone. No conversation. No opportunity to ask questions. No goodbyes.

Weird, inappropriate, strange, awkward...? *All* massive understatements which didn't seem to do it justice.

Of course, in the time he had been afforded to think between the call and the scheduled meeting, he had considered several times ignoring the ludicrous and highly irregular command. It was so far outside his job description, it was on a different page. How could he be ordered about like this, in today's age? Ridiculous. And the threats she made were just outright bullying. If he could prove it, he was a sure thing on any tribunal.

However, he knew he could *not* prove it. It would be his word against hers at the end of the day. And of the two, hers carried way more weight. So, he decided eventually that he had worked too hard and for far too long just to throw his career away now, when he was approaching a well-earned and eagerly anticipated retirement. And he had been left in absolutely no doubt whatsoever that he would have been severely censured, persecuted in fact, for non-compliance. It did not do to make such powerful enemies.

Consequently, here he was; sitting outside an almost empty café, waiting for his unknown and unwanted contact to hopefully enlighten him.

The hushed growl of a voice sounded again. There was enough gravel in that tone to cover his drive. 'How long have you worked for the Prison Service, Ian? I can call you that, can I? Don't like to take liberties.'

More unexpected civility.

'I… I don't care what you call me. I just want some clarification and I want it now. I'm tired of being taken for easy prey. Being ordered about like a servant. There are limits and I have reached them. But, if it leads to answers, I've been in a little over thirty years.'

'That long?'

He straightened a little in his chair. This nice guy act was a ploy to make him feel at ease and something told him this guy knew perfectly well his entire life story. The name of his grandma's budgie. Probably what he had for breakfast. Still, he would play along, for now.

'Yes. I suppose some would call me, *old school.* Joined as a youth and worked my way through the ranks. Officer, Senior Officer, Principal Officer, Governor. Blood, sweat and tears. Finally made it to Governor of Norgate two years ago. But why? And who are you, to know so much about me? We don't advertise where we work.'

The drinks arrived at that moment and the man fell silent. He waited patiently for the waitress to disappear, eyeing Ian up and down in a well-practised manner, as if fitting him for his coffin. A faint breeze caressed them both and once she was out of earshot, he continued.

'Enough pleasantries. Ground rules then; I am not going to give you my name. It serves no purpose. Put simply, you do not need to know. This is not about me. And it is not about *you*, either.'

Ian was comforted by that last remark. It brought him immense relief. 'Oh. So, what, or who, *is* it about?' he asked.

'Take a sip of your drink. Don't want to waste it.'

It was more like a command than an invitation and to his consternation, Ian found himself complying immediately, without thought or repost.

Am I that easy to manipulate?

This did not bode well.

'Good. That's better,' the man said smugly, as if talking to a child, his whole demeanour changing slightly. 'We are going to ask you to do something for us, Ian. Well, I suppose *ask* is not really the correct word. We rarely *ask*. You need to understand this so I will give it to you straight; you are being tasked. You have been selected for a special kind of assignment. Acquiescence is obligatory, so don't try to fight it. You cannot tell a soul either. You are forbidden to breathe a word of this to any living being. Not your wife, your friends or colleagues, your lover…'

Ian's eyes widened in astonishment and alarm.

If they know about her, what else do they know? And how?!

The man before him merely continued however, without displaying any sign of acknowledgment or concern, having probably seen and heard it all before.

'Should you ignore the rules as I relay them to you, your life as you know it will be over. Demolished. That is all there is to it. Do not test us. You will lose. On Monday next, you are going to receive a new recruit. This officer has passed the training course the same as all recruits. She has seen action and been through a rough time. There are some dangerous individuals who wish her harm. So, you are going to watch her back for us. You are going to warn us of any new developments, any potential issues or problems, so to speak. Any strangers hanging around her. Or prisoners paying her too much attention. Okay?'

Ian nodded. He was primarily thinking of himself and he began to relax a little. Was that it? Was that all he was being asked to do? He had been working himself up into a frenzy for this? It was a huge relief to know he was not in hot water for some unknown action or crime. Not being blackmailed for instance. Though, he did not like some of what he had heard so far and resolved to make changes to his personal life from now on, to minimise the ammunition available to those prying eyes.

'Yes, I think I understand. Witness Protection gig. You want me to babysit a new recruit for you. But why me? And who is she? Who has she upset? Just how serious are we talking here?'

'You, because you are in a position to receive reports on her performance and activities. A privileged position of power. Because you can go anywhere at any time. Because we think you ideally qualified for the role. And most importantly, because we said so! Her Prison Service application and record, including her back story, are all here in this file.'

He slid a well-thumbed brown envelope across the table.

'It is all complete and utter bullshit, of course,' the stranger added.

'Of course,' replied Ian, picking up the unknown package without peering inside. 'I would have guessed it, but thanks for the honesty. Only, why tell me anything at all? Why not just place her with us, without our knowledge, given that she has done the course like all the others?'

The man stared him straight in his eyes, unnervingly burning a hole in his composure in an instant.

'*Exactly*. That was my thinking, initially. I was overruled. Rightly, as it turned out. Nobody in her circumstance fares well on their own. We have learned that the hard way. She is going to be completely unaided, Ian. Though she may actually prefer it that way, it is not to her advantage. Nobody can maintain three-hundred-and-sixty-degree vision all of the time. It is impossible. To see every danger that presents itself in time to counteract it, from outside or within. Every potential threat. Even the greatest of us needs support. Trust us; we know what we are doing.'

'You do? I'm glad to hear it, because I have my fair share of doubts.'

The outsider suddenly shuffled his chair backwards, preparing to leave.

'Wait! Can you tell me anything about the danger she is in? Where is it coming from? Is it here in the U.K. or abroad? Any known enemies?'

A solitary shake of the head again. He was nothing if not consistent. It appeared as though the conversation was over but then, he seemed to have a change of heart.

'Look, it's better for you if you do not know, believe me. It may colour your perceptions, blind you to the truth. Take my advice; I suggest you consider everyone and everything a possible hazard from here on, at least until you know better. Now, you are going to have to meet with her regularly. You'll need to invent a plausible reason for that. She knows your role so she won't resist. At least, I don't think so. She will know it's beneficial to have you on overwatch and her survival instincts will kick in. Learn all you can, but remain calm and do as she instructs. Remember, she is the expert here, not you. And rest assured, we will be watching, and listening.'

'Does that mean…? Fuck me! The wife is *not* going to like that, I can tell you. And there you go again. I wish you'd just say it. Who is *we?*'

'Do I need to, really? All you need to know is that we are the good guys. *She* is a good guy. She's been winged a little, that's all. And there are those of us who want to protect her. She will never admit to it, but she needs your help. Now, I really have to go. I've said too much already. Here, if you absolutely have to, in your direst hour of need, ring this number and ask for Stan.'

He passed a black business card across the table. It had only one number on it, written in small, white ink across the centre. No name. He stood up to go and looked down on the slightly bemused governor.

'Cheer up. Nobody has died yet. Not many people are inducted into my line of work, you know. You should feel honoured. You are joining an elite club. You're going to serve your country, Mr. Townsend. You are now protecting one of its most valuable assets. There is no insertion this time because you are already in play. And that greatly reduces the risk to you both.'

He was usually mild-mannered and prided himself on the control he maintained over his emotions. But all of this absurdity had thrown him completely off-balance. His head was crammed with too many thoughts and questions he could not ask. They were rotating so fast inside his mind that he had a headache. The only thing he knew for certain now, was that he wasn't himself.

Which probably explained his ill-advised outburst.

'Now you just wait a minute!' he rasped, rising to challenge the verbal affront, the words leaving his mouth before he realised he was talking. 'I *have* been serving my country for thirty years! Maybe not in a war zone like some, being shot at, but me and my staff face confrontation and intimidation every *single* day of our lives! Do you? How many soldiers can say that? We wear the crown with pride, every one of us. When society locks up these bad boys and girls where do you think they go? There is no death penalty here, which means some poor soul has to look after them. They don't simply vanish into thin air you know. Someone has to control them, police them, nurse them, rehabilitate them… Yes, that's right, because almost all will return to society one day. That tends to be forgotten. It's no picnic when you're facing ten, thirty, forty or seventy hostile prisoners, and you know you only have three colleagues on the wing with you. When they are armed with weapons, drugged up, drunk on hooch…. We do our bit and we get precious little respect in return. The forgotten service, time and again. Out of sight, out of mind. So don't talk to me about duty! I will do my bit, as I always have. Because I am professional. Because I swore to serve, just like you. This is crazy shit you've all dreamed up here, but if this is what is required of me now, I'm your man. Though, I will *not* have you looking down your nose at me!'

The man from wherever was visibly shocked. It lasted exactly two seconds and it was perhaps the only emotional reaction he displayed when a faint smile appeared on his lips.

'Monday then. Look after our girl, Mr. Townsend. Good luck.'

Chapter 2 - Present Day

She studied the face in the mirror for a good half hour. Scarcely recognised the individual staring back at her. Wondered how much truly remained of the person she was. The turbulent existence, the traumas, the wear and tear, the physical injuries and mental scars... all left indelible marks over time on people like her. They warned her of that from the very outset. Baggage, they called it, because you carry it with you wherever you go. Some bags were heavier than others. Too heavy. Most eventually broke under the enormous strain, succumbed to the inevitable and just burned out. Or ended things in the only way they knew for sure was permanent, removed any variables in favour of a dead cert, you might say.

Humans are frail creatures.

Well, not her. Not this girl. She was made of different stuff.

It was not that she was displeased with her reflection. She knew this version of herself was still a solid nine out of ten in anyone's books. It was not regret or sorrow neither. It was just that it always took a little time for her to adjust. To come to terms with the changes required for another new mission. Another new identity. Another role to play.

What a rollercoaster ride her life had become. She was without doubt the real-life star of a thriller more exciting and dangerous than any best-selling novel or blockbuster movie could ever be. She had already consigned to memory countless people, names, jobs, cities, corpses... They were all a blur to her now. Tiny stains on her subconscious barely worthy of recollection.

And now there were more changes ahead. More

friends to make. More hearts to break. Be it ally, comrade, quarry or lover, somebody was *always* hurt. That much was a given. It was okay though. Part of the job. Unlike many, she would lose no sleep over the inevitable consequence of her chosen profession. Hurt was like death; unavoidable. An occupational hazard. Almost always a desired outcome in fact. Pain and heartache followed her wherever she went, like a stray hound begging for scraps. It was the natural order of things.

That did not mean she would not change it if she could. Of course she would. Who wouldn't? She wasn't completely heartless. But her life from an early age was too hard and uncompromising to be concerned for others, if it wasn't a viable option. And it rarely was. *She* had had to be her top priority and that meant hardening her heart with fatalistic acceptance. Learning to make the hard choices and compartmentalise. There were no laws in her jungle, just survivors and prey.

She knew which one she would be almost before she could walk straight.

Childhood and adolescence had been one battle after another so there was a need for a few necessary evils from time to time. Become ruthless or become a victim. Consequently, the adult she eventually became had evolved to be hardened, tough and free of inhibitions. She no longer flinched at the unspeakable things she was often expected to do. Just smiled and got the job done. Not for her the ghostly echoes of memories rebounding in the dreams and recriminations of a thousand sleepless nights. Others endured the nightmares and post-traumatic stress disorder. She slept like a babe.

It was the secret to her unrivalled success. She

survived and thrived in her cut-throat world because she possessed no conscience. No debilitating sense of right or wrong. No hangover. No principles or ethics battling frantically for survival within her soul, struggling desperately to surface against the odds, to remind her from time to time that she *was* still human, still capable of love, trust and commitment, when she had been conditioned to distrust and shun those feelings and beliefs to her very core.

She was dead within. It made her a better killer. Any residual flickers of humanity had been cast aside by choice, or trained out of her years ago. She was a machine now. A perfectly tuned instrument of death. When others hesitated, she launched into action. She performed to the highest standards, driven hard by her self-centred obsession with being the best. She made it to the top despite monstrous odds and was intent on staying there. Having doubts of any kind was a weakness she loathed, because it hindered her, reduced her efficiency. And she had analysed herself enough times now to know that she possessed only one such flaw, if anyone could call it that. It was a defect in her make-up she had dissected, examined, accepted and understood; she detested betrayal. Was consumed by the thought of it to the point of obsession. To a disproportionate degree which left her susceptible to making rash decisions. Acting in the moment without thinking things through. Taking unnecessary risks. It was in real danger of fast becoming the one weakness which could derail her, if she allowed it to take hold. Could be the death of her one day.

That was really messed up and she knew it. It would never change though. It was ingrained in her psyche and it was the one thing she could not control. So, she just had to conceal it. She was not about to let anyone know, just so some hotshot shrink could make a name for themselves at her expense. No, the tiny chink in her otherwise impenetrable armour could and would be suppressed, buried. She was an accomplished performer after all. That was a large part of her training. And she was now a vastly experienced operator; the hardest of the few. As icy cool as could be under fire, undercover too. She'd proven that time and again. Yes, in every aspect but one, *she* set the standard.

Kirsten. It was as good a name as any she had known. And Moore was a decent English surname she thought. It would raise no suspicions anyhow, no awkward conversations about heritage. Anonymity was crucial to the success of this next venture so she wanted to arouse as few misgivings as possible. After all, she had no way of knowing how long she would have to remain, Kirsten Moore. This new identity could last a lifetime if things did not go to plan, for the assignment was open-ended. Fluid. She knew it and had willingly signed on for the long haul regardless. All she had to do now was keep her head down and stay out of trouble. Easy enough.

Oh, and pray that trouble didn't find her, for once.

She was twenty-seven now, in her prime. Though in truth she felt way older. She had crammed so much into her relatively short existence to date that she had lived enough for two lifetimes, almost all of it on the edge. Taken risks no man or woman should ever have to take. Confronted her demons. Seen and done terrible deeds which would have destroyed the minds of lesser beings...

*

Past events shape us all. And she was no exception. Her

youthful innocence had not lasted long. Tragedy found her early when she was orphaned at just three years of age. Both her parents, her only family, were mysteriously killed in a car crash in Berlin, the exact circumstances of which were still shrouded in secrecy to this very day. Several inquisitions and years of vociferous protestations from the British intelligence services had still not managed to unearth the truth. Or at least, that was what she had been informed.

She suspected there was more to tell but it was no longer an issue as far as she was concerned. She had not known her parents. Not really. They were strangers to her, snatched away before any of her earliest recollections. She had no memory of them and so therefore she had formed no attachments, no bonds. And it is nigh on impossible for a child to love a photograph.

She should know. It was all she had of them. She possessed maybe five faded shots in total of them together. Which, she presumed, reflected perfectly how little they were actually at home with her when alive. Or how little they had actually cared for her. Either way, it was the reality she was left with and she had processed it all over many years of painful soul-searching. They had left their only toddler to struggle and survive as best she could in a hostile world. Without help. Without love. Abandoned and betrayed. In her mind, her parents were chiefly responsible for the nightmare existence which ensued; her childhood.

The tiny infant was thrown to the ravenous beasts. Which was how she described her career as a charge of Social Services. Foster parents and care homes came and went in the blink of an eye, there were so many. Some were good people, good homes. Some, not so much.

She was moved continuously. Most of it her fault, she knew. A great deal, however, was blame to be laid at the feet of the criminals who were practicing legalised torture and prostitution right under the noses of the authorities in those days. In plain sight of the very civil servants who were meant to protect her.

Was it any wonder she defied them at every turn?

A disturbed, troubled, lonely, volatile child, never able to settle in one place, lacking peer support and guidance, friendship, routine, love...

The endless reports said it all and more.

A pocket dynamo of short-fused explosive energy. Combustible rage in a petit package. Adorable to look at but dangerous to know. Full of attitude...

They were some of her favourites.

She preferred the company of animals to people, for she decided early on to give up on the human race. After all, it had given up on *her*, hadn't it? Anyway, animals enjoyed a better existence.

She was bright though, if only she could be interested enough to apply herself. She showed distinct promise early on in a number of subjects. But, inevitably, something bad always happened, after which she was moved on quickly to become somebody else's problem. That was one thing they *were* good at.

By the time she was thirteen, the general consensus was that she was heading for only one place; prison. Unless, of course, death found her first. And the smart money was on the Grim Reaper. Many thought she would perish violently at the hands of some gang she'd pissed off. Others believed it would be as a result of a downward spiral into alcohol or drugs. None actually gave her a chance of surviving her teenage years.

And then came the turning point.

One fateful day in March, just short of her fourteenth birthday, she was summoned to yet another headmaster's office, in order to receive yet another expulsion. Only this time, the head teacher was not alone. Standing silently in the corner of the room was the man who would change her life.

Retired army colonel and part-time spymaster, Michael Dunbar, was also on the Board of Governors at the school. He had heard for himself the trouble this young girl was making and a professional curiosity had gripped him. It was born mainly from a fantastic notion he had, as well as a devout wish to please his superiors.

What if he could save this one?

He determined that he just had to meet her and as soon as he set eyes on the little bundle of sheer defiance when she, the condemned, strode confidently into the meeting which would decide her future seemingly in complete control and without a care in the world, he knew deep inside that he had unearthed a golden nugget of raw potential. The makings of a very rough, exceedingly uncut and almost unbreakable diamond.

She had surveyed the room as if she were queen, much to the frustration and anger of her teacher. And very much to Dunbar's amusement.

The educator she knew. The spy she most certainly did not. And it did not faze her at all.

'Well, let's get on with it then,' she demanded.

Such insolence. Such boldness.

Dunbar was already impressed.

'Mind your manners! We have company.'

The headmaster was fuming, and embarrassed.

She shot him a look of thunder. She hated all that man stood for. He was nice enough she supposed, but she had already decided it was all an act, to condition the pupils into doing whatever he wanted them to. Herding his lambs towards the wolves no doubt. Who knew the depths of his depravity beyond that mask he wore? It did not work on her. He demanded conformity. She desired freedom.

'Given your history, you should by now realise why you are here. And what is about to happen. We have tried our best with you at this school. Heaven knows how hard we have tried, but… Well, you just won't be helped, will you?' the tutor began.

She gave no reply, either verbally or by any other means. Her only response was a few sly glances at the well-dressed stranger.

'I regret to say that it is out of my hands now, child. This latest incident is one too many, I'm afraid. Most of our children have a one- or two-page file in that cabinet behind you. *You* have an entire drawer! Your folder is like a doorstop. We have to use a trolley to transport it.'

She gave a faint chuckle at that.

'This is no laughing matter!' roared the exasperated professional. 'You are almost fourteen now. You have very little time left in school. You will soon have to enter the big, wide world and then what? What are you going to do with yourself? How are you going to survive? Unlike the others, you have no family to help you. You are a ward of the state and once the money stops…? Well, what I mean is, you have no prospects without a good education, which we are trying to give you. You are quite clearly able to do the set work, so why won't you even try?!'

Silence again. Nothing. She actually had the audacity to look bored.

'For Pete's sake! Talk to me?!'

But she did not flinch. This was nothing new for her. It was just another betrayal, that's all. They were washing their hands of her again, as they always did. Giving up on her was their speciality.

'Oh, what's the use?! So be it. You are out of here. I'm going to leave you now in the hands of Mr. Dunbar here. Maybe he will have better luck trying to reach you.'

He shuffled some papers on his desk and then hurriedly left the room, casting a quick look at his visitor which silently conveyed, *'Told you so.'*

As the door closed, she sat in silence, expecting him to speak. She was ready and waiting for another pep talk, another lecture, another motivational epic. She had already decided that *whatever* he said, it would not work. He would just be going over old ground. However, to her growing unease and discomfort, he simply stood there leaning on the filing cabinet saying nothing, eyeing her slowly up and down, though somehow not in the creepy way she was used to. Until finally, she could take the quiet no more.

'Well? What are *you* looking at?! I should sell tickets the way you're gawping. Take a good look. This is it though. This is me. No party tricks here.'

'Come now, don't sell yourself short on my account. I have read your file. Pretty interesting stuff. There was the time you took on three of the football team and gave them all black eyes. When you broke out of one of your care homes for the umpteenth time and shinnied down the drainpipes, from the third floor. The incident in the headmaster's office you broke into. The explosions in the chemistry lab. The time you punched your foster parent on the nose. How you aced the first part of your English paper at ten, top of the entire class, but then declined to show up for the second half.... Do you want me to continue?'

She shrugged. This was new though. He was a suit like all the others, but nobody had ever taken such an interest in her before.

'Makes no difference to me what you do. Do what you want, I don't care. And I broke his jaw, *actually*. The foster... It was a fraction of what that perverted letch deserved! You call him a parent? I say he was a ...!'

'Yes. You are right,' Dunbar interrupted. 'You *were* right, to chin him. You may like to know that he is in prison now, where he belongs. For a very long time. I wish I could say that for all of those who hurt you. He escaped lightly. I can't change that but I *can* arrange to have him visited, if you'd like?'

That caught her attention alright. This guy was different gravy.

'Good. Yes, please? A little bit of real justice goes a long way.'

Dunbar smiled. There was a spark inside her alright.

'Rather a grown-up thing to say? Is that really how you feel? Because, I have to say, one look at your resume tells a different story. You don't appear to believe in anything, or anyone?'

That elicited a quick and irritable response, just as it was designed to do.

'I believe in me! The only person I can trust. The

only one who won't let me down. You don't *know* me. That file isn't *me*. It's words on a page, that's all. Just words.'

'You are letting yourself down right now with your fondness for failure. You are selling yourself short, because you are capable of so much more. Though, you are correct again, when you say I do not know you. It might surprise you to learn that I would like to change that.'

She shuffled uncomfortably in her chair. 'Here, what's your game?'

He raised both hands slowly and took one step closer. 'No games. Not now. Not ever. I promise.'

She was silent once again, unsure what was happening here and how best to respond. Seeing the change in her, Dunbar finally approached the chair and sat down.

'Before I begin, I want to make you another promise. You will hopefully come to find that I am a man of my word. And I swear here and now, that I will always tell you the truth. As I know it anyway.'

His face was sincere. There was nothing in his eyes but honesty as far as she could discern and she was intrigued.

'Okay...?'

'As was so eloquently described to you by the former occupant of this office, your life is going nowhere good. And you are approaching the final destination fast. You're on an express train to Loserville, lassie. You are out of control, running downhill with no breaks. Except for this one I am offering you right here, right now. You can halt this slide into oblivion you're on, if you want to? Once I leave this office however, the offer I am extending to you now will expire. Take that in, if nothing else. This is a one-time deal. I know how young you are, but it has to be this very instant. Once you enter the Criminal Justice system, and that is where you are destined to go on your present course, we won't touch you. Then, you'll be on your own.'

Nice. The truth. Cold and hard. Just how she liked it. *How refreshing.*

'We? What are you, a spook?'

'Ha, ha… You have been watching too much T.V.'

'Yeah, course. I'm thirteen. I'm right though?'

Dunbar nodded and smiled warmly. He spoke in a soft Scottish accent which was mesmerising to her.

'Yes. I work for our nation's interests. Though, I will deny this conversation ever took place if I am forced to. If you repeat what has been said here you are liable to find yourself returned to some cesspit of a foster home in double quick time. Do I make myself clear?'

He was deadly serious, she could tell.

'Alright. Jeez, I won't say anything, I promise.'

'Fine. Let me ask you this; if you fell off the face of this planet tomorrow, all trace of you gone, who would care? Who would you be leaving behind?'

Her face hardened a little.

'Stupid question. You already know the answer, so why ask? Nobody.'

'Yes. And that is *exactly* what makes you so attractive to our organisation. To my superiors. If you agree to it, you will leave this school with me this second. No goodbyes. You will leave everyone and everything behind. When we arrive at our destination, you will be given a new identity, new clothing and belongings. All you have known up to this point, you will have to abandon and you can't go back. It will be as if you have vanished to them. As if you never existed.'

As young as she was, she took only two seconds to decide her future.

'I can do that. I'll go with you. As you said, I have nothing, so what do I have to lose?'

Dunbar was as experienced as they come but the utter self-confidence of this youngster, the carefree abandon and speed at which she made such a vital, momentous, life-changing choice, it knocked him sideways.

'Are you not going to ask me where we're going? Where you will live?'

Another impressive, instantaneous reply.

'No. I've faced enough firing squads now. Where else is there for me? I've run out of lives and I know it. No school will touch me around here. And I'm a target in the system. After you?'

Chapter 3 – Present Day

The weekend came and went in a flash, as it always seemed to do somehow. The meeting at the café had troubled Ian Townsend deeply once he had re-run the content through in his mind. Sleep was hard to find and every waking minute invaded by thoughts of his infidelity. The impact it would have on all parties if the truth were ever exposed, especially on his wife. And their privacy being violated in ways he could hardly comprehend. Nothing, he knew, would be sacred now and she did not deserve that. She deserved way better. Better than him.

He made up his mind to end his extra-marital affair without delay and found it a tremendous release. Felt as if a great weight had been lifted off his shoulders, even though he still bore the secret and the guilt. He could not recollect for certain why it had begun, except for the obvious physical attraction of a younger girl. To his great shame, he had been tested and failed miserably. He knew in his heart that what he had done lessened him as a man. As a human being too. He had betrayed the love of his life.

However, he also realised for the very first time that their marriage was probably over. They had been going through the motions for years, blind to the truth, or too afraid to acknowledge it. Shared a loving relationship, but the physical side of things had waned. They hardly ever kissed now, scarcely hugged. Had become best friends rather than lovers. It wasn't enough for him, so why should his wife feel any different?

He decided he would tell her *everything* as soon as he worked up enough courage and found the right time.

It was a welcome distraction when Monday morning finally arrived and brought with it an air of anticipation and mild excitement, despite his initial fears. In his own miniscule way, he would be part of a secret, clandestine world now which was usually concealed from the likes of him. It was an interesting development for a guy who had achieved his life's ambition when he became a prison governor. For the first time in many years, nerves actually made the hairs on the back of his neck stand to attention.

He left his wife in bed, having said his goodbyes with the customary kiss on her cheek. The drive to work took a little over twenty minutes and was without doubt his favourite time of day. He loved the solitude in the country lanes and the chance to relax listening to music. It did not matter to him that to others outside of his vehicle he looked like a fool, as he sang out loud at the top of his voice to almost every track. Songs he knew and loved warmed his soul and he did not care who knew it. His well-worn C.D. collection was his pride and joy. He had two full cases with fifty discs in each in the passenger foot well of his car and he rotated these with four more similar cases at home. He deliberately chose not to update his vehicle even though he could easily afford to. This model, unlike newer versions, was blessed with the all-important C.D. player. In that regard at least, he was proud to be called a dinosaur.

He took a left onto Kings Road, slowing to take the speed bumps at a sensible pace he hoped over time would not destroy his suspension. The lane led directly up to the prison and the adjacent staff car parks, situated opposite the exterior wall and impressive gatelodge. The sight never grew old and anxiety soon gave way to pride. This was his baby. His world. The culmination of his life's work. The post he had earned through years of honest endeavour and sacrifice.

Her Majesty's Prison Norgate was a hybrid. The original wall, gatelodge, older wings, administration offices, works department and several smaller buildings were built by the Victorians. This section of the prison had been scheduled for demolition and replacement for many years now, but the finances had never been secured. There were always higher priorities it seemed for successive governments. Additionally, the constant population pressure had meant that the old wings, as dilapidated as they were, were still needed.

A and B wings therefore housed a mixture of remand and convicted male prisoners, as HMP Norgate serviced the courts. Beyond these wings, adjacent buildings and exercise yards, the old wall had been extended by the addition of a vast perimeter wire fence, adorned with barbed wire. Within its confines were the newer structures; the remaining wings, yards, workshops, healthcare centre, education departments, programmes department and sports field. The whole complex was vast. It housed just over a thousand prisoners in total. Staffing numbers were harder to pinpoint because of the number of civilian employees, temporary contractors and volunteers, but the figure easily ran into the high hundreds. And Ian Townsend was in charge of the lot.

He parked in his reserved spot and exited his car. Fumbled for his key chain and unhooked his tally. Several members of staff greeted him with a, 'Morning governor,' or just plain deferential, 'Guv,' as he approached the Gate. He smiled and acknowledged each in turn, proceeded through the electronic gatelock and threw his tally down the key chute. Collected his radio and keys and turned to enter the prison itself.

Before he could open the final gate, a face he knew appeared from around the nearby entrance to the old locker room.

'Sorry, Boss, this way please?'

Officer Garbey, or 'The Garb' to his mates, was a member of the Security Department.

'Almost got away with it this time,' Ian joked, smiling. 'Come on then.'

Random searching was supposed to be just that; random. So how come they had to select *him* every day? They were trying to prove a point; that nobody was above being searched.

The search complete, he continued to his office situated in the old Victorian admin block just off A wing. His full-time secretary and invaluable assistant was at her desk in the adjoining room, controlling access to him as usual like a faithful hound.

'Morning, Kath. How was your weekend?' he enquired politely, as he entered his office and hung up his coat, before returning to hear her reply.

'Yes, good thanks.' She smiled graciously. 'Yours?'

'Too short, as always. How come the week days don't go that fast, eh? Where *does* the time go?'

'I know. We went to a christening. My little nephew. He'll be shaving and going to college before I know it. It was a good day though.'

'I'm glad you had a good time. What's on the agenda for today?'

She opened the diary on her computer. 'Let's

see… Senior Management Team meeting at nine. Then you have a meeting with the Chair of the Independent Monitoring Board at eleven thirty. Hopefully, you won't run late, so you can get a gym session in over dinner. At two o'clock you're meeting with the new starters. One cook, a librarian, one admin grade and three new officers. Then, you asked me to arrange a meeting with the Heads of Residential and Security, to discuss recent gang issues on D wing. I thought I'd try for around four?'

Kath had not quite grasped the use of the twenty-four-hour clock.

'Hmmn… Any further issues over the weekend, do you know?'

'Not on the Daily Briefing sheet there wasn't,' Kath replied.

'Right. Then, no. In that case, we'll do that tomorrow. I've decided I need to be more invested in our staff. Get to know them a little better as individuals. I'm going to start today. Let Training know for me please that I'll have these new starters longer than usual. Then they can get some orientation in at their new workplaces. Meet some of their new colleagues on an informal tour.'

'Sure, it's done.'

Ian thanked her and then walked to his desk, closing the door to his office behind him.

That didn't sound too unnatural, did it? he asked himself.

He strode over to the coffee machine and made himself a drink. The first cup was always bliss and he sighed with satisfaction as the liquid warmed his throat.

After being briefed on the events of the past few days in the morning meeting and following on from the various discussions which ensued, the rest of the day passed without incident. To his gratification, he managed to spend around an hour in the gym over lunch, pounding the treadmill, cross trainer and lifting a few weights. He was suitably showered, refreshed and dressed when a knock on his door interrupted his concentration shortly afterwards. It was exactly fourteen hundred hours.

'Enter.'

The door opened slowly and Kath's head appeared. 'Governor, I've the new starters for you, if you are ready for them?'

Ian removed his glasses. With the door now open he could see a group of nervous-looking individuals standing behind his secretary. Most looked as though they had only just finished school. He wondered when he had become so old. Put down his pen and walked to the door.

'Morning. Come in.' He ushered them into the small office. 'Welcome. That's it, move along the bus,' he joked. 'Standing room only I'm afraid. It's a bit cramped but there are only six of you.'

He made an instant decision.

'I tell you what, as you were. Let's move this to Boardroom One. Come on, follow me.'

He led the whole group down the corridor the short distance to the large meeting room.

'Okay, that's better. Come in and take a seat. Take your coats off too, if you'd like.'

He pointed to the chairs situated around the huge centre table which dominated the room. The employees all did as instructed, the occasional, 'Thank you' whispered quietly in response. As they settled, he gazed around the room. There was no mistaking which one was Kirsten. Though he tried his hardest not to linger his stare on her, any more than the others.

'Well now, I will say it again; welcome to Norgate. I'm delighted to meet you all. Firstly, because we need new staff. Secondly, because you have all chosen this path, this career. You are all like me hoping to make a difference in someone's life. That is immense in my book and earns my complete respect. I hope you will be equally as happy as I am here, for many years. My name is Ian and my door is always open. If you can get past Kath first, that is.'

A ripple of polite laughter eased the tension a little.

'Being serious, I will expect the highest standards from you while you are here because I want us to be the best. But I also want you to have fun, as we try to navigate together what can be a very challenging and demanding profession. Security will always be the number one priority for me, but in amongst that we also have the chance to change lives. Experience has taught me that some, but by no means all, of these men can be reached, inspired, influenced by the examples you set and the opportunities you provide. Never lose sight of that fact. Now, let's go around the room. I want you all to tell us who you are and where you will be working. And throw in one interesting fact about yourself. It can be anything. I have signed the Official Secrets Act after all. Let's begin with you,' he stated, pointing to the lady he presumed correctly was the librarian.

They each tried their best to answer the questions in an interesting, jovial manner. Several small discussions followed. Kirsten waited calmly and patiently and was fourth to speak.

'Hi everyone, I'm Kirsten Moore. I'm a little

older than the other two officers, though I won't say how old, if you don't mind? I think… I have been informed rather, that I'm going to B wing. Looking forward to it. There's nothing really interesting about me. I'm rather dull, truth be told. I enjoy keeping fit. Does that count?'

'Ha! A girl after my own heart. Me too. Sure, why not?' said Ian. He moved the conversation on quickly. Once they had all finished, he said, 'Thank you. Now, this is your opportunity to ask me anything you'd like, anything you want to know.'

For the next ten minutes or so, a barrage of questions followed ranging from the prison's history to car parking, shift times, use of gym, catering facilities for staff and camera coverage… Finally, the questions ceased and he allowed the civilian staff to leave, having first radioed through for an escort. The three remaining officers chatted quietly amongst themselves as he left the room briefly, only to return moments later having contacted a colleague on each of their wings.

'I have arranged collection. You will now be taken to your new places of work so you can meet some of your new colleagues. Use this time wisely. Ask them for a tour. Get a feel for the place and the people you will be working with.'

They chatted some more as they waited for the escorts to arrive. One by one the officers left, until Kirsten and Ian were alone. The door closed and they waited in silence for a few seconds to ensure they would not be heard.

'I'll begin then,' stated Ian, when Kirsten did not speak. 'How do you want to play this exactly? I mean, what is it I am expected to do? How often should we meet and where? I suppose what I am asking is, what do you need from me?'

Her eyes moved over him swiftly as she sized him up.

'Zilch. I need nothing from you. You have been briefed. You are to watch my back, that's all. Just give me as much warning as you can of any possible issues. You'll know when the time comes, when something just doesn't feel right. Don't hesitate then. Trust your gut and find me, no matter the circumstance. You don't want to get too involved, trust me. Keep your distance, okay? As far as you or anybody else is concerned, I'm just another member of staff.'

Ian did not know quite what he had expected from her, but this was somewhat of an anti-climax. He was feeling a little deflated all of a sudden, which both perplexed and surprised him. And as for being, "just another member of staff?" Well, that horse just wasn't going to jump any fences.

He drank in her astonishing beauty. Surely it was not fair for one person to be so blessed? She was medium height with penetratingly dark brown eyes that looked as though they could pierce your soul. Her hair was shoulder length, wavy and free. It appeared to be so soft, he just wanted to lean forward and smell it. Her flawless skin was the colour of NATO coffee and leant a Mediterranean look to her appearance and appeal which was enhanced by her athletic build, clearly the result of countless hours working out. In truth, she looked as though she would be equally at home in the Amazon Rainforest, on an athletics track, a catwalk, a royal gala or a tennis court. She was wearing no make-up at all and yet it was perfectly clear that she needed none. No amount of covering could improve on the vision before him. She was perfection itself, would look absolutely spectacular wearing a hessian sack. And at present, she was really, *really*, wearing that uniform. If ever he needed a poster girl for the modern service, in different circumstances, she was right there. And he realised immediately that her astonishing beauty would bring with it, its own set of unique problems.

'Forgive me? I don't mean to sound rude, but do you really know what you have let yourself in for here? We have a lot of long-termers and you are going to attract a lot of unwanted attention from staff and prisoners, looking as you do.'

'As I do?' she asked, playfully.

The older man blushed a little, uncertain if he had overstepped the mark. 'Yes. I am only trying to warn you. I meant no offence. Please take it in the spirit it was meant? I was told to look out for you. There are lots of men here who don't have much in the way of female contact. Lots of testosterone flying around. And you're… you're…'

Kirsten displayed no outward reaction. 'I'm... what?' she said, feigning ignorance, enjoying his obvious discomfort.

'Well… gorgeous, alright? You're gorgeous.'

She was smiling inside now. 'Thank you. A little inappropriate, but I'll let it slide. Do not concern yourself though. I am not alone and it is not the problem you make it out to be. Not if I act professionally. *Do* you question my professionalism, Mr. Townsend?'

Ian backed off a little, realising that he had not made the best first impression. 'No, no… I…'

'Because I can take care of myself you know. I will be careful, I promise. Now, won't it be noticed that we have been in here a while?'

'What? Yes, I suppose so.' He reached for his radio and asked B wing to send an officer. 'We have a few minutes yet before they come. Can't you tell me more of the problems you have had, or may face here? It may help me to understand why they have chosen to place you with us, for it makes no sense to me?'

'No. Not possible. You do not need to know. What makes no sense to you exactly? Here, is as good a place as any, isn't it?'

'Yes, I suppose. But why a prison? There are far quieter, safer places, if the object is to hide you away?'

'I have to *live*, Mr. Townsend.'

'Ian, please?'

'Ian then. I have to be able to forge a life for myself. Use my existing skill set. What else was I going to do? I would not be happy in an office. Not normal you see. I crave the occasional adrenalin fix. But I am used to working with people of all backgrounds. I know I am good in a crisis. I don't scare easily. I react well to stress and cannot be intimidated. I have good communication skills. Can you think of a more perfect role for me? Of a more qualified recruit?'

He had to admit, she made a convincing argument. 'No, I reckon not, to both questions. But, will your being here expose my staff to any danger? Because I won't have that.'

She smiled again inside.

He cares.

That was unexpected. And pleasing.

'I don't see why it should place them at any extra risk. Though, I am sure you understand that I can make no guarantees, given the nature of what I do. All I can promise you is that I will be doing my best not to let that happen. I will try my utmost to blend in and not raise suspicion. If you do as you've been asked, between us we will spot any danger before it becomes a real issue. And then, no doubt, once my superiors are advised, I will be whisked away to healthier climates before any threat can catch up with me.'

He felt better having heard it from her in person and relaxed a little.

'That's all I wanted to hear. I will do what is required of me but I want to meet regularly. We have to learn to trust each other. Can't do that if we're strangers. We can say you are considering applying for the Accelerated Promotion Scheme, and that I am mentoring you? I have performed that role many times for staff before.'

'Okay, sounds reasonable. Seeing as we are bonding so well, you may as well know that they have found me a flat to rent. Not in my name of course. My mobile number is on here.' She passed him a scrap of paper. 'Use it only if you have to. And for heaven's sake, don't let your wife see it? I can do without the drama.'

He blushed again.

Does everyone know?

Just then, there was a knock at the door. A short-haired officer poked his head around. His eyes widened and his jaw dropped a little when he caught sight of the new officer he had come to collect. Clearly, he was impressed.

'Alright, Guv? You called?'

'Yes, thanks Cookey. This is your new starter on B wing. Take her back with you and show her the ropes, will you? Her name is Miss Moore. Kirsten, to the staff.'

Chapter 4 - Training

Roughly sixty miles northwest of Scotland's Outer Hebrides lies the Isle of Herik; the most remote land mass in the British Isles. It is a rocky, windswept crag of an island, an inhospitable atoll jutting out of the North Atlantic Ocean, an insignificant pinprick on any map, and a place best avoided if at all possible. For Herik is guarded jealously, defended with lethal might by multiple branches of some of the best forces in the world, in a shoot first and don't ask later, sort of way. The British Government's most highly guarded secret is so covert in fact, that very, *very* few actually know of its true nature or purpose. Of its existence.

It was inhabited by a number of families in years gone by; hardy souls, generations of tough sea goers, the last as recently as 1913. The final residents inevitably succumbed however and abandoned all hope of eking out a living in the energy-sapping, morale-beating climate and conditions.

It lies far from the main shipping lanes due to the deadly and numerous jagged rock formations which ring its shores. A solitary lighthouse dominates the skyline. Built on the highest peak of one of several small mountains, it enforces the fifteen-mile exclusion zone easily, with no more than a rotating beam of intense light. The isle is also some distance away from regional flightpaths for civilian aircraft, though several oilrigs situated further north of its position are visited occasionally by helicopters ferrying supplies and men. Events which provide perfect cover for the comings and goings of airborne visitors to Herik, as a slight deviation almost undetectable on radar is all that is needed, the minor variance in direction virtually undetectable, particularly when the pilot hugs the sea for added stealth at the right time, below the radar.

The one large structure on Herik other than the lighthouse is invisible to the human eye from land, sea and air. It is circled by a nest of high peaks and the much extended and altered installation is brimming with highly sensitive electronic jamming devices, sophisticated counter-measures which easily deceive any spying satellite overhead. The entire isle indeed is covered by a net of sensors which detect and block intrusion by reflecting an image of Herik back to any observer; the benefit of secret and extensive collaboration with NASA and stolen technology. To any foreign power conducting surveillance in the area, any nosy civilian passing by, nothing lives and breathes on that island but wildlife. And the one or two unlucky souls who have inadvertently penetrated the great veil of secrecy over the years, were soon discovered and disposed of. Disappeared without trace. Written off. Designated collateral damage.

She was still in her school clothes and it was approaching dusk. Her eyes were heavy and her stomach protested loudly. It had not occurred to her that she had skipped lunch and tea. Not until just now that is. She was ravenous, though she soon became grateful for her empty stomach as the chopper veered violently to the right and screamed towards the landing zone, scarcely above the waterline. She looked out at the pilot's view. The many rock formations came up on them so fast out of the waves that her heart hit her mouth each time, but the expert aviator weaved at the final second as if he had flown this route a thousand times, and could do so with his eyes closed.

Saliva vanished from inside her mouth and her head began to feel way too light. She became afraid that she was going to throw up at any moment. But then she saw Dunbar and she sucked in a large drag of fresh air, determined not to make a fool of herself. Not in front of him.

The old Scot was sat in the opposite corner, stretched out as if on his couch back home, like he did not have a care in the world. His eyelids were closed tight but she just knew he was fully conscious and missing nothing. She just knew.

When Herik came into view at last, she gasped. This grabbed Dunbar's attention and he sat upright. All she could see through the side glass though was water, rocks and grass. Every glance tugged hard at her upset stomach, reminding her in no uncertain terms that she had not yet shed the infliction of motion sickness. However, as the helicopter slowed and made its final approach, descending slowly to ground level, the optical illusion before them was miraculously exposed and she forgot all about her tender state.

A giant mansion, grey and imposing, seemed to rise out of the ground like a phoenix, as if summoned by some magical power way beyond her comprehension.

'Clever,' she said, to her new benefactor. 'The roof. It's made of some kind of Astroturf, isn't it? It looks like grass.'

'Not quite Astroturf, but its infinitely more expensive cousin, shall we say?'

Dunbar stepped down from the great machine and helped the youngster to disembark, concerned that she may miss a step in the fading light.

'This is your new home; Grexley Manor. It does not look like much from the outside I know, but it is far, far bigger than it appears. There are several levels underground, tennis courts, swimming pool, leisure room, and a whole sniper course out the back. It was used during World War Two to train operators from the Special Operations Executive. You will learn about them soon. Though, back in those days, most were parachuted in. Far safer. The journey by boat is a deadly peril in itself, not for the faint-hearted and just as likely to kill our people as the missions they undertake.'

'Brill,' she exclaimed, as they made their way to the entrance.

Dunbar began to wonder if *anything* intimidated this youngster.

'When are you going to explain it all to me? What you want me to do for you to earn my keep?' she asked.

'Soon. Let's get you settled in first. It's late. We will talk further in the morning, when you meet your fellow students. I'll arrange for some food to be brought up to your room.'

That was music to her ears. She barely noticed as two desolate souls ran past her at high speed, towards the waiting chopper, having barely registered that the motor was still running, even with the incredible noise and buffeting. She had just become used to it and tuned it out.

Within seconds the engine screamed, the wind grew almost unbearable and the mighty contraption ascended into the growing darkness. As they turned to go inside her eyelids suddenly felt incredibly heavy and she had to fight to keep them open. She was desperate now for food, bed and sleep, in that order. It had been quite an extraordinary day.

The following morning, she awoke bright and early and was immediately in awe of her new surroundings. She had been assigned the penthouse suite alright. She must have been. Her room was larger than some of the flats and houses she'd been made to live in at times. It was old too, with high ceilings and coving, skirting boards and sash windows. She was lying in a gigantic, double-poster bed, underneath the grandest quilt she had ever seen. She raced to the window, adorned with curtains so fine she could picture herself tearing them down if she ever needed a ball gown. The view from the top floor bedroom was spectacular. Grass and snow-covered mountains and hills surrounded the entire installation. Every now and then they parted to reveal tantalising glimpses of the mighty ocean beyond.

She felt like she never had before and could not quite define the sensations she was experiencing. It all resembled something out of a high-class holiday brochure for the rich and famous and it was all hers, at least for now. Her heart felt like it might explode with joy.

Putting aside the obvious downsides to her current situation; the lack of freedom, playmates or friends her own age, money, clothing, toiletries, possessions, information, things to do… She thought she could be very happy here.

Two quiet knocks on the door interrupted her delight.

'Yes? Come in.'

Dunbar confidently entered the room in high spirits. 'You're up, I see. Good. I thought yesterday might have taken its toll. That you would be sleeping in. Coming to breakfast?'

She did not need a second invitation and began walking to the bathroom. 'You bet. Give me two minutes to throw some clothes on,' she said, then stopped in her tracks as she suddenly realised something. 'Wait. All I have is my school clothes?'

He looked at her as if she had let him down, like she had to do better than that in future. 'There's a walk-in wardrobe next to the en-suite. I took the liberty of phoning ahead. You will find several outfits in there that should fit. Be quick though, I'm famished.'

This was unreal! Christmas come early for a child who had had nothing all her life.

She was about to race in and choose her ensemble, when she stopped herself again. 'Hey! Is this for real? This *can't* be all mine? Are you going to take it all, move me, or move someone else in?'

He could appreciate that question coming from her. She had known no stability to date. Zero kindness. Disappointment and rejection had become her default positions. They were all she knew.

'No, it is all yours,' he replied. 'For as long as you are with us. But, remember, I told you before, this is a pass or fail course. Succeed, and you will be one of the team. In that scenario we will look after you and we will always be there for you. Fail however, and…? Well, let's just hope it does not come to that.'

There was something sinister, ominous even, in the way he spoke. And in the manner in which he deliberately halted himself from going further. The significance only really registered with her later in life. It would have explained so much, had he elaborated.

He waited outside and several minutes later they passed through wide corridors adorned with exquisite paintings and huge chandeliers. Stepped down double-bannistered staircases carpeted in imperial Axminster. Finally, they reached an over-sized door with a sign on it which read, *Dining Room.*

Dunbar pushed it open and the most wonderful aroma assaulted her olfactory senses. Tables and chairs were everywhere along with numerous individuals of all ages, shapes and sizes.

Tutors and students, she realised.

'It's self-service,' Dunbar said, gesturing towards the serving station laden with all types of cooked food. 'Go ahead. I'll find us a table.'

She attacked her first mission on Herik with gusto and a minute or so later, returned to the table with the largest plate of breakfast goodies any teenager had ever attempted.

'What the…?!' exclaimed the elderly Scot. 'And just where are you going to put that lot?'

She just smirked a little at him as she chewed on a sausage she had already placed into her mouth.

When they had finished eating, he gave her a map of the school. Instructed her to meet him in the room designated *Nelson* at nine thirty, explaining that all the classrooms were termed after famous British military leaders.

'That gives you around thirty minutes to do some exploring, if you like?' he added, sensing her inquisitive mood.

She gulped down the rest of her orange juice and headed eagerly for the exit, almost crashing into one of her fellow students in her exuberance. The young lady looked about a year older than her and was tall and gangly.

'Hey! Watch it!'

She was about to reply defiantly, even though she knew she was in the wrong and at a height disadvantage. It was just the way she was wired. She bit her lip though, showing hitherto unheard-of restraint, as she thought better of making enemies if she could help it on her first day.

'Sorry. My fault. Need to slow down,' she muttered.

The older girl looked her up and down as she decided whether to accept the apology.

'You're new.'

It was not a question. It sounded more like an accusation.

'No harm, no foul though. I'm Jessica, though everyone calls me, Jay Jay.'

'Hi.'

'Well? Carry on then. You evidently have places to be so don't let me stop you. We'll be seeing a lot more of each other, I am sure. This place is too small not to.'

She bolted through the door and for the next half an hour she tried to take in as much of the place as she could. Raced through the corridors, stuck her head into open rooms, cupboards, toilets… She learned that if she took the stairs on the second floor at *Montgomery*, they led down to the main entrance. However, if she turned left at the first-floor staircase, walked through the corridor past *Wellington*, *Marlborough* and *Wingate*, she reached the rear staircase, which led down to the hindmost exit.

She opened the door and stepped outside, taking in deep lungfuls of cool sea air.

Everything, she thought, *is different here.*

The time vanished before she knew it and she had to run back to her classroom to avoid being late. She opened the door without knocking first, force of habit, and interrupted a conversation in full flow between Dunbar and the seated students before him. Another man stood next to the Scot and all eyes fell disapprovingly on her.

'Ah, come in. It's okay,' said Dunbar, breaking the awkward silence. 'We can pick this up later. Take a seat at the front.'

Oh great! The front. Teacher's pet. No hiding there.

She reluctantly did as she was instructed, without argument. This was clearly a day of firsts. She gazed around the class of fresh-faced students and calculated quickly that there were around twenty in all, most aged between fifteen and seventeen she would say, with Jay Jay and herself visibly the youngest. That did not faze her in itself though. She knew from experience she could hold her own in an older crowd and self-confidence was not usually one of her shortcomings.

'Now we are all here,' Dunbar began, once she was seated, 'we had better begin with introductions. Class, this is your newest recruit. She will choose her name in due course, as per protocol. She is the youngest we have ever selected, so please make her welcome. Introduce yourselves after this lesson.'

He turned to address her directly. 'This is the latest intake. You are the final addition. They are already three months ahead of you in their learning, so you will have to play catch-up, okay?'

She nodded to signal her acceptance of the challenge without hesitation. He was really stacking the odds against her now though. Competing with older, fitter participants when they already had a distinct advantage? Was he deliberately setting her up to fail?

'I'm sure you'll be fine. This prime specimen beside me is one of your tutors. He goes by the name of, Mr. Green. As per usual, that is not his real name. All the instructors here have fictitious names, most of them a colour. It makes it easier for the students, I'm told. Those you see in this room are your classmates, but know that on *this* course, they may also be your competitors. It depends on the situation. Consequently, you are warned not to grow too many attachments while you are here. Despite the thorough selection process, the pass rate at Herik is around fifteen to twenty percent, so I expect to see only three or four of you left standing at the end.'

She gave another short intake of breath. That few? Was he joking? What had he seen to make him believe that she, of all people, could emerge from these trials victorious?

She had no idea. But an inner resolve suddenly gripped her. She did not like to be beaten at the best of times and never had anyone show such faith in her and her abilities. She would prove to all those who had wronged her that she could make something of herself. Only, what *exactly* was she expected to do?

It was as if Dunbar had read her mind.

'There is no set length for the course. It ends only when the instructors feel you are ready, or we have run out of recruits. You are now a government asset. Well, a trainee at least. Vast sums of money are going to be spent on you. We are going to teach you all the skills you will need to survive and thrive in the most hostile of environments. We will forge new identities for you, qualifications, complete histories and references, with the full backing and knowledge of a select few patriots at the very summit of power. You are going to learn so much with us. But you will be expected to study, to grow as an individual, to function as part of a team in certain circumstances, to develop a set of skills which will render you extremely adept, useful.'

'Useful? To who?' she asked.

'To your country of course.'

She gulped. Just hearing the words again in this setting brought it all home.

'So, what are you going to teach me, exactly?'

Mr. Green stepped forward. He was in his mid-thirties, quite good-looking with mousy blonde short hair and clear green eyes. Excellent physique.

'As well as a,' he held up two fingers on each hand to simulate quotations marks, '*normal* education - I do so detest that word - you will receive training in languages, etiquette, cultural differences, geography, economics, politics, espionage, history, weapons, physical endurance and resistance to interrogation, pain management, first aid and more. Oh, and of course, you will be taught numerous ways to kill. Silently, painlessly and otherwise. The curriculum is not rigid. We tailor it to each intake, each pupil, dependent upon their attributes, skillset or deficiencies, assignments etc.'

'I suppose I was kind of expecting it, but we are assassins, yeah?'

Mr. Green looked sympathetic but resolute. 'When we need to be. Why? Is that a problem for you?'

And there it was; her first major test. If she hesitated now, it would demonstrate weakness right from the very beginning, a fatal flaw she would probably never eradicate. She had considered the question in bed last night. It had kept her awake despite her extreme fatigue. In the end though, regardless of her youth and immaturity, she knew for certain that she had it within her to take a life. If it was sanctioned. If it was under orders. The why's and justifications were for others above her to contemplate and determine. She would do whatever she had to in order to grasp this chance she had been given, to escape the god-forsaken hell she was living.

So, she looked him straight in those beautiful eyes of his. 'No problem. When do I get to fire the weapons?'

'Ha! So be it. Good for you. All in good time. Under strict guidance and supervision, we will teach you to master a variety of weaponry. Also, to respect it. And in time, various forms of hand-to-hand combat. I came from one of our frontline regiments. Some of my colleagues served in the Special Forces. Some were Military Intelligence. We have *all* seen active duty, taken lives. There are no passengers here. Your childhood, such as it was, is over. Here, you will be treated like an adult at all times. Expected to behave like one too. From what I read in your file, I would have thought that quite appealing to you?'

She nodded in agreement again. 'Sorry, but, I was only recruited yesterday, so how did you read my file?' she asked.

'You are sharp. Dunbar. He's been watching you for weeks, compiling a dossier on you. It makes for good reading.'

She cast the canny ex-spymaster a quick glance but he did not acknowledge her and Mr. Green turned to address the whole class. 'That's enough talk. We have to move on. The formation of S.O.E. Take out your text books and turn to chapter three.'

He gazed at her and pointed at her desk. 'You will find a timetable of sorts in the bag at your feet. Also within, is all you need in the way of stationary, writing and reading materials. If you feel you require anything more, just ask. I am not going to recap what we've covered so far. I suggest, in your own time, you read and assimilate chapter's one and two.'

It was school all over again. Only, it wasn't. It was so, so much more.

Dunbar made for the exit but halted directly in front of her. Looking down, he whispered, 'I'm going now. I'll be popping in from time to time to see how you are faring. I have stuck my neck out so far for you, lassie, I actually have cramp. Don't mess this up, please? You are *my* recommendation. There were many dissenters. Many who thought your age would be a problem, that you were not strong enough. I have ignored those voices and given you a clean slate. It is up to you what you do with it. Your existence has been erased from every record we could find. This is your opportunity to be someone. Prove me right. Be all you can be. Goodbye.'

She felt like she should thank him but the words just would not come. He was right in everything he said. She knew that now. She had been destined to waste the only life she had been given. Here, she had purpose and a family of sorts. That was all she had longed for. The outside world had forgotten she was human, treated her worse than most decent people could imagine. Starved her of affection and kicked her hard in the head when she was down, time and again until all she had left in her was rage and fight. They had placed her in harm's way whether they knew it or not. At least these guys were being honest about it. At least here, it served some part of a higher cause.

Yes, she would give it her absolute best. And if that wasn't good enough in the final reckoning, at least she would have the satisfaction of knowing she tried. If she failed, it would not be for lack of effort.

She looked up into his steely blues. 'Bring me a present next time you come, for my birthday?' she said, smiling.

'Ha, ha… I can do that.'

The door closed silently and Dunbar was gone. The next chapter of her life had begun.

Chapter 5 – Present Day

'…And then he said to me, *"You know, I have a soft spot for you, Miss Moore. Right at the bottom of my garden!"* Ha, ha…'

Kirsten had been a prison officer for just short of three months. Despite her unique background, it had still proven to be a difficult, varied and challenging experience. To her surprise, it was also enjoyable and rewarding. There were highs and lows almost daily. Times when she felt anxious and cornered, vulnerable and inadequate. Moments too when she really did feel she was making a difference which brought a warm feeling of contentment inside.

She had met at least once weekly with Ian, who was operating in his guise as her mentor, ensuring all was well but at the same time checking that no perceived threats had emerged. Their relationship as a consequence was blossoming into one of healthy, mutual respect and trust. They were now in his office. The door was closed, the coffee fresh, the biscuits in plentiful supply.

Ian laughed along with her, completely at ease in her presence. 'Ha, ha… Congratulations! You've made it. You have finally arrived, Miss Moore.'

She appeared puzzled and put down her drink. 'What? What do you mean by that?'

He paused slightly, choosing how to word his explanation.

'We are none of us born officers, you know. We all have to take the time we need to settle in at first, to adapt from civilian life to this. There's a world of difference between the two. As a member of the public, you would not be expected to understand our hidden world; a domain where people are killed for half ounce of tobacco. The things we see and are asked to do on a daily basis. Just as you had to become acclimatized here, it takes time also for the prisoners to get to know you and your levels. Where you personally draw your line in the sand. We all must have one to be effective but it takes a while to find that out for yourself. For you to get to know prisoners, how to interact and show you won't be intimidated, and for you to learn how to instil discipline. I, for instance, found out quickly that a no said with a smile, *still* means no. It carries no less weight because of your civility. Something to consider. Though, it sounds to me as if the prisoners have already accepted you; that you can't be played with. Sounds to me like you've earned yourself some respect, Boss.'

The first four weeks were the hardest. She had undertaken a two-week Induction Programme during which she mostly shadowed a more experienced colleague. A vast percentage of her time was spent on her own wing but she also conducted part of her shifts in additional areas she would soon be expected to cover, including Segregation Unit, Visits, Reception and Safer Custody. She hated being the new recruit all over again, having to rely on others for guidance when she had devoted so much of her life to perfecting the art of self-reliance. And to make matters worse, Ian had done her no favours at all with the single decision he had made.

Word soon spread amongst the staff that she was an Accelerated Promotion candidate. It singled her out as special in the eyes of management and possibly believing herself to be better than anyone else in the minds of some staff. A probable management spy. Many thought they had to be careful what they did and said around her at first. It was a clear and obvious barrier to acceptance she could have done without. And one old sweat pulled no punches as he commented one evening.

'That's all fucked up, that is! The whole idea is absurd. What other organisation would choose to place all of their eggs in one basket, eh? Spend all of their limited resources on one individual, just because they have a degree in Sports Science or Sociology, Knitting or something? To the detriment of the other ninety-eight percent of their staff. Does it make them a good officer if they have a degree? No. You can't learn this job in a classroom. Any more than you would grab a scalpel and start operating. You learn it out here, on the landings, getting your hands dirty. And to manage effectively you need to know the job. Will they never learn?'

All she could do was sit and listen, feeling small. It was unnatural for her not to fight her corner but she was not about to defend a policy she did not fully comprehend. All she knew was that the anger she felt that day was directed at Ian, who had put her in this position. He had invented the cover story just so they could meet regularly, seemingly without any thought for how hard it might make her assimilation into the ranks. She was supposed to be blending in, after all.

In their next meeting, she gave him both barrels.

It meant of course that she had to try even harder to earn her colleague's respect. And she did. She took to the job from the off. Her aloof, reserved, stand-offish nature actually served her well for once, at least in the beginning, helping to maintain a professional distance whilst she watched and learned from experienced officers. She soon gained a solid reputation. She was firm but polite, treated all prisoners the same and always employed the golden rule; she *never* promised anything unless she was certain it could be delivered. She learned the hard way that it was far easier saying yes after you had said no, than trying to do it the other way around.

The physical stuff, Control and Restraint, had come easily to her, though she had to be very careful not to divulge her secret ability and to stay within the Code of Conduct and C and R manual the service adhered to. She was itching to become involved in every incident but she deferred to others, remained silent and awaited the call.

Her first chance she supposed was some kind of test. The guy they had to restrain and re-locate was massive, a man-mountain if ever there was one. He was threatening staff from behind his cell door with a broken table leg. This was what the staff called a planned scenario; a static situation which they could manage on their terms and in their timeframe. Kirsten was chosen to 'kit-up' and be part of the team. She donned the blue overalls and protective gear with confidence. With the aid of a shield, they entered the cell and quickly disarmed and restrained the perpetrator. It was a textbook takeout and it gave staff the confidence to use her again and again. She never declined.

Other aspects of her role began slowly to unearth another, more compassionate side to her personality. She was acting she knew, but she hardly recognised herself. She helped those in need to write letters, complete applications, word responses which would be used when addressing parole boards etc. She found to her amazement that these tiny shreds of decency and humanity she was displaying without thought came easy to her.

She was still green in so many ways, still wet behind the ears and learning her craft, but Miss Moore was a decent officer now, fully at home and content in her work environment.

Ian was delighted to hear about and witness her progress. He had maintained a watching brief but it was almost to the point of obsession. He used any excuse he could to visit the wing, checked visitors to the unit, the observation book, orderly officer logs, incident reports, security briefings, CCTV… He also requested weekly reports from her custodial manager, as part of his mentoring role. However, so far, he had unearthed nothing which would indicate a specific, targeted threat towards her. All the reports he had received on her progress were extremely positive.

'I have to admit to you, I was concerned at first how you would adapt, fit in. It seems like I needn't have worried?' he stated, bringing the meeting to an end. 'Your colleagues can't speak highly enough of you. Well done.'

She sighed contentedly. 'Thanks.'

'That's enough for today. What are you on this afternoon?'

'My detail has been changed. I'm now on visits runner.'

Detail changes were common and new officers regularly pulled that duty as it was a great way of learning the layout of the prison, as they ferried the men to and from the visits hall, from all areas.

'Okay,' he replied. 'Have fun.'

She left and returned to her wing. At thirteen forty-five hours she began collecting five prisoners from B wing who had booked visits. She unlocked each in turn and instructed all to wait for her on the one's landing, the lowest level next to the exit off the wing. The door and gate opened out onto a long corridor which led to the walkway beyond and finally the hall used for domestic visits.

As she approached the group and reached for her keys, it did not occur to her that there might be an issue. Perhaps, it *should* have, in hindsight? Maybe, she *should* have paid more attention to the list?

It was not often that a random group was comprised entirely of long term, violent offenders of the same faith. All under thirty serving over fifteen years for serious and organised crime. Two serving Life. All with a string of assaults against staff and prisoners whilst in custody. Had she been more attentive, more experienced maybe, she may have sought assistance with the move.

Rookie error.

She placed her key in the lock but was hailed from above.

'Miss Moore!'

She gazed up to see a large prisoner she knew to be named Baxter. He was hanging over the two's railings.

'If you're going to Visits, can you take me over?'

Baxter was a complete unit. A bodybuilder and powerlifter, he spent a vast part of his time in the gym, or doing in-cell workouts. The remaining time he was employed as visits redband; a trusted prisoner who helped in the tea bar and with the cleaning. He was a Cat D walking, the lowest security category. He had demonstrated a good attitude and a mature outlook in prison. Working as a nightclub bouncer, he had killed a trouble-maker with one punch and was now serving Life with a tariff of six years for Manslaughter.

'Sure, come on then,' answered Kirsten.

He ran down to join the group, arriving just as she finished searching the last guy.

That was when she first sensed trouble was brewing. She gave him a rub down search also and turned to lock the door and gate behind them. Her instincts had not been dulled by the prison environment and she could almost smell the tension. She had noticed quickly the uncertain looks cast between the others as Baxter joined the party. She registered the silence too. No group of prisoners walked to visits in complete silence. It was highly unusual.

Something was about to go off and she had a pretty good idea who was being targeted.

She positioned herself perfectly, assessing quickly that a large Lifer named Iqbal would be likely to instigate proceedings. He was vocal and belligerent at the best of times, disruptive and generally not a nice guy. He had appointed himself as the unofficial leader in many minor disturbances previously. Half way down the corridor, he stopped and turned to face her, aware just as she was that there was no camera coverage in that area, a fact known by all prisoners and raised repeatedly by staff as a serious security concern. Cameras had now been ordered, received, but not yet fitted.

It was just her luck.

Kirsten knew she was in a very tight fix. The confined space to work in, numerical disadvantage, possibility of weapons and mismatch in strength and power, all had her slightly concerned. She determined quickly that she had to strike first. Strike hard and fast. She had no idea of their motive, their plan, but if the first words from his lips were hostile, Iqbal was going down.

Hang the consequences.

'That's far enough,' demanded the menacing brute, extending his arm to stop her. 'You...'

The speed and ferocity of Kirsten's response was astonishing to behold. She knocked his arm away with her left hand, whilst striking at his throat with her right, crushing his windpipe a little.

She spun on her heels and the man on her left fell crashing to the floor, as she kicked off his kneecap.

The third attacker was behind her almost instantly and her weight was shifting away from him but she managed to kick out with her right leg. Her boot hit him squarely on the jaw with a loud '*crack.*' He bounced off the nearby wall, unconscious before he fell.

She swiftly stood upright to face the final two assailants. Another Lifer she knew as Hussain threw a swift punch aimed at her nose. She easily slipped it with a jerk of her head, as if it were thrown by a sloth. Off-balance now, he made easy prey. She crashed her elbow down onto his extended arm and broke his radius in two, fracturing the ulna for good measure.

The final goon was backing off at this point, but her blood was up now and she was enjoying herself.

Big boy's games, big boy's rules.

She punched him hard in the solar plexus. As he doubled over and the shock to his system caused a temporary shortage of breath, she brought up her elbow and cracked him on the jaw also. Blood oozed from his mouth as he bit his own tongue in two.

Kirsten turned towards Baxter, hands raised, deadly weapons poised to strike. But he had taken no part in the intended attack. He was now standing up against the wall, open-mouthed, aghast.

What had he just witnessed?!

Broken bodies lay all around them. In the space of only a few seconds, the quiet corridor to visits had been transformed into Armageddon.

He stared at the perfectly calm officer now standing before him. She was hardly out of breath. It terrified him; what he saw in those eyes. A ferocity which could only come from a killer. He knew for certain that these prisoners, these so-called hard men who were so feared on the wing, were only alive now because *she* had allowed them to be. They would recover from their wounds in time, but only because she had decided it would be that way. She was the one who had chosen to hold back, to use non-lethal force, he was sure.

What kind of officer was this?!

The cat was well and truly out of the bag now.

Realising Baxter was no threat and that time was short, Kirsten tried briefly to question any who could talk. There weren't many. It was a pointless exercise so she decided quickly on the next best course of action.

'Listen, I'm going to radio this in,' she instructed Baxter. 'I'm going to say and report that these five thugs tried to assault you. But that you used your strength to fend them off. I will emphasize that you acted in self-defence, okay? You are heading for Cat D and no governor is going to find you guilty of *anything*, not after the report I'm going to submit. Five against one? You'll be a legend.'

Baxter gave an uncertain nod of his head. 'But, what about them?' he asked, pointing to the shattered remnants of the gang which had targeted her.

'Don't worry. They are not about to admit that they were beaten up by a girl, are they? If the truth ever surfaces, it will be their word against a proven officer and a Cat D prisoner. This way, they can save a little face, and you become a machine nobody will mess with. It's win-win.'

'Okay, Miss. If you say so.'

Ian was informed of the incident by the duty governor, who phoned him around twenty minutes later. He was instantly consumed by thoughts of failure, guilt. He could not accept that he had not seen the attack coming, had not been able to warn her of danger, as he was supposed to.

'Really? Baxter, eh? Wow! Who'd have thought? Big guy though. Probably does some Korean martial art or something? How is Miss Moore? That can't have been pleasant to witness, especially for one so junior in service. Have her call me when she can please, so I can check on her welfare?'

'Right, guv,' came the reply.

After briefing the duty manager, completing her incident report, injury forms, computer and penning adjudications for the five prisoners guilty of attempted assault on Baxter, Kirsten found a quiet office to phone Ian.

'So, what happened really?' he asked. 'Are you alright?'

'Better than *they* are,' she answered. 'Thanks for asking.'

'Were they going for you, specifically?'

'Yes, I should say so. This was a planned hit alright. They were taking no chances either. Five onto one is good odds any day. And there were supposed to be no witnesses. Baxter was a mistake, a last-minute addition to the list. They knew there were no cameras too.

All that for an officer of my size? It's overkill of the grandest order, unless you know my history and the threat I pose.'

Ian was still not convinced. 'They *can't*, surely?'

'Loving your naivety. It is charming, but I think we have to at least consider it. Also, my detail was changed. Was that a co-incidence? We *may* have a mole.'

'No! No way. I'd stake my reputation on my staff. They are not bent,' Ian declared, defiantly. 'Though, I'm going to check the cameras on the wing, before and after, see if anything strange leaps out at me. Just to be on the safe side.'

She hung up and resumed her duties. Later that evening she was relaxing in her flat when her mobile rang.

'Hello, it's Ian. I've found something. Can I come round?'

The reply was immediate and firm. 'No. The less you know, remember? I'll text you a meeting place.'

Ian left work and drove to the rear of a large, abandoned industrial estate as directed. The whole place was deserted.

Nice spot to meet, he thought. *No witnesses, no cameras.*

As he waited for her to show, he began to feel a little anxious. Three minutes later though, a small hatchback pulled up alongside his car. Kirsten was driving but she did not leave the vehicle. Instead, she lowered the electric window.

'What was so important?' she asked, without delay.

'You were right. There is something fishy going on here. The guys who were going to attack you - good luck with that by the way - they were all Muslims. That is strange; that they would launch such an unprovoked assault when you have had no issues with them or any faith. It got me questioning things. I checked, and both before and after the incident, they can be seen on camera associating - well, more like being visited by - two lower end thugs called Briggs and Carter.'

'So?'

'*So*, they are known associates, runners and enforcers, for Tommy Nylander. And they are known racists too.'

Kirsten straightened in her car seat as the revelation grabbed her attention. She verbalised her thoughts. 'Racists visiting Muslims. Before and after the event. And you used a first name. There is more, isn't there?'

'Yes. I'm surprised you didn't recognise the name. Though, he usually keeps a low profile and has others doing his dirty work. Tommy Nylander is the man at the very top of the hierarchy on your wing. He's behind everything. His family practically run this city. They are our very own version of the Mafia, into extortion, blackmail, drug dealing, gun running, prostitution and heaven knows what else. Now that Tommy is banged up for a twelve stretch, his brother Ryan is the main man outside. They are seriously bad news.'

There was another short silence whilst she processed it all.

'Right, let's deal with what we know. We have a planned hit, an unusual association or collaboration, and a reluctance to use their own men… They were trying to pin the blame on the Muslims. Probably paid them to take me out and take the fall. But why would they risk so much? Unless, they divulged my true vocation? That all fits.'

Ian was enjoying playing detective, being the Lewis to her Morse. 'Yes, looks like it. But where does that leave us?' he said.

'They tried to take me out, but they also distanced themselves and used a scapegoat or five. That is not standard behaviour. Probably under orders. We need more to go on. I'm not certain exactly what happened, but I think we're close. We need to know who was really behind it, and I'm going to find out. If you're up to playing chauffeur tonight and watching my back, I think I need to pay Ryan Nylander a little visit.'

'What?! Are you sure? He will be swarming with protection. These are *not* people you want to make enemies of. Especially if you are trying to keep a low profile.'

'Yes. Agreed. But it's what I do and I think we may be past that now? Someone wanted me dead, I know it. Were prepared to sacrifice foot soldiers to achieve it. Has the ability to recruit anyone it seems and strike behind the walls of a prison. Nobody goes to those lengths unless they are taking out a high value target. There is too much exposure. They obviously believed it was a guaranteed killshot and worth the risk. Kirsten Moore is not worth that risk. But *I* am. And how did they know my identity? Besides, having failed with their first attempt, what is to stop them from trying again? I'm a sitting target in there. Face it; we're blown.'

Ian shrugged his shoulders because he knew she was right and he had no answers. 'Okay. They seem to hold all the cards, don't they? What can we do?' he asked.

Her eyes were alive now. She looked possessed.

'We can move to the offensive.'

Chapter 6 - Training

Grexley Manor on Herik Island, along with a sister building in the Western Highlands named Arisaig, was requisitioned during World War Two as a training base for agents from the Special Operations Executive. This clandestine force which operated behind enemy lines to cause mayhem and confusion was the brainchild of Winston Churchill. It had an immeasurable impact on the outcome of that conflict which was certainly out of all proportion to the actual size of the unit. After the war, no longer required, Grexley Manor had been mothballed whilst a suitable buyer was sought. However, Churchill became Prime Minister again in 1951 and at the time it was still lying empty. Two soviet spies were exposed that year in Great Britain, Donald Maclean and Guy Burgess, but both managed to escape to Russia. An infuriated Churchill knew for certain that there were others out there yet to be unmasked and apprehended. He was subsequently proven correct. His obsession with Soviet expansion and infiltration led directly to the formation of a new, ultra-secret network of British agents. Once again, it was Winston's original idea and it was codenamed Operation Szabo, after an SOE agent who had been caught and executed by the Nazis.

The aim was to covertly supplement the ranks of MI6 with a completely different type of agent. An altogether different type of unit. A force so secretive in nature and conception, that even the intelligence services would be unaware of its existence. A battalion of expert killers which could be relied upon to do the unthinkable and beat the enemy at their own game. Invisible assassins trained to the highest possible standards who could eliminate the untouchable. Impossible to identify or detect. Spies and executioners who could be disavowed, if necessary, in an unofficial policy of plausible deniability.

Churchill began by recruiting from retired SOE agents, SAS and the Commandos, the instructors he needed to make it happen. He brought in retired spies and experts like Bill Fairbairn, who pretty much developed the hand-to-hand combat methods used by Special Forces during World War Two. The first recruits and therefore agents were mostly orphans from the war, for they were in plentiful supply and had no family to miss them, should they suddenly vanish. Children were abducted from several European countries decimated by conflict and far too occupied with survival to notice, or even care. Grexley was stealthily re-instated onto the active-duty roster. The complex was expanded, enhanced, protected by state-of-the-art technology and shrouded in secrecy. And the entire project was assigned mountains of funding from a secret account controlled only by Churchill and his chosen successors. A limitless pot of gold which had literally been taken at gunpoint from the Nazis, liberated by British forces at the P.M.'s command to fight communism after the war. Only a fraction of what was seized was ever declared. Even less was eventually returned to the rightful owners. The spoils of war.

It was wrong. Szabo insiders knew that the whole thing was unspeakable, but they did it anyway. Because they believed sincerely at that point that the enemy was *already* within. War was upon them. It just hadn't been declared yet. These were desperate times. Britain was under attack again, having just come so close to defeat and subjugation. Desperate measures were being employed to meet the emerging threat and in the eyes of all, the ends justified the means.

Due to the very real fear of infiltration and leaks, Churchill and his chosen staff had to start again from scratch, vetting everyone involved in any way, two hundred per cent. A rigorous and thorough screening process ensured that only those very few individuals who absolutely *had* to know of the programme's existence were brought into the fold. This did *not* include the Cabinet or the sitting Prime Minister, excluding Winston. It was essential that he or she could deny any incident or scandal, genuinely believe it was the work of a rogue nation or organisation. The appointments were never political for that reason. The top-secret committee which decided such matters knew that difficult decisions would have to be made. Decisions most politicians would never contemplate. There could be no such weakness this time around.

Dirty tactics were needed for a dirty war.

Presently, Operation Szabo was being commanded by Sir Crispin De Wigt, Permanent Under-Secretary at the Foreign Office, and Sir Charles Munford KCB, the National Security Adviser. The only other persons who were aware of its existence or activities were active or retired agents, or those involved in training, supply, transport, defence etc. All of whom knew the *severe* and relentless consequences should the truth *ever* be divulged.

She would tell you if she could that her recollection of her fourteenth birthday was her happy place. The thought, the memory she was encouraged to find, the haven she defaulted to, in times of direst need.

Whenever she was so utterly miserable that she craved a mental escape from the hazards of her current reality, it was always there to call upon. The one comfort which would never let her down. She had deployed it in action many, many times and it had worked time and again. It was the chief weapon she brought to bear in order to maintain her sanity when all seemed lost. It enhanced her will to survive and preserved her tenuous connection with humanity. At several crucial junctures, when seriously wounded, under torture, awaiting execution, it literally had been her one and only friend. The difference between life and death.

The slight teenager was five weeks into the most gruelling of training programmes. Her mind ached at this point almost as much as her battered and bruised body. She had thought of giving up so many times that she now dismissed the notion in an instant, as nuisance value only, an irritating, buzzing insect circling her constantly which was to be ignored, or swatted into oblivion.

She had achieved only one thing of note to date, as far as she was concerned. She had decided on her name. Erin. She had always loved it. Once knew a care worker called Erin who was somehow not as horrible as the rest. Her paperwork was in the surname of Thompson. This she gave because it was in her view, ordinary and common. Most lists were held or compiled in the format of initials and surname. There were lots of Thompson's in Great Britain. Anyone searching for her would therefore have to trawl through a larger pool of potential aliases. Simple.

Coursework was tough. She was playing catch-up alright. She soon realised how much she had missed in those opening lessons. How much the other students were already ahead of her at the beginning. However, instead of allowing the daunting realisation to consume her with doubt or melancholy, she decided to use it as motivation. As inspiration. She hit the books harder than she ever had, studying every night, often into the small hours of the morning. She concentrated and listened in class, asked questions, researched, hit the library, watched tutorials, sought the assistance of classmates, tutors… Anything she could to close the gap.

Jay Jay was a constant and willing source of help. They shared the disadvantage of their years, as well as several personality characteristics such as extreme willpower, drive and energy. She had been warned not to become too attached to other students but with Jay Jay, that was one battle she knew she was destined to lose.

Erin learnt in that first month or so that, with a whole shit-load of determination and the right application, she could just about compete academically with anyone on the course, despite her youth. Physically however, her frail and growing body was just not up to it. Not yet anyhow.

At the beginning of the fifth week, she attended her third self-defence class. The first two sessions had not gone well but it had not dampened her enthusiasm or confidence. Much to her frustration, she had quite naturally proven to be weak and predictable. She was young and untrained, so what did they expect? Now, it was the turn of the expert instructors. Trained killers. The best of the best. And the first of these was a large, brawny hulk from the Royal Marines.

'Right, listen in!' he bellowed, bringing the group before him to an instant state of attention. His eyes fell immediately on the two younger girls. 'First off, you may as well know that I have been ordered to treat you all *equally*. For the uneducated among you, that means I will not go lightly on you for being small and pathetic, supporting Man United - which is just as inexcusable in my book - or any other affliction or characteristic! Understand? For the real simpletons, I have just warned you that I will *not* pull my punches. So, it follows that if you are hit by me, it is going to bloody well hurt! You are going to *feel* it a little. Or a lot. I suggest therefore, that you try your utmost, *not* to be hit!'

Erin swallowed the lump which had just appeared in her throat.

'Now then, whilst we are on the subject of fighting and being hit, do not go believing all that crap you see in the movies. Or read about in books. No soldier in his right mind *chooses* to enter into a stand-up fight with another human being. Unless they are crazy. Or playing for the cameras. Those of us who intend to complete our mission and return home unharmed, not in a body bag, are seeking a quick and painless kill every time if we can. Painless for *us* I mean, not the enemy.'

Trading blows with anyone is simply affording your opponent an opportunity to land a lucky punch. Hit someone in the right place, no matter how small you are and how large your opponent, and you can bring them down. Though, I warn you, enter into a brawl with the likes of me, or someone of my size, especially if they know what they are doing, and you're likely to need transport to the hospital or the morgue in short order.'

Erin had always been impulsive. In her mind she was a streetfighter. Had to fight back home with the bigger kids and some adults just to survive. In the care homes the bullies said she was fast. She was completely engrossed now and before she knew it, her lips were moving and the thoughts in her head were no longer confined to that safe location.

'I reckon I'd last a while. I'd be too fast for you. I'm not sure I'd have the power to take you down mind.'

The hardened warrior removed his green beret and smirked.

'Is that so? Confidence. I like that. Hold that thought.'

That sounded ominous and her heart rate jumped.

'Class, we are often asked which is the best of the martial arts. Well, forget Karate, Kung-Fu, Judo and the rest. The *best* system is a combination of the finest elements from each. Whatever works for you. That is why you will be instructed by experts in every discipline known to man. Then, you will do what we do. You will choose the teachings from each tutor that suit your style, height, strength, speed... Okay, time for a demonstration. Where's my little Miss Cockiness? Ah, come on then, front and centre,' he said, looking straight at the shaking youngster.

Erin was really wishing she had not spoken now, but moved gingerly to the front. She was scared and a bead of sweat trickled down her forehead. She was also determined to show what she could do, in spite of her trembling hands.

'Let's see what you've got then. No quarter, remember? You need to hit me three times to win. Head shots. Any hit counts. I hit you once though, it's game over. Understand?'

She nodded. Three to one. Sounded reasonable, given his size.

'Begin.'

Erin was immediately up on her toes and dancing around him like a firefly before he had finished the word. Four attempted punches flew past her ears as she dodged, ducked and weaved. Her fellow students cheered each time the instructor missed. She struck him lightly on the nose with her fist, aware only too well that he would hardly feel it. It counted though.

One.

She felt a surge of confidence and shortly afterwards a second blow followed, this time on his jaw.

Two.

She turned swiftly to follow it up and finish the fight. And walked straight into his right cross!

Game over. Endex.

An explosion of pain. She reeled backwards and caught sight of something flying off her body. She bent over and breathed deeply, trying to stop herself from fainting. Blood poured from a wound in her mouth. She placed a hand instinctively up to her swollen lip, pulled it away and saw instantly that it was covered in claret. Her hazy gaze turned towards the direction of the flying object. It was now nestled firmly at Jay Jay's feat. A look of absolute horror overcame her friend as she stared down at it.

Her tooth!

Far from feeling defeated, Erin raged inside and she bolted upright, determined to continue the fight.

'No! As you were! Stand still!' roared the marine. 'One strike, remember? I win. That's enough for you today. Good fight though. Great effort for a beginner. You have real potential and a good heart. Control that anger though and don't be so overconfident. You had me, if you had just measured your blows. Don't lose that speed. The power and accuracy will come in time. Okay, off you go. Go see the dentist. Take that tooth with you. He'll fix you up. See you next lesson. Each instructor has you for as long as needed.'

For some strange reason she did not understand she bowed her head to him, feeling like it was the right thing to do. Then she reported straight to Healthcare.

The complex boasted state-of-the-art facilities, no expense spared, it had fully equipped operating theatres, treatment rooms and a recovery ward with physiotherapy on call. The medical professionals were all leading specialists in their chosen field. They included surgeons, dentists, plastic surgeons, psychologists... Those who were not retained full time could be flown in at a moment's notice. It was a lucrative appointment for the lucky ones chosen; a hefty retainer was paid into their bank accounts yearly to secure their loyalty and silence. A not-so-subtle reminder of the vulnerability of family was also given as an added incentive.

It all served to ensure the shelf-life of the government's most valuable assets, the agents, was extended as far as possible.

Her birthday arrived three days later. The tooth had been re-attached, stitches inserted and the bruising and swelling had reduced somewhat. The day began like any other birthday, without so much as a card or a song. She was not concerned though, for it was the norm and she attended her lesson in *Stirling* classroom without dwelling on it. The secure vault of a room was a top-secret treasure trove of newly developed or modified weapons, devices, contraptions and explosives. The remaining lessons that day included the most widely used poisons, infiltration and extraction methods, human biology and a good hour on the shooting range with the Heckler and Koch MP5 sub-machine gun.

They were dismissed shortly before tea and Erin retired to her room for a quick shower. She had completely forgotten it was her birthday by then. She opened the door and threw her jacket on the bed. It landed next to an unknown package. She looked around, wondering who had been in her room and if this was a distraction technique, designed to fool her whilst a would-be assassin crept up on her from behind. Just to be on the safe side, she swept the entire room, checking all areas. Then she locked the door.

She approached the parcel cautiously, as if it were a bomb. It was exquisitely wrapped in expensive paper and had the cutest little pink bow. She stared at it in awe. A small card was protruding from the top. She reached down to retrieve it and read the writing.

Promises are meant to be kept.
Happy Birthday.
D.

She glanced at the card with tear-laden eyes. He had remembered. Somehow, he had arranged this surprise just for her. She clutched the card to her chest. Nobody had ever made her feel this special. She was overcome with emotion. She couldn't have cared less what was actually inside the wrapping. He had taken the time and effort to let her know she was in his thoughts.

That wonderful, wonderful man!

She carefully removed the bow and placed it into her pocket. Then she did the same with the paper, taking great care and an absolute age. Finally, she opened the cardboard box with extreme care and peered inside.

She pulled out a beautifully ornate, silver box, engraved all the way around with intricate patterns and flowers. And etched in the centre with an inscription.

It is not in our power to anticipate our destiny.

It was delightful. Though, she really had no idea what it was. A piece of writing paper was lying in the bottom of the box. She reached for it, unfolded it and choked back more tears as she read Dunbar's handwritten note.

Hi. Hope things are going well. Wasn't sure what to get you. Not really a shopper. Saw this and went on impulse. Open it.

She wiped away her tears and carefully prized open the top. As she did, a soft melody began to play. She listened for a while in ecstasy and then picked up the note again.

It is, 'I vow to thee my country.' It was one of Winston's favourites. They played it at his funeral. The inscription is his too. I like to think it means you never know how great you can be. What you are capable of. It's a jewellery box. I thought...'

'Yes. Yes, you *did*, didn't you? I love it!' she cried out loud, before quickly finishing the letter. Her tears were in full flow now, making it hard to read.

'...you could use it as you grow. Something to

remember me by and your first birthday with us. I just wanted to let you know that you are no longer alone. Not this time.'

She pressed the letter to her heart and lay backwards on the bed, the music still playing softly. What a feeling! Erin had never known anything like this before. She was giddy, as if she were dancing on air.

Chapter 7 – Present Day

An eerie silence descended on the abandoned estate as Ian tried to make sense of what he had just heard. What the hell did *go on the offensive* mean? Just how far exactly did Kirsten expect him to go? He was a pencil-pusher, for heaven's sake! Not some gun-toting avenger. Sure, in his younger days he had seen plenty of violence, but he was more at home now with budget meetings, paperwork and key performance indicators, rather than the rough stuff. There were plenty of younger staff for that. And the thought of locking horns with criminals the calibre of the Nylander's, really concerned him. There's was an entirely different world altogether compared to his. A dangerous, shadowy world. Though every fibre of his being wanted desperately to help the young agent, knew it was his duty in fact, Ian Townsend was beginning to feel very, very afraid.

He hadn't agreed to become involved on this scale. He was supposed to be a lookout inside the prison, that's all. He knew he could leave at any time, cut her loose and return to his nice, safe day job. To the career he loved and was rewarded handsomely for. She wouldn't be returning to the prison now anyway. That was for certain and she herself had said as much. The smart play surely was to admit his fears, shake her hand, start the engine on his car and get out of there as fast as he could? Run like hell and live to a ripe old age in relative comfort, on the pension he had worked so hard to amass.

He gazed down at his trembling hand.

'Get in,' she said, opening the door to her car.

This was it. Possibly, the defining moment of his life. Decision time.

Yes or no, Ian? In or out?

This was his opportunity to walk. Perhaps, his only chance. Was he content to abandon her though, knowing she was being hunted and had nobody else she knew she could count on? Was he that guy? Would he be able to live with himself afterwards, if he left her?

He couldn't say for certain why, but he exited his own vehicle, locked it and sat down in hers.

'Okay, I'm in. Where are we going?'

'Not yet.'

She reached behind her and retrieved a small holdall from the rear seat, pulled it onto her lap with some difficulty. Unzipped it fully, allowing Ian to catch sight of some of the contents. Inside were several large bundles of different currencies, notes in pounds, euros and dollars, the unmistakable silhouette of two handguns, half a dozen loaded magazines and a wad of identification papers and cards, including passports and driving licenses…

'What's all that for?' he asked, thinking she had all she needed in there to disappear or start a small war.

Kirsten continued rummaging around the bottom of the bag as she replied, searching for a particular item. 'This is my go bag. Have to be ready and able to move at a moment's notice. My life can often depend on it. I'm just looking for… ah, got it!'

She pulled out a small, high-tech, state-of-the-art, super-fast computer and communication device. 'Burner. It operates without a Sim. Untraceable. Pretty handy bit of kit.'

She turned it on, waited thirty seconds and then punched in a sequence of numbers. Ian heard it ring twice, then silence.

'Obsidian 554,' she stated into the device, staring at him. 'Asset requires access to Meridian.'

The person on the end of the line simply replied with one word; 'Hold.'

Ian looked blank. He had no idea what was happening but he had the good sense to remain quiet. A minute later, the voice returned with another abrupt command.

'Send.'

'Search parameters. Nylander, Ryan. My location. Possible associates. Criminal history. Current whereabouts and target acquisition package... Yes, I'll wait.'

She kept the device held to her ear but addressed Ian while she waited for a response. 'Shouldn't take long. They are accessing some of the most sophisticated systems in existence. The algorithms they have created enable them to retrieve vast quantities of data in minutes, seconds even.'

'Oh. *They* are certainly bods you want on the home team. Listen, should you really be telling me this stuff? I'm hardly…'

'They made you my partner when they brought you in,' she interrupted. 'They knew I would need someone to watch my back. Besides, you only know what any enthusiastic schoolboy could read up on. I think we passed your original job description when they tried to have me butchered, don't you? Your fate is linked to mine now. We have to make a plan, decide…'

The voice on the phone sounded once more and Kirsten responded. 'Yes, secure line confirmed. Begin... What time? How many? Good. Strength and calibre? Weapons? Send the schematics through. No. No backup required at this time. Standby for CFA. Asset going dark. Out.'

When she had finished speaking, Kirsten immediately switched off the device and removed the battery.

'CFA?' asked Ian.

'Sorry, we keep transmissions short and sweet if we can. Harder to intercept that way. Call For Assistance. That's you. If needed.'

'I thought you said they couldn't trace it? Why are you turning it off?' asked Ian, pointing to the device.

'Saving the battery. Besides, I'm not certain who I can trust at this stage. I've already divulged our line of enquiry. No need to give them our exact location.'

'But they already know where we're heading?'

'Yes, but not *when*. It's not much I know, but they will expect me to do a thorough recon before infil or assault. Standard practice. They won't expect me to act so soon. If there *is* an issue at our end, that is. I needed the intel so it was a calculated risk.'

'Okay, so what did you learn?'

'Ryan Nylander is a real piece of work, you were right. He spends his days up to all sorts. No set pattern, so it will be hard to pin him down. Most nights though, he can be found at his nightclub; Dreams. He launders a lot of money through it and conducts the majority of his business from there, as well as enjoying the VIP hospitality suite. He's a real ladies' man by all accounts. Can't keep it in his trousers. That's the best way to get to him.'

'How?'

'Simple. I'm going to walk in through the front door as a paying customer. Sometimes you are best hidden in plain sight. Meet me back here at twenty hundred hours. I'll steal another car and you can drive me to the club. Bring a flask. You're COP. That's observation only. Nothing tricky, alright? I'm not sure how long it will take but I need you to warn me if the place gets rowdy all of a sudden. If anyone who looks like trouble shows up. Particularly, if they are mob-handed and looking to fight. You'll know if that happens. I'll bring earpieces so you'll be able to listen to what is happening inside. If it looks like I need help, you can phone for the cavalry. Ring Stan.'

Ian retrieved the card he had been given from his top pocket to check it was still there. 'Yeah, I can do that. Just sit in the car and watch. I think you're mad, but I can do that.'

Ian pulled onto the old industrial estate a little before eight pm. The butterflies in his stomach were merrily conducting a little jig by this time. His bladder control was being severely tested and his throat was incredibly dry. She was already waiting for him in a new five series BMW, having changed the plates of course. She was wearing a wig and sporting coloured contact lenses which somehow transformed her entire face. She looked absolutely stunning as a redhead. Really high class.

He drove her to the nightclub and she slowly exited the vehicle. Handed him his earpiece and donned hers. Then she took off her coat and Ian's breath vacated his body all at once.

'Wow! Just spectacular. Wow!' he exclaimed.

She was a vision of perfection. The dress fit her perfectly, showing off every inch of her delightful curves and though he knew it was ill-mannered, he just couldn't help but stare.

'Thank you. Again. Though, keep your mind on the task at hand, please? I'm relying on you.'

And with that she strode confidently away.

She entered the venue and immediately several heads turned in her direction, as they always did. Kirsten had not always had such a dramatic effect on the opposite sex. She was somewhat of a late developer. However, somewhere around her sixteenth birthday, she began to become aware of how men would stare at her, look her up and down whilst trying not to be noticed. How they would behave differently in her presence. How the most obvious would make fools of themselves or drool. Nowadays, it was no exaggeration to say they were putty in her hands. Most of them anyway.

She headed for the bar and ordered a drink. A large scotch, single malt. Neat. She sipped it slowly and took in the view.

The club was only half full but several people were already on the dancefloor having a good time. A few groups of partygoers were already drunk, even at this early hour, and very loud. Somewhere off to her right a glass smashed, followed by the obligatory, 'Waahaayy!!'

Moments later, a young man in a dishevelled state was carted off by the bouncers in arm locks. An early end to his evening. Probably a good thing, before things became messy.

Over the next hour or so, numerous men approached her and asked if they could buy her a drink. Par for the course. Some tried awkwardly to engage her in conversation despite her clear reluctance, and failed. She was polite but firm and she knocked them all back as she tried to hook the big fish. Ian sniggered each time as he listened in.

Those fools. Those poor misguided fools.

Behind the glass of the upstairs VIP area, she spied several men in suits pointing her out. She turned her gaze on them deliberately and flashed them a smile. A little over two minutes later, the bartender took an internal phone call. He placed the receiver down and approached her.

'Excuse me, Miss?' He smiled and gestured towards the upper level. 'I've been asked by Mr. Nylander to invite you into the VIP room?'

Kirsten casually sipped her drink. 'No, not tonight. I think I'm okay, thanks.'

The barman appeared nervous all of a sudden. 'I can't tell him that. It doesn't do to refuse a man like him, take it from me. It was not an invitation. It never is.'

'Oh. Well, in that case, I'd be delighted.'

She picked up her drink and walked slowly up the stairs. At the top, two huge muscular bouncers grinned, undressing her with their eyes before opening the glass door.

The room contained maybe eight small tables, surrounded by soft leather seats. Four of the tables were empty but at the others, several groups of men were being entertained by scantily-clad women. Clearly hostesses of some sort. Prostitutes maybe. A short but powerfully built man introduced himself as Jimmy. He said he was Mr. Nylander's associate and escorted her to his table. As they arrived, the two ladies sitting next to him were told to leave, much to their annoyance.

'You are a hard man to say no to, I hear?' began Kirsten.

'So I've been told,' replied Nylander, smugly. 'I'm Ryan. And you are?'

'Thirsty.'

She downed the rest of her drink in a seductive manner and placed the glass down. Nylander raised his arm and the barman brought over a bottle of Louis Roederer Cristal Champagne, with two glasses.

'Please?' he said, indicating that she should take the seat next to him.

Kirsten was perfectly calm. She sat down slowly. This placed the others in the room at ease and they all moved away in order to afford their leader some privacy, as had happened a thousand times before. Nylander reached forward to open the champagne. He poured two glasses, placed one in front of her and sat back.

Kirsten glanced around her and performed a rapid risk assessment. Time to act.

'If you want to live, you will do *exactly* as I say!' she hissed, menacingly. 'Look down, slowly.'

He did as he was ordered. Kirsten moved in closer and placed her arm around him. Pushed forcefully into his waist was a suppressed Glock 26 pistol.

'I need you to remain perfectly calm. Just smile and relax. Pretend we are hitting it off and I'm a sure thing. In some ways, I am. I assure you, at this point I only want to talk, but I will kill you if I have to. That is no idle threat. Say yes, if you understand.'

'Yes. Who are you? And how do you seriously expect to leave here alive, after this?!'

Kirsten smiled slightly. 'Unless you have a death wish, Mr. Nylander, you will hear me out. Then, I'll take my chances. But you are focussing on the wrong subject. You should be more concerned about yourself. Your odds of surviving this encounter depend entirely on what you say next. Or don't. There are several ways this can play out. Know this though, before you go making any rash decisions; the first to die in a shootout here, will be you. And I promise I will take several of your second-rate men out before they can even draw their weapons.'

'So, *talk* already!' Nylander whispered, angrily.

'Okay, but first, laugh for me and take a sip of champagne. Make like you're enjoying my company. Men usually do.'

Nylander clearly had unrealised acting potential. The remainder of the room showed no signs of being aware that their boss was currently enduring the worst night of his life.

In her own time, Kirsten continued. 'Your brother, Tommy.'

'Yeah? He's banged up. What about him?'

'He tried to have someone killed today. I have it on good authority that it was on your orders.'

'I...'

He was about to voice a denial, an objection, but the gun was being pushed so far in to his ribs now that it made him stop and think better of it.

'Was that you?! Damn, girl! That was some killer shit you pulled. Glad they weren't my men you humiliated.'

'So, you don't deny it?'

'Why should I? Look, I'll kill you if I ever see your face again, but today? That was a *paid* job, that's all. It's nothing personal. You know the score. It's no secret I will die for anyway. Some whack job from London, big suit and tie type, posh accent an' all, he left very clear and precise instructions how it was to go down. And fifty large.'

'Pardon? You were paid fifty thousand to off me?'

'Yeah. Only, there were strict conditions. We had to use another crew. That much he made clear. We weren't too keen on that but there was no wiggle room. They got fifty too. So, a tonne, all in all. What did you do to put such a price on your head, eh?'

'You never asked him?'

'Wasn't really interested, until now. Money talks. Okay, I've played your game, now...'

'Enough!' she hissed, pushing the gun even harder into his side. 'Tell me more about the man who paid you!'

'I'm no snitch.'

She moved the gun down to his groin. 'If you ever want to have children, I would reconsider your answer.'

He shifted nervously in his seat, weighing up whether she had the audacity and courage to fire. He remembered the reports he had received; how easily she had fought off five burly assailants in prison. This was no ordinary girl he was dealing with. This was a trained professional of some description.

'Okay, okay! Blonde hair he had. Broken tooth up front. Kind of stood out. That's all I have, I swear. He paid in cash. You survived the attack somehow, but he hasn't asked for the money back. Not a single penny of it. That's odd, no?'

'Yes. *Very* odd. I'll tell you what's even *more* odd though; *You*, believing you can try to kill me, threaten me again in this club, and think that I will still let you live. You're a dreamer, Mr. Nylander. You just *made* it personal.'

Nylander's face instantly reflected the terror he felt as he looked into her eyes. All he saw was immediate confirmation that he was dealing with a tough and determined, experience murderer. It dawned on him like a haymaker and he could not help but flinch slightly.

It was an involuntary reaction. Hardly perceptible to any ordinary, untrained eye. But to Kirsten's heightened senses, it appeared as though he could possibly be making for his gun. The Glock in her expert hand moved immediately to his heart. A fraction of a second later, a one hundred and fifteen grain jacket, hollow-point bullet tore a hole straight through his chest.

If you seek peace, prepare for war.

Chapter 8 - Training

The training regime on Herik was full on. It was long and arduous by design, intended to weed out the weak and identify the strong, of mind and body. Only the toughest recruits would pass the course and by doing so, each would demonstrate the proven reserves of stamina, courage and conviction necessary to complete future assignments. The trainees therefore undertook schedules which would break most human beings. Each week was rammed with coursework, arduous exercise, demonstrations, punishing tests, gruelling endurance marches and lectures from guest speakers. Days off were rare. But then, what was there to do anyway for young people on a miserable, windswept island in the North Atlantic?

The swimming pool, firing range and gym were some of the few leisure activities available for recruits in their downtime. But these were used extensively on the course and mostly packed with students undergoing lessons. The solitary pub, if you could call it that, was the one place they could relax with a drink in a social setting. Though, no matter how hard they tried, the conversation always seemed to revert to work-related topics, seeing as it was the only thing most of them had in common. So, for Erin and many others, a good read, the peaceful seclusion of a long walk or run around the island, or a challenging climb in the steep mountains, was their only escape from the relentless pressure.

And it was unyielding. Cranked up a notch every single week. Not surprisingly, it soon began to take its toll.

By the third year of Erin's intake, just twelve of

the original twenty recruits remained. Twelve of the fittest, toughest, most resilient young adults in Britain. Of those who had fallen by the wayside having failed the stringent standards, quit or left in disgrace, nothing was ever heard of them again. Nothing. Not a single letter, phone call, text or postcard. It was a taboo subject which was never raised in conversation.

That was not to say that the trainees did not ever leave the island. Introduced into the curriculum in year two were a series of practical examinations in the community, conducted under simulated and also authentic, stressful conditions. These methodically planned tests of endurance, courage, intellect, adaptability, skill and tenacity were thrust upon the unsuspecting recruits without warning. They began one Tuesday morning when Mr. Black, the espionage tutor, halted his class and stared out of the window into a burgeoning blizzard, at the mountains in the distance. Eventually he addressed the class, though he did not avert his gaze for a second.

'We have worked you hard for a year now. Time for some fun-filled exercise. All of you, leave your things and report directly to Stores, right now. Draw winter gear for climbing. That small rise you see ahead of you,' he stated, pointing to the nearest mountain, 'is called McGregor's seat. Don't ask me why. You won't like the answer. Somewhere on that slope is a red flag. You are all to find it, touch it, and return here. The last to do so will have failed this course. Unless, by some miracle, the *entire* class complete this task in under three hours.'

That was three hours of sheer hell right there. Fighting the students as they raced for kit, the elements, the slippery conditions, and the freezing cold.

Clambering over jagged rock formations at full speed, ignoring the cuts and bruises as she fell, her aching muscles. Fighting desperately for oxygen, the burning agony in her lungs… But, to her surprise and amusement, even as she pushed herself to the point of absolute exhaustion, close to collapse, Erin discovered to her delight that she was having the time of her life. She absolutely loved the whole experience, felt exhilarated, euphoric, free.

Everything about her was growing and blossoming now; her physical attributes, her mental endurance and resolve, her fortitude… Although, to her intense fury she limped home two places behind Jay Jay, her ninth-place finish was a very credible performance for one so young. And she knew it.

From that moment on, she began to eagerly await the next practical with excited anticipation. They soon became the best elements of the entire course for her. A chance to prove herself. To test how far she had developed. To compete against the rest and close the gap to the top. She relished the break in routine, the dangers, the excitement of the unknown, the challenge. They gave added purpose to her existence and focal points she could use for motivation.

The tasks they were set grew more and more complicated, more intense, as the years passed by. Mountain climbs became so easy they were soon considered by most to be routine, boring even. So, the instructors raised their game. Soon, they were being dropped into Catterick Garrison in Yorkshire for a weekend of Basic Training with the Royal Regiment of Ghurkhas. These fearsome warriors were absolute gentlemen to Erin whilst she was there and she grew to both love and respect them all. Their fearless attitude to soldiering and complete loyalty, their obvious sense of honour, warmed her heart. That weekend, meant to be physically and mentally draining, would become one of her most treasured memories.

She was sixteen when her and Jay Jay were set loose in the middle of London for forty-eight hours. They had no identification on them, no phones, money, maps, or food. Just a list of eight objects they had to acquire from various locations around the city, without being discovered, before reporting to an unregistered safe-house. The objects included a button from a tunic worn by any of the Guards regiments, a photo from inside the Tower of London, with extra credit if it was of The Crown Jewels, any artefact from the China exhibition in the British Museum, any item from Churchill's War Rooms, and any dinosaur bone from the Natural History Museum. The two intrepid teens were the only recruits to achieve all that was asked of them and they eventually strode confidently through the doors of the safe-house with thirty-five minutes to spare. They were exhausted, ravenous and thoroughly expecting to be arrested at any moment. They were not.

Another of Erin's favourite exercises was the short-duration, high-intensity parachute course with the Red Devils; the Parachute Regiment display team. Though, a close second was the week they spent learning to ride motorbikes with the White Helmets; the Royal Signals' expert riders.

Weeks became months. Months became years. The two friends grew alongside each other in size, strength and beauty, as if it were another competition. They were both high class students and nearing the end of their training. They had used their friendly rivalry for inspiration. Erin had begun at last to match Jay Jay in every aspect. Though she was younger, she became determined to overtake her friend and be the best.

One morning when she had not long turned eighteen, Mr. Red, Political Science tutor, instructed them to change into smart but comfortable civilian attire. Once they had, they were to report to the helicopter pad.

'What, all of us?' Erin asked, looking around the class at the five remaining students.

'No. Just you two,' replied Mr. Red. 'The others have different assignments.'

Around thirty minutes later, the two girls boarded the chopper and donned headphones so they could hear the briefing they were about to receive.

'Your papers are beside you. Driving license, utility bill, purse, phone and money too. And a crucifix. You are both English students at Bristol University. Catholics. You are eighteen and from Bristol itself. Best friends. Erin, your name is Sophie Jones. Jay Jay, you are Michelle Davies. You will be dropped somewhere in Northern Ireland. We want you to make your way to the Falls Road area of Belfast.'

Erin's heart skipped a beat. She knew from her history classes that the troubles had ended in 1998 after years of bloodshed. Northern Ireland was therefore far more peaceful now than it had been until recently. Still, there would be no love lost for the English in that part of the city, which boasted a fiercely proud catholic community that harboured many grudges, and plenty of current and former members of republican paramilitary organisations. She looked over at Jay Jay who was obviously having similar concerns.

We'll be lynched.

'You are to go to a pub called, The Black Swan. We are combining training with intel-gathering on this one. Concerns have been raised that it is a meeting point for terrorists intent on breaking the ceasefire, and undermining the peace process. I don't need to tell you of the potential misery that might cause. We want to know who goes there; names, pictures, any information you can gather. Now, at ten-thirty precisely, you are to start a fight with the locals. You will win that engagement and exfil by any means. Then, you will make your way to the British mainland, where you will report to any British Army base, ask for the guard commander and give him the password; Marauder. All bases will have been briefed and warned to expect you. However, be on your guard just in case. They will place you in a cell whilst they check out your story. They will be told nothing. And they have been ordered not to engage you in conversation in any way. We will collect you when able. Questions?'

Erin looked at Jay Jay again. This seriously ratcheted up the risk levels. This wasn't *training*. It was a sink or swim mission. Do or die. False identities and no local pickup? They would be lucky to survive, be disavowed if caught, probably killed as spies. The British government couldn't afford such a scandal on its own doorstep. The newsreel image they were shown of the two soldiers caught at an IRA funeral and dragged from their car, killed by the mob, ran through her mind. They would probably be tortured for information, subjected to horrendous treatment, exposed online...

And the instruction to fight?! That was just ludicrous. It made them cannon fodder. It wasn't essential to the success of this mission. They were playing games with her!

'Just one question,' she said, accepting her fate was in her own hands. 'Rules of Engagement?'

Mr. Red shook his head slightly. 'Yeah. Hard bastards, the Irish. Tough as nails. Non-lethal force only, I am instructed to tell you. We are no longer at war. Just gather the intelligence, have a little fun, and scarper! Understand?'

At eight-thirty pm two pretty, young English students walked through the doors of The Black Swan. As soon as they did, all conversation stopped and every set of eyes in the place bore down upon them. The cars passing by on the road outside suddenly sounded like tanks, it was so quiet in there. The tension was so thick for a minute or so, it was palpable. They ignored the blatant and hostile stares and approached the bar.

'Hi,' said Erin.

The barman eyed them slowly up and down as he continued wiping a glass with his towel. Erin was wearing a peroxide blonde wig which made her look a little like Marilyn Monroe. She was pleasantly surprised to find that she was not at all nervous. She had expected to be. But she felt supremely confident of her abilities. Trusted in the training they had been given.

When the bartender eventually spoke, it was with a slow, measured tone and a thick accent.

'Ay, 'bout ye?'

'Fine, thanks. Err… half a lager for me and a Bacardi and coke for my friend, please?'

He moved slowly to fetch the drinks and a few conversations started up again. Most the regulars however, continued to stare and listen in to the encounter.

He hadn't even returned with their drinks before a young man in his early twenties appeared at their side, standing unnaturally close. Erin could smell the stale tobacco and beer on his breath.

'I'll get these, Paddy. What's the craic? I'm Tommy Coyle. What are yous two up to then?'

He had blurted out his name as if it was supposed to mean something and carried some weight in these parts.

'I'm sorry?' asked Erin. 'We're just here for a good night. A few days sightseeing, you know? I'm Sophie and this is Michelle. We're on a break from Uni. Heard Belfast was the place to be?'

Tommy and a few of the others scoffed at that. 'Aye, twenty years ago maybe. Yous have had a different welcome then, so you would. What…?'

'Houl yer whist!'

A strong, commanding voice exuding extreme authority stopped the youngster from finishing his sentence. They turned sharply to see an older man in his mid to late forties approaching. He was easily six feet five. A large scar sat menacingly over his left eye.

'Now don't you go frightening these wee young 'uns with your bluster, ye buck eejit! Off with yous. Them times have gone. Come, sit with us ladies?'

He gestured to a table around which six men of similar age were gathered, staring. Two stools were pushed out invitingly.

'That's most kind, thank you,' Jay Jay replied, smiling politely.

They left the younger man at the bar, humiliated and angry. He had clearly been ordered to stand down by a superior. The discipline was there for all to see.

They were introduced to the others and memorised every name, every detail of the conversation in the next two hours, every face, birthmark, scar… As the drinks flowed, a few lips loosened a little and it became obvious that the group had been active during the troubles. Probably still were. The girls casually asked about Tommy and his friends and were informed that he was related to convicted prisoners and some who were considered martyrs. He was himself thought of as extremely dangerous because he was a loose cannon with several axes to grind. But also someone the disaffected youth had migrated to in recent times. He romanticised the troubles even though he wasn't there and had played no part. Part of a new generation which saw advantages to being associated with the IRA.

At ten-thirty exactly Erin stood up as if to go to the toilet. Jay Jay was now on high alert as her partner walked towards Tommy and his friends. He rose as she approached, intending to stop her. But Erin punched him hard on the nose without warning, before he had the chance to speak, catching him completely by surprise. His head jerked backwards and a spray of claret covered his motionless and shocked friends. They stood up quickly, hesitating for a split second due to unexpected events and possibly because their leader had just had his nose broken by a girl.

Big mistake.

Erin took full advantage. She kicked the stool into the nearest man and upturned the table violently, sending glasses and bottles flying in all directions. And whilst the shell-shocked group were trying to shield themselves from flying debris, she put years of martial arts training to good use.

Jay Jay too launched into a furious frenzy of action. She grabbed the drinks tray from the table and took out two guys with it, ramming it into their throats in quick succession before throwing it into the face of a third. She followed this up by rendering him unconscious with a front kick as he lunged at her.

Before long, most of the regulars had exited the pub in panic to form a crowd outside out of harm's way and only the fighters remained. Many of those were upon the floor and able to play no more part in proceedings. Erin and Jay Jay now occupied the centre of the room, standing back-to-back, easily fending off anyone brave enough to close within striking distance. The whole place was a complete mess. Injured and unconscious locals lay everywhere amongst the spilt beer, smashed glass and bottles.

Erin caught sight of something black in the barman's hand with her peripheral vision. She reached down and drew the knife from her ankle strap, threw it immediately, then watched with satisfaction as the bartender dropped his pistol, the pointed blade embedded painfully in his forearm.

'Time to go,' she stated, coolly. 'After you?'

Jay Jay moved quickly for the exit and was delighted to find nobody trying to bar their way. The small crowd waiting outside began to jeer as they emerged unscathed but their stolen car was only yards away and they had disappeared before the expected local reinforcements arrived. By the time the police showed up, they were long gone.

The Garda were at a loss to explain what had happened. There were numerous eye witness reports of two unknown British teenage girls ransacking the hardest pub in Belfast. Taking out two well-known gangs. It was laughable. Though there was indeed evidence of an almighty fight, the Garda believed they were being misled. The incident couldn't have happened as the regulars had told it. Surely it didn't go down like that? It was more likely to be another instance of infighting amongst the catholic paramilitary groups. One faction trying to assert its dominance over the rest.

The young Szabo recruits spent the next two days on the run, avoiding detection and capture as their training had taught them. They acquired three different vehicles and stayed off the main roads, running two unofficial roadblocks without firing a shot. They slept in the cars and stole what they needed to survive. On the third day, they entered the village of Cushundun and commandeered a small fishing vessel. The crew were held at knife and gun point and forced to sail to Scotland. They were warned to remain silent and released. Another car was acquired and they finally reported to an army base just north of Kilmarnock. They were asked several questions by the soldiers in command but gave only one word to the ranking officer: Marauder.

They were held in the cells overnight and at nine-thirty the following morning, a familiar face greeted them as the door opened.

'Morning,' said Dunbar, as if he were out for a stroll and just happened to be in the vicinity. 'Don't talk, just listen. Don't say a word until we are out of here. Quite a show you two put on. Caused a bit of commotion over the channel, I can tell you. Good effort.'

He grinned like a Cheshire cat; immense pride evident in his eyes. 'Let's get you two out of here.'

He ushered them out of the guardhouse without a

word and showed them into his waiting car.

'Home, and debrief.'

Chapter 9 – Present Day

As she walked up the stairs heading for the VIP area of Dreams nightclub, Kirsten's highly trained eyes had already spotted the unnatural bulges in the jackets of the two bouncers guarding the entrance. Was this usual attire for an inner-city venue these days, or were they expecting trouble? She was permanently on a high state of alert which came with the territory, but the presence of lethal weapons in a civilian setting such as this, in Great Britain, that spelt trouble with a capital 'T.' Mentally, she had instantly upgraded herself to a war footing before they even opened the door.

As she was shown to Mr. Nylander's table she conducted a quick visual recce and counted only four or five guys who looked as though they were also carrying. After surviving so long as a top agent, completing so many successful missions and having undergone such rigorous training, detecting the players in the deadly game was the easy part. Simple. Second nature. Stopping them could often prove more problematic though, depending mostly upon the two unknown variables of quantity of combatants and reserves, and quality of opposition.

Adding her escort, Jimmy, into the mix, that gave her an estimated enemy force still standing of eight. The Glock 26 she held in her hand boasted a ten-round magazine, though it was now minus the one bullet she had spent sending Ryan Nylander to oblivion. The remainder of the VIP guests in the vicinity she calculated would either panic and rush for the exit, or freeze out of fear and the basic human instinct of self-preservation. People often believed when involved in a violent incident for some reason that an attacker would not shoot if they did not move. If they remained perfectly still. Seemed like an enormous gamble to Kirsten. One she would never make. Still, their life; their choice.

At the very least, it lessened the hostile targets if they made like statues, and the confusion. It was about to kick off big style either way. It would be quick and it would be chaotic. No avoiding that. Too many variables for it to be cut and dried. But then, the ability to react swiftly and adapt to ever-changing scenarios had always been one of her strengths.

Let the dice roll. She would just have to make every shot count.

Nylander's lifeless corpse had only just begun to fall when Kirsten selected her primary target. The boy Jimmy was wired. Like a squaddie on patrol, just waiting for contact. Eager to prove his mettle. All muscles, sinew and brawn, keen to please and fiercely loyal. She knew the type. Could see it in the way he carried himself. She'd dealt with his sort a thousand times and dropped most of them.

And, just as predicted, he was the first to react.

He was also the closest. He reached for his weapon with rapid reactions but still he was too slow. *Way* too slow for an agent of Kirsten's calibre. A round from her pistol hit him squarely between the eyes before his hand fingered metal, ending his life before it had really started.

Sometimes, you can be *too* eager. Flag yourself as a major player. A threat.

Huh! Not so wired after all. Life choices.

A quick glance to the entrance told her that the two bouncers had failed to enter the room before the first of the panicked guests and hostesses rushed to leave.

Amateurs!

That gave her a little extra time. All the clubbers below were now scrambling for the exits, screaming and shouting in fear. The scene was one of pure bedlam. The two large bruisers had drawn their weapons but their pathway was blocked by several panicked revellers and they could not bring them to bear. This rendered the five potential combatants in the room the immediate threat. Those holding their ground. The trick would be to take them out before the two at the doorway entered the fight, or were presented with an opportunity to engage her with a clear field of fire.

Her astonishing speed was once again her saviour.

The first two henchmen were easy to dispatch. They were the nearest to her still breathing and both were struck high in their centre mass within seconds. They fell awkwardly onto tables adorned with glasses and bottles and the dead weights easily smashed through the lot.

Number three had his weapon drawn by now. An Uzi nine millimetre. Weapon of choice for many in the criminal fraternity because it was small, compact and gave a lot of suppressing firepower at short distance. However, to her amusement and surprise, the hired henchman appeared to be clumsy and awkward with it. Not skilled at all, as expected. His movements were unnatural and he was thinking too much. Clearly, he had spent no time at all on the range.

You get what you pay for.

Kirsten found herself chuckling inside at the absurd scene. Never one to miss an opportunity, she darted to the left and fired though, straight into his stomach, denying the pathetic wretch the hope of a lucky kill. He began to fall but did not release his weapon. His finger tightened around the trigger and the sub-machine gun emptied its magazine into the floor. She finished him off with another round to the face.

A sudden rush of air passed her cheek and the unmistakeable sound of a bullet striking brickwork informed her in no uncertain terms that she had just escaped death again, by the smallest of margins. How arbitrary this game of life and death she played was. A slight adjustment here or there and the mystery shooter would have made himself a hero.

Too bad. He had missed and she instinctively calculated the trajectory and probable direction of his round.

Her eyes locked onto a lean man in his early thirties. Another who oozed military bearing. Knew what he was doing. A second bullet was therefore probably already on its way and she threw herself violently into the open area ahead of her, presenting a swift moving target which was difficult to hit. She rolled quickly and heard another shot miss. Exited the evasive manoeuvre as fast as she could and pulled her trigger, the very instant her gun felt like it was on target, relying on pure instinct this time.

The athletic-looking gunman reeled backwards in shock. He dropped his weapon and clutched at the gaping hole where his windpipe had been. However, his frantic efforts to stem the blood loss were in vain and he bled out within minutes.

The final mobster was just a boy really, not yet in his twenties. Experience had taught Kirsten however that these youngsters with something to prove were often the most fanatical in a fight, and therefore dangerous. History lessons in training on the SS Hitlerjugend came to mind; how tough the allies found them in battle, how hard they fought for every inch of ground. This youth had his weapon drawn and pointed directly at her. She was in his sights and if he had any skill at all, he had a clear shot before she could respond, though he was on the other side of the room and she was dancing from side to side to make things difficult for him.

He pulled the trigger and nothing happened. Tried again and again. He had committed the cardinal sins; rushed and panicked. He was out of his league in this tussle and his confidence was draining fast, having already watched his more experienced comrades die. Never an easy thing to do at any age. It dawned on him now that he was about to join them. She saw it in his eyes. The fear and sense of immediate doom. The desperation.

'That's a Beretta 92 you're carrying. It has a manual safety. You have to disengage it to fire. But then, you probably knew that and just forgot? Well, you made your bed. Maybe I would have spared you, if you hadn't tried so hard.'

At that range, she couldn't miss. She felt no pity, no remorse. No forgiveness. Not from this girl. In the moment, she did not think at all. At the wrong time, thinking could get you killed. No, she acted and reacted. She executed a plan. She got the job done.

Right between the eyes again. Cold and efficient. She favoured that shot because she was good enough to pull it off. Not many were. And it always neutralised the target in a split second. No chance of return fire. Minimal risk.

Two bullets remaining.

She scanned the area but there were no more targets to be engaged, just a few frightened civilians cowering under tables and behind chairs, snivelling, praying, throwing up.

The bouncers at the entrance had fled, along with the panicked VIP's and nightclub workers. So much for the muscles. They had presumably thought better of entering into a firefight with such a proficient killer. Brawn don't mean a thing when you're facing a Glock.

She raced to the bar area and looked for the rear service entrance which had been displayed on the building plans she had been forwarded on her device. It led down a flight of stairs to an emergency exit. She moved swiftly, anxious to leave before the police or any more gunmen showed up.

She crashed through the doors and out into the night. The car park was almost full now. She could hear the screams and shouts of those fleeing the club by the front entrance. She quickly located the five series. Ian had the engine running and his phone was pressed firmly to his ear. His lips were moving rapidly and he appeared animated, his arms flailing around unnaturally.

He's phoning for help, she realised.

She threaded her way through the parked cars as quickly as she could. At every given moment however, she scanned elevated locations, looking for snipers. It was instinct, training, due diligence. But it was also more than that; a nagging feeling she could not shake that she was being watched. Targeted. That she was *already* in somebody's crosshairs.

Half way to Ian and the relative safety of the car, she spotted a shadow move on the roof of a nearby third storey building. She hated being right at times like these.

Just once she would like an easy day. Or night.

She immediately grabbed a passing woman to her left, as if to give comfort to the distraught girl, but really hoping the human shield she presented would limit her exposure and deter the gunman.

Within moments however, a searing pain coursed through her left arm and the girl she was holding fell to the ground, shot through the chest, the through and through having sliced open Kirsten's flesh also on the way out.

She had only her Glock pistol and two rounds with which to return fire. It was pointless at that range, but she fired her last two bullets anyway, hoping to unnerve the shooter for a moment as she made a run for it.

Years of gym time enabled her to accelerate like an Olympic sprinter. She covered the distance in no time and was grateful that Ian, seeing her dash, had already opened the passenger door. Bullets smacked into the tarmac, sending sharp fragments flying up into legs.

'Drive!' she barked, even as she was still in mid-air.

More rounds hit the bodywork and windscreen as they sped away from the scene at high speed, the onlookers parting hastily for them in order to avoid being mowed down.

Ian was white now. He genuinely looked like Casper and she would have laughed if the circumstances were different. His expression was an accurate depiction of disgust and shock. He was also shaking uncontrollably.

'What the fuck?! You… you've been shot!' he yelled, a thousand thoughts he was attempting to convey suddenly interrupted by genuine concern for her welfare. 'I heard all those gunshots and screaming. I thought… I didn't know what…'

Kirsten patted his arm gently with her blood-soaked hand. 'Calm down, Ian. It's only a flesh wound. That girl took the full force of it. They missed the bone, and anything important. I'll be fine.'

She was completely unruffled. Her breath had somehow already returned to normal and she actually looked as if she had enjoyed scaring him to death. Her arm was caked in blood, which had also splattered her from head to toe, so Ian was only too aware of how close she had come to being killed. He felt awful that the young clubber had not been so lucky.

'You say it like it was nothing. That girl was innocent! All she wanted was a good night with her friends. That was somebody's daughter, you know. And now she's dead. Do you not feel anything?'

She looked deadly serious all of a sudden. 'Yes, of course I do. I'm glad it wasn't me.'

He shook his head in revulsion and disbelief. She was a different breed altogether this girl.

'What happened in there? I didn't sign up for this! What were all those shots? You killed Ryan, didn't you? Why? You were supposed to be after information. Dead men don't talk. Did he have to die? I heard that one, but what about the rest of them?'

She answered flatly, as if she were choosing which filling she wanted on her sandwich. 'Same. All dead. Those who stood and fought anyway. As usual. That's the game, Ian. I had to send out a message. Let whoever it is behind all of this know who they are dealing with. The deed is done and word will spread pretty fast now. It won't be so easy for them to hire local goons in future. The risk level has just sky rocketed. They will have to hire a pro now. Pro's cost serious money. And within their circles, they talk. Everyone knows everyone in this business. Believe me; this benefits us.'

Ian shook his head again in disbelief. 'Oh my God! What have I gotten myself involved in? I'm not cut out for this. I'm a prison governor. If they...'

Kirsten grimaced a little as she interrupted him.

He might as well know the truth.

'Wise up, Ian! Switch on, for fuck's sake. You can't just pick up where you left off. Not after all this. You've been associated with me now. There would be an investigation or an enquiry if you returned and they would find evidence of your complicity. A traffic camera or mobile footage. CCTV from the prison. Records of our meetings. Witness statements. That's how things go. Face it, that career has gone. It's over. They know who you are. You've already become a legitimate target, just like me. Your face will have been circulated to every corner of the country by morning. They don't know how much you've been told, so you are a loose end to them that needs tying off. A potential threat. And they won't want anything left to chance, anything which could expose them. That sniper wasn't part of any local gang. They were set up like a pro. No, this was planned. It was a trap. They despatched an assassin to take me out. No doubt you were the secondary. I'm sorry to tell you this but they would have targeted you next.'

Whatever faint traces of colour were left in his cheeks vanished. 'Oh shit! Well, that's just great. What am I supposed to do now?'

'You… We, have only one choice; we have to

finish this. Find those responsible, the decision-makers at the top, and bring them down. Lock, stock and smoking barrel. It's the only way. Maybe, when the dust settles, someone with power and influence can intervene on your behalf, I don't know. But the life you knew has gone.'

A minute or so of silent contemplation followed. No matter how hard he tried, he could see no way out of his current plight. If they were able to target a trained agent inside a prison, they would think nothing of finding him, wherever he was, and taking him out. His best and only chance as far as he could reason, was to hang on to Kirsten's coat tails for all he was worth and hope for the best.

Eventually, once he had calmed down a little, he said, 'So, who was that shooter, the one on the roof?'

'I do not know. Could be anyone. But I think there is something I should tell you. I knew what was coming.'

'I'm sorry? Knew? Knew what was coming, the sniper?'

'Yes. *And* the attack at the prison.'

'Seriously? How?' he asked, bemused.

'You were right all along. You should trust your instincts more and not be so trusting. I could have been placed in a quieter profession as you said, hidden away in some office backwater, but then…'

Ian looked over at her as the penny dropped. He was dumbfounded. 'Are you saying that you *wanted* to be found? That's crazy. Why?'

She took a deep breath. Let it out and looked at him like a woman about to divulge she had been unfaithful.

'Keep your eyes on the road and listen to me. We

have lost six agents recently to targeted assassinations. All killed by an unknown professional. We have enough evidence to suggest it is the work of one individual, but no idea who they are working for, their true objective or motivation. I was inserted with you at the prison as bait. It was thought that if I proved hard enough to kill, I could lure the assassin out of hiding.'

'Bait? You used me, and us, put us in harm's way to entice this mayhem?!' he roared in fury.

'Yeah. Sounds pretty cold when you put it like that.'

She was always annoyingly calm, no matter what he said or did.

'Well, you certainly seem to have achieved your goal. Congratulations. You're out of the closet now and no mistake. We both are. I suppose I ought to be grateful nobody was… Just a moment, when you were in trouble back there, I rang the number given to me, as instructed. I asked for Stan as I was told to do.'

Kirsten remained quiet. She knew what was coming.

'Only, I tried my utmost to explain how urgent it was, but I was met with complete silence. Nothing. They were there alright, I know they were there, but they just flatly refused to help us. What does it mean?'

She rolled her neck and stretched her muscles. 'It means that, as suspected, we have trouble inside the wire. Big trouble. The kind that gets you dead real quick. Strap in, because we are on our own.'

Chapter 10 - Training

She was nineteen now with the kind of looks and figure that usually adorned the cover of a high-class glossy magazine. Stronger, healthier, fitter, quicker and tougher than she had ever been. Years of strength conditioning and continual physical exercise, resilience training, punishing trials and mock assignments had combined to produce one of the finest recruits the instructors of Operation Szabo had ever fashioned. She was ruthless, determined, resourceful, relentless, strong-minded, robust, formidable and fearless… Every perfect inch the model agent. The ultimate assassin.

However, one final hurdle now lay in the path of the remaining recruits before they could be considered operational. The most daunting examination they would ever face. And the pressure was on. All were expected to pass this last trial having performed so valiantly to date. Despite the fact that they were now about to throw themselves head-first into a whole new world of hurt. Face a test very, very few were brave enough to undertake; Special Air Service Regiment, Escape and Evasion training.

It was a minor part of what SAS applicants had to endure to win the coveted beige beret, that was true. But it was designed *specifically* to weed out all but the very best troops. To sort the wheat from the chaff.

Many of the tutors at Herik were ex-regiment and rightly proud of their service. Badged members of an elite club. Agents often collaborated with Special Forces on missions. Members of the two units therefore shared a common bond strengthened by the knowledge that they both operated in a world of complete secrecy, at a level unparalleled elsewhere. SAS candidates were warned at the very beginning of selection to expect fleeting visits from newcomers to the course. Unknown attendees who would arrive without warning, stay briefly to undertake elements of the training and vanish just as swiftly as they came. They were instructed not to speak to these strangers or question their origins for their enquiries would be reported and constitute a breach of the rules. And whilst they participated in each gruelling phase of selection, the anonymous 'guests' were afforded the exact same treatment as any other volunteer, without favour or allowance.

Army four-tonners were not built for comfort. She was being thrown around in the back of one now like a rag doll, barely managing to cling onto the side rail in order to stay upright, just like everyone else. She had bounced so hard and so often on that plank of wood they termed a seat, that her arse was seriously beginning to hurt.

It was early, dark, wet and miserable. Her clothes were already damp when she was instructed to put them on. A fact the instructors had found mildly amusing for some reason. They were now completely drenched, cold, incredibly uncomfortable and very, very heavy. Ironic really, seeing as she had been stripped naked at the beginning and searched in every possible way to ensure all she had on her was her watch, button compass and the sketch map they had all been given. The vintage World War Two British army gear she wore by command was designed for ease of mass production in a time of dire need, rather than for comfort or functionality. It itched like crazy next to her smooth and pampered skin. The large greatcoat was several sizes too big for her. She was sure there were quite a few creatures sharing it as well. She could still remember the instructors belly laughing when it was issued. She might have discarded it in different circumstances, but she knew it was her only protection against the elements. And the windchill factor was bound to drop the temperature rapidly to well below zero at night, in the exposed, open expanse they were about to traverse.

The rear of the truck had nineteen luckless souls crammed in so tight she could smell what most of them had for breakfast. And tea last night for that matter. Erin and Jay Jay were the only females. The other three potential Szabo agents, Rob, Neil and Steve, were interspersed with the army candidates. Silence reigned as they all contemplated what lay ahead, no doubt planning their next moves and considering the best tactics to avoid being caught too early, potentially extending their interrogation phase. Which was never a good idea.

Several sets of intrusive, inquisitive eyes moved slowly over Erin and Jay Jay from all quarters. Erin flashed a supportive smile to her friend. It was returned gratefully, but she could tell that Jay Jay was not looking forward to what was about to happen.

Most prospective agents and SAS recruits dreaded this test the most. Unlike her. She relished the idea of being matched against the *best of the best* for the next three days, which was how long she had to evade capture if she could. A hunter force comprised of expert trackers and elite soldiers would be on her tail from the very beginning. She was the fox and they were the hounds, but these pursuers had been handed every possible advantage on purpose. She had been provided with no useful equipment; no warm clothes, decent boots, sleeping bag, torch, binos, matches for example. Whereas they, on the other hand, were given transport, radios, phones, surveillance gear and most worryingly of all, dogs. And to hand them an extra edge as if that wasn't enough, each escapee was expected to rendezvous with instructors at several checkpoints and specific times, thereby deliberately revealing their presence and probable direction of travel. Nothing like fair competition.

Then again, *life* was neither easy nor fair, was it?

'So? Adapt and overcome,' was all Dunbar had said when she had moaned to him about the lack of symmetry.

The brakes to the old vehicle suddenly screamed in protest and the lorry shuddered to a halt. Two doors opened and slammed in quick succession and the tailgate was lowered before she could blink.

'Out! Get out, you 'orrible lot! Out now!'

The deep roar of a voice instantly engendered fear and respect in equal measure. The entire contingent scrambled to exit the vehicle as quickly as they could and lined up on the side of the road without instruction.

'Spotty Dogs! Scum! The whole lot of you! Filth! Well, let's see how many of you we can bin then!'

His chiselled features rapidly turned red with exertion as the corporal in charge blew for all he was worth on his whistle.

The candidates for selection moved off swiftly and dispersed in each and every direction, trying not to bunch together and seeking their own path. Erin raced for Jay Jay as planned. They headed swiftly for a tiny copse on the horizon, silhouetted against the rising sun. It was their intention to remain together for as long as possible, having decided beforehand that the clear risks of doing so were outweighed by potential benefits. At least in the beginning. They would present a larger target to locate no doubt, but two pairs of eyes ensured a constant vigil could be maintained at all times, as they rotated the watch when in need of rest.

They sprinted across the open ground as fast as they could to put distance between them and the drop-off point. By the time they reached the trees, the sun had just crept above the horizon and the temperature was beginning to climb a little. Though the wind remained biting and their saturated clothes made for painful, demoralising conditions.

They paused to catch their breath.

'Phew! Glad to be off that old boneshaker anyway. To think, all those other poor sods have volunteered for this,' said Jay Jay, once she had recovered a little.

Erin scoffed at the absurd observation. 'Yeah? What are *we* then? What have we been doing these past five years, eh? We made our choice. There are far easier ways to make a living. You never thought of leaving, becoming a clerk or something?'

'Who, me?' her friend replied. 'You must be joking. And miss all this? I'm livin' it large, I am.'

Jay Jay had grown up poor on a council estate near Dagenham, brought up by a single mother struggling to cope with four children, from four different fathers. Her career prospects had been slim, despite her high intelligence. Her family life violent and volatile. Had it not been for the ever-watchful eyes and timely intervention of a certain Mr. Dunbar, the teenage runaway would most likely have succumbed to the same fate as many a lost soul.

'Yep,' replied Erin, chuckling. 'That makes two of us. Living the dream. Now, remember, we keep low on open ground and we watch our silhouette. We look for unlikely cover, spots to hide which are too small for the others maybe; ditches, streams, gulleys, dips in the ground. We stay clear of anywhere too obvious. Here, rub some dirt into your face, neck and hands. They're bound to have dogs. They will smell these rags a mile away. So, we're going to be compromised at some point and will have to move fast when we are. We split up on contact if needed. And I'll see you in T.Q.'

'Yeah, I remember. All for one, and that one is me. Let's go.'

Tactical Questioning was the worst part of SAS selection for many. Once caught after evasion, the interrogation phase was renowned for its brutality and effectiveness. Trained professionals employing tactics the majority of which were outlawed by the Geneva Convention and struck fear into the hearts of potential recruits. The horror stories told by many veterans did nothing to alleviate their anxiety. Three more days of mental and physical discomfort inflicted on would-be operators when the mind and body were *already* weak and hurting. Hell. Tests of stamina and endurance. Relentless questioning where only the 'big four' could be volunteered in response; name, rank, number and date of birth. Any other reply, any other utterance but the one pre-determined, sanctioned, universal response, usually constituted instant failure.

Nothing was for certain though, because the SAS had their own set of rules.

And so began the escape phase. The two trainee

agents and their three colleagues had been grouped with some of the toughest soldiers in the British Army. To even apply for SAS selection was a monumentally brave thing to do. To put yourself through the hardest selection process ever conceived. That took real guts deserving of utmost respect. And the Szabo novices soon learnt that the training was tough for a reason. Train hard, fight easy.

It was bitterly cold in the wind and frequent rain, which was sheeting down almost sidewards at times. They were constantly wet and dithering. The ceaseless chattering was in danger of loosening fillings and cracking teeth.

Bet the local dentists around here drive expensive cars, Erin thought. However, having been trained in far worse conditions on Herik, the Szabo agents easily put it out of their heads.

The two girls heard rather than saw the chasing troops, the noise carrying on the wind as they hid beneath their greatcoats to gain some rest. Shouts and cries of frustration betrayed the capture of many army personnel, most of whom roared with disappointment and anger when detained. Eventually, the first checkpoint time arrived and the two fugitives reluctantly broke cover.

'Alright darlin'?' a cocky Sargent with a sardonic grin enquired, as he leant back against a tree, hands shoved deeply into the warm pockets of his combats. 'Don't suppose you wanna jack it in, do ya? Do us all a favour?'

She seethed inside but showed no outward sign of emotion.

I'm not your darling, numbnuts. At the very least, I'm your equal.

'No thanks,' she smiled.

'Okay,' he said, and listed off a grid reference. 'Be there by eighteen hundred.'

They took off again as soon as they could, travelling in the opposite direction, throwing in a huge dog leg to confuse any pursuers. Searching for available cover once they had placed an acceptable distance between them and the checkpoint.

And so it continued; four such RV's were successfully completed. They avoided capture by moving often and stealthily creeping from cover to cover, occasionally bursting into a frenzy of action and dashing over open ground when required. At night, they huddled together for warmth as their energy levels dropped dramatically due to the freezing conditions, lack of sleep and food.

What I wouldn't give for a cuppa and a bacon roll!

Erin shuck off the notion. That was weakness creeping in. She was better than that and she knew it.

On the third and final day, the hunters closed in on their position as they watched from a concealed hide. The soldiers moved closer and closer until finally, the two runners decided they had to make a break for it. Like speeding gazelles, they leapt from cover and sprinted in opposite directions. The four squaddies hunting them did likewise and Erin found herself trying to evade two very competent individuals, clearly fit, motivated, elite troops. Paras.

For two hours she ran and hid, then ran some more and hid again. She heard Jay Jay's capture, the sound of her anguished cry and the dogs barking.

Poor cow, she thought. *She's in for it now.*

She remained concealed however in thick gorse as the trackers struggled in vain to locate her. Now, she was glad for the thick, oversized greatcoat. She did not know it at this time but she was the last of the candidates still at large. The intense cold had invaded every bone in her body and she wondered if she would ever feel warm again.

After hours of fruitless searching, she saw one of the soldiers radio for assistance and heard him speak.

'Get the dogs up here ASAP. The bugger's somewhere in this gorse field, I know it.'

She knew she would be discovered sooner or later, but it amused her greatly to eke out every possible minute she could until then. Her heart raced with excitement. They had to be nearing the end of the evasion phase, surely? The final checkpoint loomed and that would be simply a handover no doubt. She therefore decided to save her strength and wait it out.

A short time later, Landrovers and more trucks drew up sharply. Tailgates dropped and swarms of troops piled out. Then the dogs arrived, all going crazy, barking loudly as if it were a competition, as they strained on their leads salivating at the prospect of hunting down and finding their quarry.

The troops formed a large skirmish line and began walking her way, clearly practiced and proficient. Though she remained concealed from sight, it was not long before they had her boxed in, trapped. When they were only ten feet away, she raised herself slowly and lifted her hands.

'What took you?' she asked, smiling from ear to ear.

The professional soldiers did not look impressed.

She was seized roughly. Her hands were immediately cuffed behind her back and a cold wet sandbag shoved over her head. It caught Erin by surprise, as everything went dark and a swift punch connected sharply with her stomach, forcing the breath from her body. She instinctively dropped to her knees. Screams, shouts, threats and insults rained into her from all directions. She jerked in agony as a size ten boot connected with her mid-section. She desperately tried to suck air into her deflated lungs. She would have vomited, if she had anything in her stomach at this point.

She was hauled up and carried face down in the handcuffs, her wrists and arms instantly on fire with pain as the metal edges cut into her skin, her feet dragging on the ground.

What is going on?! she thought to herself, shocked by the severity of the violence being dished out. *This wasn't in the brief!*

Erin was picked up by several pairs of hands and literally thrown into the back of another truck. Her hooded head banged off the cold metal floor. She tried to right herself, but another hand grabbed her head and slammed it back down, forcefully.

'Stay down! Stay fukin' down!' a voice bellowed in her right ear.

She remained completely silent, catching her breath and too terrified to move. More soldiers piled into the rear of the truck and those who could, placed their muddy boots all over her body.

The interrogation phase had begun.

She was still smarting from the treatment she had received on seizure when the vehicle stopped. They hoisted her up and frogmarched her into a building of some sort. It sounded echoey, like a hanger or a warehouse. They moved rapidly through several pairs of doors, along corridors, until they eventually stopped. Her legs were unceremoniously kicked from under her and she fell to the floor. It was cold. So very cold. A knee dropped down hard on the back of her neck. Another was rammed onto the rear of her thigh. She struggled for air. It was all she could do to remain calm, to avoid panic, to scream or try to fight back, but she knew it would be counter-productive.

Stay composed and be compliant.

If she made no trouble for her captors, gave no complaint, she knew she was less likely to receive another kicking. So she hoped, anyway.

The wet clothing was cut off her with Emergency Medical Technician scissors. She was soon left naked apart from the bag covering her head. Her exposed body shivered uncontrollably on the cold floor as her watch was ripped off. Then she was ragged to her feet and forced to stand. Her head was dizzy now.

What the hell is going on?!

This was way rougher than she had been expecting.

Another heavy slap across her face brought her violently back into the moment.

'Feet apart,' a voice boomed. 'You are going to be searched. Do not resist.'

From her rear there was a sharp tug of the bag on her head, so hard she was forced backwards and off-balance. She recovered with some difficulty and sensed someone step in front of her. She gulped. A pair of gloved fingers slid insider her and moved around. She'd been subjected to a full search by the Medical Officer before she boarded the truck, three days ago, but nothing like this.

The invasive digits lingered far too long. Then they moved to her back passage. She flinched as the fingers rummaged around. Finally, satisfied that she had nothing secreted, the hand withdrew.

'Mouth,' a voice in the background called.

'Oh God!'

She knew what was going to happen next. The grip on the bag was relaxed a little and she was able to stand upright. The sack was lifted up revealing her mouth. Her jaw was closed, teeth gritted tight. She began fighting inside, struggling with every fibre of her being not to butt them with her head, or deliver a knee strike against the unknown sadist performing this exam. She knew it would only result in further pain.

'Open,' a voice whispered quietly, inches from her face.

Slowly, reluctantly, she opened her mouth, as a torch clicked on.

'Bite me, and you lose your teeth! Understand?'

The grips on her arms were tightened. The same gloved finger slid into her mouth and felt around, exploring every possible part, all of her teeth.

'Tongue up,' the voice commanded.

She did as she was told. Finally, after what seemed like an age, the hand withdrew.

'All clear.'

She tilted her head forwards to spit onto the floor, hoping she could get it through the gap in the bag.

And soon wished she hadn't.

A huge fist came hurtling down onto the back of her neck. When she opened her eyes, she was prostrate on the floor. The ringing in her ears was deafening, the pain intense. The handcuffs were removed abruptly and even this simple action hurt like hell.

'Don't fuck about. Don't touch the hood. Now get dressed.'

The voice was monotone and constant, filling her with loathing. It called again and a bundle was thrown at her feet. She followed instructions and slipped with great difficulty into an oversized boiler suit, without standing up.

'Good,' the voice said.

Then the guards moved to replace the handcuffs. She was pulled to her feet then pushed through a door and along a lengthy corridor. She strained to hear every word emanating from several rooms on either side of her. Loud and intense bawling. Repetitive questioning. Answers. Screams. Shouts. Sobbing.

The others. At different stages of the process.

Eventually, she was launched through an open doorway and fell awkwardly onto the floor. She struggled to regain her balance and rise to her knees.

'All yours,' another voice said.

A sense of dread consumed her as the door closed shut.

'Stand up straight!'

She did as ordered, pushing herself up to her feet with a monumental effort.

Give them no excuse.

A different voice now sounded, softer, calmer.

'I want you to tell me what you are doing on my land? Where do you come from? And who is your friend, Jay Jay?'

Erin inhaled deeply. Exhaled slowly.

'I'm sorry, but I cannot answer that question.'

And so it continued. For the next few hours, a torrent of queries was asked, bellowed and finally screamed at her. Sometimes right into her face from an inch or so. But Erin had regained much of her composure and offered the same exact reply to all, just as she was meant to do.

Eventually, the interrogator changed tactics. 'Okay, you leave me with no choice. Remember, you brought this on yourself. Staff!'

The door opened immediately. Whoever entered, grabbed her by the arms and spun her around, slammed her up against the wall. Her head cracked off the brickwork. She felt blood running down her face, the copper taste on her lips. She had no time to dwell on it, as two large hands turned her head, placing her forehead against the wall. Her feet were then kicked backwards and apart, until she was leaning at a forty-five-degree angle, her weight pushing forwards and her neck and shoulders aching instantly in protest. She could do nothing to alleviate the excruciating pain. She just had to endure it.

Before long, every single muscle and nerve in her body was screaming for mercy. But no respite was forthcoming. The guards just sat and watched. Waited. Occasionally, they called out, 'Give up. You know you want to. Come on, do it!'

She remained in that agonising position for what seemed like an eternity, sweating, shaking, and crying inside. She focussed on the day of her fourteenth birthday and Dunbar's music box. It helped a little. The thought took her away to better times, at least for a while. Temporarily, it was instrumental in relieving a tiny portion of the stress and pain. She would use the same tactic several times over the next two days or so.

After what seemed like an eternity, for she had no idea how long it had been in reality, she was really beginning to struggle. She moved, desperate to alleviate some of the pain.

Searing hurt shot though her whole body as the stun gun connected with her lower back. She jerked violently and fell to the floor again. Tears streamed down her face.

'Aahhh! Fuck!' she screamed.

Two guards dragged her upright, turned her around and removed the bag. Her eyes hurt from the changing light. Once they had adjusted, she gazed around the room.

Empty, save for her, the two guards, both bald in black and wearing ski masks, an interrogator in a suit, easily recognisable as the woman who had been asking her the questions because she was sitting behind a desk, pen and paper on show. A single lamp hung overhead and her features were obscured by shadow. A woman in her early forties maybe, well dressed in a smart Chanel suit, blonde hair, fit, intelligent, kind-faced.

'Release her.'

The two guards let go of her arms and she fell over. They removed the handcuffs and she instinctively rubbed her wrists. Her hands were purple and swollen.

'Get out, all of you,' the lady said. The room cleared. 'Sit down,' said the woman, standing and positioning a chair for Erin. 'What have they done to you, you poor thing? Can I get you a drink, a cigarette perhaps? Some food?'

Erin looked at the suited female as she sat down.

She was wearing a pair of black La Boutons and a Rolex Oyster Jubilee.

What was the time?

She couldn't see. Slowly, she shook her head.

'I'm sorry but I cannot answer that question.'

'Don't be so silly. There's no need to be like that with me. What have they done to you?'

'I'm sorry but I cannot answer that question.'

The woman in the Chanel suit was good, and very persistent. She attempted to coax Erin into saying something different, anything, for a long time, but to no avail. Though she was in complete rag order, on her chinstrap, the young apprentice agent did not deviate from her instructions.

Eventually, the woman sighed, smiled and nodded. 'I'm impressed,' she said, and moved to the door. 'But it won't save you. They all break in the end. It's just a matter of time. And copious amounts of pressure.'

Without another word, she left the room. The black-clad guards returned, only this time they were wearing ear defenders and carrying three feet lengths of hosepipe. She was cuffed once again and moved swiftly to another room, thrown down on to the floor and given a few extra kicks to the ribs for good measure. Then she was sat upright. Her legs were manhandled and crossed for her. The palms of her hands were placed flatly on the top of her head. Speakers in all four corners of the room erupted with a cacophony of static.

White noise. My God, this is agony!

'If you move from this position, you get this.'

Thwack!

A length of pipe smacked against her back with a

thump. She bolted upright in anguish at the sharp explosion of pain.

'Ahhhh!' she gasped, then bit her tongue to cut off the scream. The pain was unbearable.

'If you inter-lock your fingers, you get this!'

Thwack!

Another sharp strike, only this time from the other guard. More pain washed through her entire body. She so desperately wanted to kill them both in that moment. But she remained silent and just tried to focus on her breathing.

In for four, hold for two. Out for four, hold for two. Repeat.

Time passed and the sensation in her arms and body moved from on fire, to completely numb. Her entire anatomy seemed to be actively punishing her for every second she remained seated. Her body was trying to protect itself, like taking your hand off a hot pan. Still, she would not give in.

No surrender! Got to hold out, she thought. *Got to hold on.*

The guards and interrogators tried and tried, hour after hour, to gain anything from her, taking it in shifts. There were several sustained periods of silence and then all hell would break loose again. Time meant nothing. Days and nights passed. She had no way of measuring it and no idea if she had lost consciousness. Beyond all expectations, she was proving to be strong and tight-lipped. This small girl was made of the good stuff alright.

As the harsh treatment continued, the hardest part for her was the sleep deprivation. After a while her body craved rest. Her eyes ached so much she was worried there would be lasting damage. She endured severe migraines for the very first time and did not enjoy the experience at all. And yet she fought and fought. The white noise was incessant. The sounds combined to work against the frequencies of her brain and she began to hear voices, noises in her head she knew were not real. She saw lights and colours, shapes and forms in that murky room which twisted her mind.

The noise eventually stopped abruptly and the lights came on. Erin's eyes burned again. The door burst open and in strode a man in a designer suit.

'Enough of this soppy bollocks!' he stated, ominously. 'Outside, now!'

He indicated to the guards. Erin was hauled up, hooded and frogmarched through the maze of doors and corridors again. Her legs did not work now as they should and they had to half-push, half-carry her. She lost track of time once more as she moved between the real world and a dream-like state. Somewhere in amongst the nightmare, cold fresh air hit her hard in the face and pulled her out of the fog of delirium.

The echo of boots on concrete sounded and she heard a vehicle in the distance with its engine running. She was back in the hanger again. She had to be! Her heart raced.

Thank God it's over. It has to be over. I'm going home.

She could barely stand. Her legs were trembling uncontrollably and she was being supported by two guards. She was totally spent and surviving now on her body's fat reserves. She had only been given tiny sips of water and barely any food. She couldn't run or fight, even if she wanted to.

She was pulled around. The man in the suit was

inches from her, his voice calm and cold.

'Alright luv. Here's the deal… Officially, we are allowed five to ten per cent fatalities on any selection draft. Happens all the time; heat exhaustion, exposure, accidents... What can you do, eh? Has to be expected when we are training killers. You are about to have a nice little accident, if you don't co-operate right now. You have took the piss so far, and it ends here.'

It was a trick. Another mind game. It had to be.

Erin's heart sank. She was sure she was through with it all. Only to be subjected to more fuckery. One last try. She didn't utter a word. She couldn't if she had tried; her throat was so bone dry.

'No? Got nothing for me?' the man in the suit asked. 'Right, let's do this.' He motioned to the guards with a wave of his hand. 'Back the truck up here.'

Erin was still hooded and forced face down onto the concrete. She could hear the lorry backing up. The engine revved as it moved closer and closer.

What the fuck is going on?!

She began trembling in fright.

'Over here,' the man shouted, giving Erin another swift kick in the side.

Shit! They are actually going to kill me. They are going to waste me and make it look like an accident! Don't want a girl passing their precious course!

The truck was danger close. The guy in the suit was bent down next to her ear.

'Last chance. Tik, tok, tik, tok…'

Despite her delirium, she could hear and sense the tyres on the concrete, right next to her head now.

Oh fuck! This is real! They're going to kill me rather than let me pass. Fucking bastards!

She lifted her head. She wanted desperately to tell them to go fuck themselves. But what if it *was* another test? She stopped herself in the nick of time and thundered out the same response.

'I'M - SORRY - BUT - I - CANNOT - ANSWER - THAT - QUESTION!!'

Then she turned her head the other way. The tyres of the huge vehicle inched closer and closer. She couldn't feel anything now though, not the debilitating pain in her arms, the guard's kneeling on her back, nothing. All she felt was a blind, all-consuming rage.

Fuck this. Fuck this life!

She began to sob. Unbelievably, that darned music box came to mind. And the man who gave it to her. It was ridiculous she knew, but it was all she could think of in her final moments on earth.

Her breath quickened, sucking in air, preparing for the inevitable as she sensed the wheels and tyres now only inches away. The sound from the engine was deafening. She gulped, taking in her last breath, then screamed loudly as the tyre actually touched her head.

She took a final gasp, ready for one last defiant cry before everything went black.

'That will fucking do! Endex!'

The voice raised above the din was like a cannon exploding. The pressure on her head was relieved soon after as the vehicle reversed and the engine shut off.

Erin shook uncontrollably, in shock.

'Get the medics in now!' a panicked voice called out. 'This shit has gone on long enough!'

Immediately, the bag was pulled off and the handcuffs were removed. She looked around in amazement, too scared and wary to say anything. Slowly, she was sat up. She could just about make out a black-clad guard with a truck tyre knelt next to her. He had his balaclava rolled up and he looked severely worried. Then she saw the four-ton lorry.

It was six feet away from her! Had been all the time.

'It's okay, Erin. It's really over this time. You can relax now.'

A man in a white coat she recognised as the doctor who had performed her original medical examination shone a pencil torch into her eyes.

'Look at the light, Erin. Follow it for me.'

Her vision was off and the world just wouldn't stay still. Her hearing was muted. Words were slurred and time seemed to be running far too slowly. Everything just felt wrong somehow.

'Get an IV into her,' the doctor ordered. 'She's severely dehydrated. Heaven knows how she's lasted this long.'

From somewhere, two medics wheeled in a stretcher and Erin was place on top. She couldn't feel her body. It was shutting down. Lack of consciousness was only moments away.

In that final minute, before her whole world faded to blackness, the outline of a familiar face appeared before her, as if by magic.

Dunbar just smiled at his protégé. 'Well done, Erin. You'll do. You're in.'

She passed out.

Dunbar looked at the experienced SAS operatives around him and beamed with pride. His girl had taken it all and then some. Everything the country's finest could throw at her. Even when they threatened to lose the plot and kill her. When they leapt from behind the desk and assaulted her so badly, she thought she would never walk again... She had *still* defied them. Beat them.

Three weeks later, on Herik, Erin, Jay Jay and the two other successful candidates, Steve and Neil, received confirmation that they were now officially badged agents of Operation Szabo.

There was no fanfare, no ceremony, no award. They received no accolade whatsoever.

Erin was shocked and stunned to learn that the successful SAS applicants had been allowed to finish the interrogation phase after the requisite three days. The agents however, had completed five.

Her training was officially over.

Chapter 11 – Present Day

Kirsten removed her wig and took out her contact lenses as the car travelled at high speed away from the city and the carnage she had left behind. She placed the articles in a bag she retrieved from the holdall, along with her phone and all of the electronic equipment, wound the electric window down and tossed the lot. Her arm hurt like hell once the adrenaline had worn off and even these small exertions caused her great discomfort. She applied quick-clot to the open wound and covered it with a dressing from the trauma kit in her go-bag. An injection of a broad-spectrum antibiotic into her thigh followed.

'We need fresh wheels,' she stated, whilst she was packing the med kit away. 'Only, they can't be reported as stolen. Any ANPR camera or PNC check will give us away. They will hack in to every speed camera there is, comb through CCTV footage, traffic lights etc. That's what we are up against now. The whole world will be hunting us. The tech gear is really useful but it gives them a way to track us, so it had to go. Don't suppose you know of anyone living nearby who is away on holiday?'

Ian thought for a moment. 'Actually, one of my senior managers is in the Maldives for two weeks with his family. He's away for another six days, I think. We're quite friendly. Me and the wife have been round there a few times for dinner.'

'Perfect. What does he drive?'

'Err… Land Rover, Discovery.'

'Excellent. That will do nicely. Garaged?'

'Definitely. It's his pride and joy. His last motor was pinched. Never shuts up about it, so he's a bit anal about security for this one. It's a bit of a standing joke at work.'

'Sounds like a knob. Is he married?'

'Yeah, two kids.'

'Okay, not such a knob then. How big is she?'

'The wife? Sue, and she's about your size I'd say.'

'Even better.' Kirsten was glad to hear some good news for once. 'Drive straight to his place on the back roads if you can. We stick out like a sore thumb in this thing. Good job the roads are quiet.'

It was past one a.m. when Ian stopped the bullet-ridden BMW a five-minute walk from the house. Kirsten grabbed her bag and slipped out into the night. Ian pulled off nice and slow. The map from the glove compartment they had both studied showed some nearby woods and he made straight for them.

At the house, within twenty seconds the expert assassin had picked the lock to the front door. It took her a further minute or so to locate the car keys. Not long afterwards, she was sat in the driving seat of the Discovery and heading for the woods. They met up fifteen minutes later at their chosen rendezvous point; a small gravel car park marked on the map, deserted and miles from anywhere.

Ian looked around nervously, terrified they would be seen. He turned up his collar.

'What's wrong with you?' Kirsten asked. 'You look a little jumpy.'

'Can't help it. You know what goes on in these places late at night?'

'No, what?' she replied, puzzled.

'Doggers,' Ian answered, sheepishly.

She rolled her eyes. Of all the things to think of at

such a time. His mind worked on a different wavelength to hers. Then she sprang into action, moving quickly and efficiently. From her bag, she produced a bottle of clear liquid and a cloth.

'What are you doing?'

'I'm wiping the car down. Any prints or DNA need to be removed. Maybe they have us on camera, maybe not.'

After less than two minutes she tossed the empty bottle into the back seat, along with the bag containing her gear. She took out a pocket knife and started to slash at the upholstery.

'What are you doing now?' Ian asked, baffled.

'Making sure it burns thoroughly,' she said. 'The less evidence, the better.'

Kirsten then took out a jet flame lighter and began to set fire to the car. They watched together as the flames took hold. Within minutes, the expensive motor was a raging inferno.

Together, they returned to the house, garaged the car once more and let themselves in. It was pitch black but Kirsten did not want to risk turning the lights on, thereby alerting any onlookers to their presence. They blundered around a little in the dark until Ian literally fell onto the sofa in the living room.

'Finders Keepers,' she said, smiling. 'Looks like I have the master bedroom. Get some rest. We both need it. See you in the morning.'

She moved silently away and the events of the day immediately caught up with Ian. His eyes closed quickly and he was fast asleep and snoring before she had even reached the landing.

Kirsten was happy to discover the master

bedroom had an en-suite with a built-in shower. She was covered in dried blood from head to toe and needed to wash her wounded arm. She took the Sig Saur P229 pistol from her go bag, checked the magazine and chamber, placed the gun on the night stand. She unplugged the bedside lamp and positioned it carefully on the floor, outside the shower for a little light. Then she enjoyed a nice long wash before finding a large man's T-shirt in one of the drawers, put it on and climbed sleepily into bed.

She woke at six. A large red stain bejewelled the pristine white sheets where her arm had bled. She ragged the sheet off the bed and took it downstairs. Found some matches in a kitchen drawer and burnt it in the lounge wood- burner. When she had finished, she found a bottle of bleach in the bathroom cupboard and walked back to the bedroom, poured the entire contents onto the mattress.

Ian was still fast asleep. He was hanging half-on half-off the couch, his bare leg exposed and his foot touching the floor. She was amused by the pitiful scene for thirty seconds or so, but then decided they had to move.

'Wake up. Ian? Come on, up you get, sleepyhead. Time to go. We eat on the move. I've raided the cupboards and grabbed a load of biscuits and crisps. We'll have something more substantial when we're on our way. The initial cordons will have been relaxed by now. Budget cuts. Police won't pay the overtime to put roadblocks in every direction. And we left the original perimeter in good time. But now, we need distance, for that sniper will be harder to shake.'

Ian shook the sleep away. He rubbed his eyes several times. Then he stared up at his younger compatriot. She was dressed in jeans and a sweatshirt that were slightly too small for her. However, somehow, unbelievably, she looked even more beautiful this morning than she had last night, dressed up in all her finery at the nightclub.

'Where… Where we going?' he asked, sleepily.

'We have a long drive ahead of us,' she replied, rubbing her arm. 'We need information. I can't go through normal channels now. I don't know who we can trust and they will track every move I make. I'm not used to running from my own people. I ditched all the tech so we're doing it the old-fashioned way. That should please you at least?'

'Huh. You know, I think it does. Not gonna deny it.'

He smiled at her and his heart fluttered a little when she smiled back. There was pure gold in that smile of hers, of that there was no doubt. If only he could bottle it. There was also more than a hint of death, pain and misery behind those eyes. But, you can't have everything.

'Priority number one is to identify the guy Ryan Nylander fingered. We're following the money. Always a good plan I've found. It is usually the undoing of most crooks. The one area they don't pay enough attention to. We're going north.'

They headed out to the garage. Kirsten backed the car out and Ian locked the double doors. He sat in the Discovery and fastened his seatbelt.

'Can I suggest something?' he asked.

'Sure. As long as it's appropriate. Go for it.'

'My sister lives about forty minutes north of here. It's not too far off our route. And she's a vet. Does a lot of house calls, so she always has meds in her bag. It's not ideal I know, but maybe she'll be able to fix up your arm?'

Kirsten was reluctant to delay their journey and involve someone else, though she could see the sense in his proposal. Any infection at this point could prove costly, if not fatal. She conducted a quick risk assessment in her head. Came up with one overriding concern.

'Tell me honestly. Do you trust her?'

'With my life. She is all I have apart from my wife. And as you may have gathered, we are not all that close any more. Marie's divorced and has no kids, so she'll be on her own.'

'That's an assumption. She may have company. It's a risk worth taking however. We go there then. Lay low for today whilst I get some attention. We travel around three in the morning. Less traffic and less police.'

She reversed out of the drive and pulled away. 'Of course, I *will* remind you always that this was your decision if things go wrong. And if she crosses me, I *will* end her.'

Ian instinctively began to laugh. A fraction of a second later however, he stopped himself, as it suddenly dawned on him that she was being completely serious. He gulped hard and said no more.

They drove to Marie Townsend's house and stayed that day. The wound was cleaned, irrigated with an antiseptic solution using a thirty-five-millimetre syringe and closed with cyanoacrylate glue. Kirsten took the spare room in the afternoon for a rest. Marie had asked a lot of questions whilst administering first aid but she was sensible enough not to push too hard for answers. It was clear that she had decided her brother's new lady friend was not a person to cross.

Maybe it was her reluctance to talk? Her cold and regimented persona? Or the Sig P229 tucked in the back of her jeans? In any case, Ian had assured her he was okay and that she was a friend he trusted. That was enough from the brother she loved.

At three in the morning, having eaten a very early full English, they were back in the car and ready to set off.

'How long will it take?' Ian asked.

'Around five hours, maybe six.'

'Right. We need tunes then.'

He rummaged through a compact disc box he had found. 'Aha! Classic. Tears For Fears Greatest Hits. Job done. Time for *me* to educate you for a change.'

The journey was largely uneventful, though it took six and a half hours in total due to the need for several toilet breaks, courtesy of Ian's weak bladder.

Eventually, Kirsten spotted a signpost she had been looking for. 'There's a left turn about two miles ahead. We're nearly there.'

Richland Bews residential home for the elderly was as pricey as they come. The yearly fees constituted a hefty mortgage for most people. A tranquil, picturesque paradise in which to spend your final years, it lay nestled amongst some of the most spectacular scenery in Scotland, just north of Aviemore in the Cairngorms National Park area of the Highlands. The region was a tourist hotspot, littered with beautiful secluded lochs, ancient forests and mountain trails.

The drive which led up to the main building was almost a mile long. And the converted manor itself was a thing of beauty, like stepping back in time a few hundred years. It was built out of old Scottish drystone and also boasted several hectares of land attached, which surrounded it for some distance.

'This is charming. Really fabulous. Oh, I want to retire here, please? Who are we here to visit?' Ian asked, as they pulled up on the visitor's car park.

'An old friend.'

Kirsten was unusually quiet. She was not the most talkative person at the best of times but she had eventually opened up a little on the journey. Now though, she looked apprehensive, as if everything she did and said really mattered, and was being judged.

They approached the reception desk and rang the bell. An elderly lady in a home-knitted cardigan several sizes too big for her with holes in the elbows rushed from a nearby room to stand behind the counter. She took a minute to compose herself and removed her glasses.

'Sorry to keep you, my dear,' she said to Kirsten, immediately recognising her. 'Good to see you again. It's, Miss Brown, isn't it?'

Kirsten cast a quick glance at Ian, then nodded. 'Yes. Yes, it is. You have a good memory.'

'Tish. Nonsense. Someone as pretty as you? Hard to forget. Michael's niece? Would you like to see him?'

'We would, if it's convenient. We have no appointment but it's been an age. I've been busy with work. I thought perhaps…?'

'Och, there's no need to explain to me, dearie. He's a lovely gent and not an ounce of bother, but you have your reasons, I'm sure.'

Kirsten sighed. 'Where is he please?'

'Well now, let's see. He'll most likely be out in the garden this time of day. At the rear. He likes the fresh air you see. Spends hours out there. Though, how much have you been told? About his current condition?'

Kirsten immediately looked concerned. 'I'm sorry?'

The old lady appeared mortified all of a sudden and cast a worrying look at Ian. 'Oh my! I thought you knew. I'm so sorry to break it to you like this. He… He had a seizure, about a year ago now. Affected him badly, I'm sorry to say. He lost all movement in his legs and the right side of his body. Hasn't been able to say anything since. We think he understands us though and he communicates well enough. Just nods and grunts but somehow, we know what he wants or needs.'

Kirsten was too stunned to speak. Ian placed an arm around her, feeling that she needed support.

'Which way to the garden, please?' he asked.

'Straight through the French doors in the sitting room. You can't miss it.'

He led Kirsten out and into the grounds. Several groups of residents were happily chatting away and laughing at tables and benches, around a large square lawn. Some were playing bowls on the green. At the far side of the square was a bench where a gentleman who looked to be in his mid-eighties was sitting in a wheelchair. He was smartly turned out in a silk dressing gown and matching cravat. A solitary male nurse sat with him, oblivious to the world, happily engrossed in a paperback.

Kirsten's eyes brightened when they caught sight of her old mentor and friend. Her pace quickened and together they strode purposefully over.

'Hello there. Are you here to visit with Mr. Dunbar?' asked the nurse as they approached, hearing their footsteps at the very last second and rising to greet them.

Kirsten didn't answer, just looked into Dunbar's eyes, searching for some flicker of recognition.

'Yes. Yes, we are,' replied Ian, for them both. 'This is his niece.'

'Oh. Pleased to meet you. I'll take off then, give you some peace. Give me a shout when you leave, please? Reception can call me if I'm not around.'

He hurried away. When he was out of earshot, Kirsten knelt down at Dunbar's side. She kissed his cheek tenderly but he did not flinch. He just stared at her, betraying no emotion at all.

'Well? Are you going to say something to me? Come on, old man. You can do better than that... Nothing? Not going to greet me at all?'

Not a thing.

'Oh, come on! Grunt. Squeak. Hit me or something. Anything!'

No response at all.

She moved to shake him but Ian grabbed her arms and stopped her. 'What are you doing?! You heard what the lady said. Perhaps she was being generous? Perhaps, he is worse than she let on? Either way, you won't get anywhere using force.'

Kirsten rose to face him with mounting frustration bordering on hostility. 'But I need him, Ian! *We* need him! He's the one person who can help us unravel what is happening. Make it right. Your only chance of salvaging what's left of your career. Possibly your marriage. Of avoiding jail time, or worse. If he can't answer my questions, we have nowhere else to go. Don't you understand? He is the one person I trust in this world. I can't…!'

'Not here.'

Kirsten was interrupted mid-sentence by a faint whisper of a voice, barely audible at all. She looked at her new ally. Ian's lips had not moved however so she gazed down at Dunbar, who remained completely motionless. His lips were crooked and a tiny bit of drool was escaping through the gap. If he was acting, he was damned good.

'Come on. We're taking him for a walk,' she said, kicking off the break to his chair.

Ian raced to catch up with her as she pushed Dunbar swiftly through a gap in the hedge, following a well-trodden trail. Soon, they found themselves on a track amidst long rolling fields of green grass broken up only by tall, majestic trees on both sides and occasional views of imposing, snow-covered mountains. After several minutes, they reached a small style which led into a forest. A lone bench was positioned neatly to mark the boundary of the care home grounds. Kirsten positioned Dunbar in his wheelchair next to the bench, looking out onto the fields. Then they both sat down.

'Okay, 'fess up. What gives?' she asked, addressing her invalided friend.

Dunbar moved slowly to take a good look around. Once he was satisfied they were not under surveillance, he shook his head and stretched out his neck, shoulders, mouth and lips.

'Aaah, that's better. You've no idea how hard it is to keep up the pretence. I have cold sores every week. They sting like hell. And the cramp? Well, that's just not nice. Hi'ya, kid. Long time no see. Things must be really rough for you, if you've come here. Who's he?'

Dunbar indicated that he meant Ian by two quick flicks of his head.

'He's my back up.'

The retired spymaster was not overly impressed, that much was abundantly clear. Years of extensive experience told him right away that Ian was a civilian, nothing more, and he began to show real concern for her now.

'Och, how bad is it? Give it to me. All of it.'

Kirsten explained everything she knew in a full and comprehensive verbal report. All that had happened so far, ending with a description of the man Ryan Nylander had stated had paid to have her killed.

'… but I do not know anyone like that. I have racked my brain and I have no idea who he is. I can't think who would…'

'I know him.'

Ian and Kirsten looked at each other with a mixture of extreme relief and surprise. They immediately returned their gaze to Dunbar, inviting him to explain his interruption.

'You sure stirred up some trouble this time, didn't you? But then, that was always your special talent. It's safe to say you've really burned your bridges as far as help goes. You know that, don't you? You can't use *any* of our people from here. Nobody operational. It's not safe.'

Kirsten shrugged her shoulders. 'Yep, figured as much. What can you do, eh?'

Ian was not so quick to accept that they were completely on their own, however. Was it so futile to ask for help?

'Why? Why is she on her own, with no support?

It doesn't work like that, surely?' he demanded.

Dunbar inhaled and exhaled slowly. 'Not usually, I grant you. But this time you have stamped on the bee hive in front of the queen. The man you are looking for works for the one person you never want as an enemy, believe me. One of the most powerful and well-connected men in the entire country. The entire world for that matter. We're not talking James Bond here. That would be too easy. You've pissed in the tea of the guy who orders 007's immediate superior to clean his boots for him!'

Kirsten suddenly knelt down and grabbed Dunbar's wrists. 'Which one? Tell me.'

Her old benefactor looked down at the ground for a moment, hoping to shield from view the resignation in his eyes. He had always known this day would come and dreaded the extreme consequences which would surely ensue. He lifted his gaze moments later and looked Kirsten straight in the eye.

'So be it. Sir Crispin De Wigt. The moneyman you described is Roger Hanson. De Wigt's Head of Security. Ex-para, ex-SAS, ex-merc. Tough nut. If he has paid that amount of money to two criminal factions to take you out, he's acting under orders from the very top. And I mean the summit. It *has* to be De Wigt. I…'

Dunbar hesitated all of a sudden. It was obvious that he wanted to say more, but something was evidently bothering him.

'What? Don't stop now. What is it?' pushed Kirsten, eager to learn all she could.

There was a long pause and they wondered if that was all they were going to get. But eventually, Dunbar continued.

'Look, I may be completely wide of the mark. I think… I think this all may be connected somehow to your mother's death.'

Kirsten was dumbfounded. She had no idea what he was getting at. That was going back so far it did not seem plausible.

'What do you mean?' she asked.

'Your mother was just like you. Szabo to the core. She told me once, not long before her death, that she had stumbled onto something huge. Something extremely dangerous that she needed to flesh out before she could air it to anyone. But that when she did, it would eclipse anything we had known or done previously if she was correct. She had no evidence to back up her claims at that time and would not talk further u ntil she had. They were unproven theories that's all. Educated guesses that terrified her. What if she was right though, and these events are linked? She was sent away to Berlin before she could investigate further and she never came back. She died before I could talk to her again. I had no idea what she was referring to so I could not…'

'They *silenced* her!'

It was Ian who interrupted. Though he only spoke out loud what Kirsten was thinking.

'Yes. It certainly looks that way now. That was my conclusion as soon as you explained things,' agreed Dunbar. 'And if someone the stature of Mr. De Wigt is involved, one of the men running Szabo free from any outside interference, you've bit the arse of a bloody great grizzly which will in all likelihood attack at any given opportunity.'

'So, what do we do now?' asked Kirsten. 'I won't roll over and play dead.'

'No, didn't think so. Not your style, is it? That would be too sensible. Well, if I were you, I'd…'

Dunbar's entire body suddenly jumped violently for no apparent reason. His chest was holed and his back exploded into a spray of blood and matter. A single shot boomed out in the distance, echoing in the mountain air and shattering the peaceful morning.

Kirsten instinctively threw herself under the table, as a second round smashed into the ground she had just vacated. She wanted desperately to check on her friend, but she was trained too well for that. Dunbar had seen to it. And it was her training which kicked in now, racing to the fore.

Sniper. Got a bead on us.

She grabbed Ian and sprinted the short distance to the style, vaulting it in one swift, effortless bound, as more bullets impacted on the ground around them.

Single shots. Lone shooter. Well aimed, but not able to predict or track my movements; Long distance!

Before long, they had reached the relative safety of the trees and crouched in cover.

'Shit!' cried Ian, shaking with fear. 'Shit! Shit! I may have soiled my underwear. This guy is seriously beginning to piss me off! What happens now? Will they come for us?'

She picked up a daisy and started playing with it like a child, as she calmly watched the horizon. 'Unlikely. Too risky. They don't know what I'm packing. That was a safe kill. Stationary target from distance. Probably scoped us from the high ridge, over there.' She pointed to the north. 'That's what I would have done. Professional. Wonder how they tracked us so fast?'

He couldn't believe how cool she was. Her

mentor had just been killed. Did she feel anything at all? Was there ice running through her veins? She was like a rock; cold and hard, devoid of life. What must she have seen and done to make her like this?!

'So, how long do we stay here?' he asked.

'Make yourself comfortable. No point risking it. Few hours until sunset.'

'Won't they have heard the shots and called the police?' he enquired, frustrated and scared.

'This is *shooting* country, Ian. Shots go off all the time out here. Nobody takes any notice.'

He sat down and huddled behind a large oak, trying desperately to control his breathing. Kirsten just sat staring at Dunbar's corpse with a blank expression. Eventually, Ian decided the silence had persisted long enough.

'I'm… I'm sorry about your friend.'

She smiled slightly and took a deep breath, looked away so he could not see the solitary tear rolling down her cheek. 'Thanks. Shit happens. He was too good to end his days like this anyway, in a retirement home. It's how he would have wanted to check out, I think. Given a choice. One thing puzzles me though.'

'Yeah?'

'Yeah. Why did he pretend he'd had a stroke and could not talk? That he had possible brain damage? I think he knew something else. We started losing agents around that time too. That can't be a coincidence. I wonder what more he was going to tell me? Whatever it was, it made him a higher priority target than me for any assassin or I would be the one dead now. He saved my life again.'

Chapter 12 - Operations

Your first kill is the hardest. Isn't that what veterans always say? Clearly, they had never met Erin.

She had not yet left the training facility on Herik Island. So, for the time being, she was still using that name. Another would be chosen upon commencement of live operations, to guard against anyone who had dealings with her as a trainee, discovering what she was really up to in the field.

Just six days into her espionage career and her whole future had already been mapped out for her, at least in the short term. Though, for technical reasons, both she and Jay Jay had been granted a brief respite before embarking upon their civilian vocations. Their official cover. The remaining agents had already been assimilated into the general population, in a variety of professions which allowed them a certain amount of freedom and the ability to access key locations, organisations, businesses and people, both internationally and in the U.K.

The huge complex seemed to be even larger with hardly any students in residence. It was eerily empty as it awaited the imminent arrival of a fresh batch of recruits. The girls kept themselves busy by training, honing their skills on the range, brushing up on languages, dialects, current affairs, anything of interest and note. But, this morning, they had received an immediate summons to the main briefing room. And it did not do to be late.

Jay Jay was already there when Erin arrived with twenty-five seconds to spare. Her only friend of similar age was seated at the large meeting table along with Dunbar and Mr. Green. The former SBS legend and

Royal Marine Commando, now Head of Training at Grexley, was stern-faced and serious and all times. The man had no sense of humour it seemed. Probably surgically removed after he was blown up by an improvised explosive device in Iraq. As Erin sat down opposite him and beside her fellow agent, the huge painting of Queen Elizabeth which was hanging on the wall behind seemed to tower above him, framing his features and increasing his air of authority. As if his many facial scars, disfigured right hand and eye patch did not do that already.

His voice was usually authoritative and unyielding. This time though, he addressed them in a surprisingly friendly tone hitherto unheard by the former trainees.

I'm operational now. The bullshit has ended at last.

'Morning, Erin. Bang on time, I see? We haven't begun yet. Make yourself comfortable and listen in.'

The newly qualified agents did their best but the chairs were hard and bare. The room smelt of polish. The walls were adorned with blown up photographs of missions from several wars, as well as snapshots Erin could not place. They shuffled slightly, gave up trying to ease their discomfort without cushions and patiently awaited his briefing.

'Firstly, may I add my belated congratulations on your achievements? That was some show you both put up on SAS selection. Especially you, Erin. Two fingers to the man. Stuck those SF assholes right in the eyes. Oh, it's okay, as a former member of the club, I reserve the right to take the piss whenever the mood takes me. It pleased me no end to hear of your progress. We will be dining out on that one at others expense for years to come, I dare say. What, Dunbar?'

The old Scottish spymaster smiled politely. 'Ay, Boss. Quite.'

Erin and Jay Jay glowed with satisfaction. To gain such gushing praise from a genuine hero worshipped by every recruit was unheard of.

'Now, to business. A situation has arisen out of the blue which we think you two can alleviate for us. It requires prompt and decisive action. We have a very small window of opportunity which we dare not miss. Hence, why we are sending you in straight away. Our sources have unearthed a Russian spy ring operating with impunity on British soil. Close to, or inside, the upper echelons of government. It will not do and we will respond to this threat with lethal force. British subjects working for our potential enemies? Selling state secrets and information vital to this country's national security? Spying on their own? In my book, there is no greater crime.'

He took a sip of tea and invited everyone to avail themselves of the refreshments provided. Nobody accepted the invitation.

'Very well, the mission... Your primary target will be a man named Richard Hamilton. He is currently the private secretary to a senior civil servant in the Foreign Office, with access to all kinds of secrets, as you can imagine; planned trips abroad, timetables, troop displacements, agendas… That sort of thing. He has been divulging information to Moscow for over three years now.'

'Three years?!' asked Erin, completely disgusted. 'And we have known about it all this time?'

'Yes,' answered Mr. Green. 'Not only known, but often encouraged and aided. Without his knowledge I might add. Fed with false intel. We've had tabs on him for a while. Traced back to where it began and hypothesised the remainder. The material he had in the beginning was low grade intel so we were not too concerned. The kind of stuff just juicy enough to bait the Russians, but hardly damaging to us in reality. Those at the very top kept him in play to see who he would lead us too. And now, it appears as if that has proven to be a wise decision. However, he has also upped his game and he is beginning to tread on too many toes. He has begun to expose facts which can and will hurt us. It appears from the outside looking in that his handler may have changed. They are now tasking him with increasingly sensitive assignments. Something big is in the pipeline and it is crucial enough for a foreign intelligence service, presumably SVR, spymaster to be travelling here in the guise of an industrialist on a business trip. They will be meeting shortly at a top hotel in London.'

'Security?' enquired Erin.

'Four usually. All former military. Spetsnaz. Typical security detail for a high-profile businessman these days, to ward off potential kidnap attempts.'

She nodded. 'Fine. You want us to take out the lot.'

Dunbar interjected. 'Yes, termination mission. Nothing more. We have a plan in place we want you to execute.'

Erin looked at Jay Jay. She was happy to partner her friend first time out.

This is it. All the years of pain and effort have led up to this moment. At last.

'Okay, let's hear it then,' she said.

The next few hours consisted of a mini lecture. A thorough and comprehensive briefing package, including dossiers to study, photo presentation and full details of contingency plans should things go wrong. They learned that Richard Hamilton was married to a wife who knew nothing of his illegal activities and had three small children. He also enjoyed the company of a very high-maintenance mistress. Surveillance operatives already in play had confirmed that she had learned of his planned meeting at the Savoy and invited him to turn it into an extended business trip. An extra night had therefore been booked and she was eagerly anticipating spending close to two full days in a swanky hotel in the best part of the city. Shopping trips. Maybe taking in a theatre show or dining out in a top restaurant. And of course, plenty of bedroom action. Two days or thereabouts when she would have him all to herself. Almost.

What Richard Hamilton was completely ignorant of, was the fact that his lover was *also* working for the Russians. She had been feeding back intelligence to her own handlers on his movements, likes, dislikes, habits, secrets… Pillow talk. Spying on the spy, for immense financial gain now held in secret offshore accounts.

Insertion for this mission had been planned and organised. It was summer and staffing a busy hotel during the main leave period was always a struggle. Szabo agents had already arranged for several of the hotel chambermaids to meet with a rather nasty man-made sickness bug, the day prior to Mr. Hamilton's arrival. When they all phoned in sick on the same morning, the duty manager panicked a little. The phone call to the employment agency which requested two temporary replacements at short notice, had followed within two minutes. Szabo agents however, had hacked the phone line. They intercepted the call and posed as agency employees stating that, as luck would have it, they had two young students on their books on a break from university who would be perfect for the job.

For this mission Erin cut her hair short. She lightened it and wore green contact lenses. She was now Jenny McAllister. Jay Jay adopted similar tactics and operated as Jill Crutchley.

The Savoy is located in The Strand and has been one of London's premier hotels since the nineteen hundreds. The grade two listed building boasts over two hundred and sixty rooms, many of which have panoramic views across the river Thames. On the first day of the mission, the two newly badged Szabo agents reported for their shifts bright and early. They undertook all duties they were assigned and shadowed experienced maids for part of the day. They were sure to give the impression that they were pleasant, hard-working and friendly. Nothing to raise any suspicions.

When the opportunity arose in late afternoon to take some food and drink up to Mr. Hamilton's room, it was too good a chance to miss and they both immediately volunteered.

The first meeting was therefore unplanned and fortuitous. It afforded the assassins an opportunity to reconnoitre the killing ground, as well as two of the targets themselves. The door opened and they wheeled the food trolley into the room. Hamilton was half undressed, his designer suit jacket discarded on the bed, his shirt unbuttoned and his shoes kicked off. He was good looking. Mid-thirties, blonde hair, with an air of supremacy about him, or extreme confidence. This lessened his attractiveness somehow.

'That will be fine, thank you. Leave it there.'

Hamilton took out a money clip from his pocket and unfolded a brand new, crisp twenty-pound note. He made to hand it over to Erin but when he caught sight of her astonishing beauty, he pulled it back a little, deliberately extending the moment and the opportunity to gaze into her eyes. An awkward silence followed as his look lingered far longer than it should have, before he eventually let go of the note.

'Ahem!'

A loud cough sounded to his rear, interrupting his concentration, exactly as intended. Out from the bathroom strode his mistress with a look of fury and jealousy, having seen the way he was drooling over the hired help.

'That will be all. You may go now,' she barked, resolutely.

Madeline Chadwick was from an upper middle class English family. She was university educated. Only, it was Bristol University, as opposed to Oxford or Cambridge. A fact which Richard Hamilton reminded her of constantly and closed many doors for her in Whitehall. She was nevertheless ruthless and highly ambitious. Tall and reasonably good-looking, there was a swagger to her movements which indicated an outward disdain for strangers. She also possessed a cold-hearted interior to match. The type of girl one could take an instant dislike to. And though they had only just met in person, both Erin and Jay Jay were now itching to punch her squarely on the nose.

For now, they contented themselves with a good

look around on exit and the knowledge that they would soon return.

Day two began the same way. They reported for duty and performed their fair share of necessary but mundane tasks. At eleven o'clock precisely, a smartly dressed elderly gentleman entered the hotel lobby. Jay Jay was watching and had been waiting for him.

'Falcon to Eagle. The Bear is in play, over,' she radioed through to Erin, using the state-of-the-art, minute, electronic microphone hidden in the top button of her uniform.

'Received. Company?' Erin responded, from the empty room situated two doors away from Hamilton's suite.

'I have eyes on two Keepers, flanking him. No, wait. Correction. Standard two by two. Repeat, four in total. The second pair are covering the exit at the moment. Watching front and rear. Over.'

'All received. Out.'

Erin did not have to say anything more. Jay Jay knew what to do. She would maintain a discreet distance but follow behind the party. What the old timers used to call, Tail-end Charlie.

They both donned their specially designed, almost invisible latex gloves and prepared for action.

The elder man approached the desk briefly before he and all four escorts made for the elevator. They rode it up to the fourth floor, where Richard Hamilton was staying.

Mikhail Semenov was an experienced spymaster, a veteran of the Cold War. He should have retired years ago but his accumulated knowledge was considered invaluable by his SVR counterparts. He had run numerous operations on British territory previously and been responsible for several coups, including high profile assassinations, a series of defections and the infamous, successful cyber-attack on MI5 some years earlier. He was therefore a priority target for Szabo operatives and a nice added bonus for Erin and Jay Jay.

Erin had been busy whilst Jay Jay was on watch. She had installed a micro camera with its own built-in power supply. It was almost undetectable as it had no leads and it was now covering the hallway and elevator on the fourth floor. It afforded Erin a perfect view on her wristwatch monitor of the Russians exiting the lift.

Semenov and two of his guards approached the door to the suite. The remaining two covered the elevator and stairs as per standard procedure. Erin quickly gathered the towels she had folded neatly and placed on the bed. She opened the door to the room she was in and casually stepped out into the hallway. Concealed beneath the towels and gripped in her right hand was a fully loaded Steyr M9A1 pistol, with a thirty-millimetre silencer attached. That gave her seventeen rounds to play with, plus the same amount in the spare clip tucked into her suspender.

The two most advanced escorts cast a quick glance over the pretty maid but were not unduly alarmed, assuming as intended that she was changing towels as part of her normal duties. As she approached, the door to the suite opened slowly.

Perfect timing.

Phut! Phut!

Two suppressed shots sounded quietly and the two Russian henchmen fell, each with a neat hole in his forehead. They were dead before they had any opportunity to reach for their weapons.

Erin was now vulnerable to shots from the other elite veterans near to the elevator but she had to train her gun on the main Russian spy, force him and whoever opened the door into the room. Essentially, she had to trust her partner to cover her. Trust her with her life. It was imperative she entered the room quickly, before the door was closed.

Within a second, two more shots were fired from the door leading to the stairs and both remaining Russian guards were killed from the rear. Jay Jay joined Erin swiftly, pausing only to place one more round into each of the dead foreigners, just in case.

Erin bundled Semenov and Hamilton into the room. She closed the door as Jay Jay entered behind her. Madeline was fetched from the bathroom and all three were sat down on the end of the bed, with their hands on their heads, fingers interlocked.

'Isn't this cosy?' began Erin.

'I do not know who you think you are young lady…'

Mikhail Semenov as it turned out spoke excellent English. Hardly any accent. But Erin was in command here and short on time. She interrupted him in an assertive tone.

'No. You're not *meant* to know who I am. That's kind of a given. Anything to say, before I can your fat arse?'

'Niet. I am prepared to die for…'

Phut!

She shrugged her shoulders at Jay Jay. 'What? He had a good run. Hope I live that long.'

And with that, she fired two more bullets into his

chest. Cool as you like. Then she turned swiftly to her partner. 'Take the floozy over the other side of the room. One to the head, remember?'

Madeline Chadwick began to holler and cry but Jay Jay hit her around the head with the butt of her gun and it had the desired effect. She dragged her to the desk and chair.

Erin believed Jay Jay would finish her swiftly so she turned to face Hamilton. The pathetic wretch was crying. Not openly snivelling, but there were definitely tears in his eyes. He knew he was about to die.

'I'm not going to beg,' he said, looking into her eyes and seeing only the soul of a competent assassin, despite her obvious youth. 'I know I've done wrong. I didn't think I was…'

'No, *traitor*, you gave it no thought at all, did you? Just looked after yourself. Your family will now have to live with the shame of what you've done. You have it easy. All *you* have to do, is journey to hell.'

Phut! Phut!

Double tap to the head. Nice and efficient. Natural, like water off a duck's back.

Erin heard the sound of a scuffle behind her. She turned and was horrified to see Madeline had grabbed Jay Jay's gun. They were now grappling with each other for control of the firearm. She raced over to the two fighters and kicked Madeline's calf hard, forcing her down onto her knee. The violent action also freed her hold on the weapon, allowing Jay Jay to recover control.

Erin stared at her friend in complete disgust. 'How the fuck did she get the drop on you?!' she demanded.

'I froze, alright? It's not training anymore. It's a

girl. Like you and me.'

Erin shook her head in severe disappointment. She could hardly believe what she was hearing. What had just happened?

'She's nothing like me! The very first test. You fell at the first hurdle, you dozy…!'

She raised her weapon, pointed it at Jay Jay's head and tensed her trigger finger.

'No, no! It's just a blip, I…'

Phut!

Jay Jay slowly opened her eyes. She had fully expected to be shot for failure. Terminated. She gazed down now with immense relief on Madeline's body. A solitary bullet had entered one side of her head and exited the other.

She stood in shock as Erin took her weapon from her and wiped it clean. Then she watched as her friend wrapped it in Madeline's hand, placed a finger on the trigger, and fired it into Hamilton's corpse.

Erin then took a fake break up letter penned in 'Madeline's handwriting' from her pocket and threw it on the dresser. It contained an admission of guilt and alluded to the fact that the Russians had a video of the two of them having sex, stating that she could no longer handle the threat of being blackmailed and the scandal which would surely follow if their love affair were revealed so sordidly.

Erin stood up to leave. 'There you go. Murder-suicide all day long. She confronted her former lover. Killed him, just as the Russians showed up, so they got it too. Wraps things up nicely. Let's get the camera and go.'

They exited the room and took refuge in the empty suite two doors down. Placed their gloves and disguises in two holdalls and changed clothes. Just before walking out of the door with all their gear, Jay Jay stopped Erin to say something.

'I'm sorry, alright? I know I let you down.'

Erin sighed. She was still furious. 'Yes. Yes, you did. Big style. That is the one and only time it happens! Clear?'

'Crystal.'

'Good. We never speak of this again.'

Chapter 13 – Present Day

Just before dark a concerned employee at Richland Bews residential home began searching for a missing resident. When she finally found Michael Dunbar's corpse in the clearing at the very edge of their land, the anguished, high-pitched scream she gave could be heard echoing in the mountains for miles around. It brought several members of staff racing to her location and within minutes they were joined by numerous inquisitive residents. Confident that a large crowd had formed and that the sniper would have vacated their position as a sensible precaution while an exit route was clear, Kirsten and Ian emerged slowly from the darkness of the trees. They were still careful however to place as many bodies between them and the shooter's location as they could, whilst they explained what had happened to the horrified onlookers. Then they stated that they were going immediately to the house to report the incident to management and await the police.

As they moved swiftly away from the gruesome scene, Kirsten noted that the nurse who had been sitting with Dunbar when they arrived had also took the opportunity to scurry away. It was a suspicious act she would have investigated further in different circumstances, had time not been a pressing concern. As it was, she was anxious to leave whilst they still could and she let it go. They marched rapidly through the home without stopping to speak to anyone and reached their vehicle moments later. Kirsten started the engine, placed the car in reverse and looked over her shoulder.

Before she could pull off however, a loud tap suddenly sounded on the passenger window. It startled

Ian a little but when he looked up, the same nurse was peering in, willing him to wind down the window and clutching an item in his right hand.

Ian pushed the button and the glass lowered. The nurse was out of breath. He gasped a large lung full of air and then talked speedily between breaths.

'Won't stop you... Mr. Dunbar, he… he knew something like this was going to happen... we became quite close, he and I... he left me strict instructions... I have this for you.'

He pushed a sealed envelope through the car and handed it to Kirsten. 'He told me, in the event of his death, to hand this to his niece and nobody else. I was to tell you to read it as fast as you can. Not to delay.'

Kirsten thanked him and then raced off at speed. She drove down country roads for around ten miles until she found a small lane leading into an area covered by trees. She parked up in the shade, confident they could not be seen from the road or above. She glanced briefly at Ian and then opened the letter, read it aloud.

If you are reading this note I must be dead. Do not mourn me. I had a good life longer than most. Longer than many a good soul I knew and loved. Know that you were the main highlight. The daughter I never had. I'm sorry I was so hard on you. Never told you. You are all I dreamed you could be, and more.

Now, time to focus. They are tracking you. All agents are implanted with a device without their knowledge. It can be activated and de-activated when needed. It is standard practice. Think. It will be very small. They must have performed surgery on you at some point to insert it.'

'Holy shit!' exclaimed Ian. 'Those crafty bastards!'

Kirsty did not reply. She was following Dunbar's instructions and thinking hard. Then, it dawned on her.

'The tooth!'

'Eh? Come again?' said Ian.

'One of my first instructors knocked out my tooth in training. I hadn't learnt to duck at that stage. They fixed it. Put it back as good as new. I've had a few upgrades too over the years. It would be the perfect place to hide a micro-transmitter.'

Ian was a little staggered that news of this nature no longer surprised him. What did that say about his current state of mind?

'Right. What do we do then? See a dentist?' he asked, naively.

Kirsten simply smiled and took out her Leatherman multi tool.

Ian's eyes widened in horror as realisation dawned. 'Oh no! I can't. I'm feeling queasy just at the thought of it.'

Nevertheless, he knew immediately that he had no choice. Kirsten fetched a half bottle of vodka from the holdall. She took a swig and washed it around her gums. Then she opened wide, pointing out the offending tooth.

Five minutes later, they had discarded the smashed transmitter in the trees and were underway again. Ian was driving as Kirsten's mouth was bleeding badly and she was in considerable pain. She stemmed the blood loss with a bandage from the first aid kit but her mouth felt like it was on fire. To take her mind off the agony, she continued reading Dunbar's letter, albeit with some difficulty.

'...insert...ah. Something is happening inside our organisation. Something bad. The winds of change have come for us and they have blown in a plague of locusts. The latest batch of recruits, they went rogue. Well, some of them did. The ones not recruited by me. I started asking too many questions. We discovered two had conducted unsanctioned ops. We cornered them both, but they killed themselves before we could determine who they were working for.

Then, someone very professional with serious talent began targeting our personnel. Taking out those I trusted. We have lost two full agents and countless support personnel as I write. Good people we cannot replace. You will no doubt be briefed on that, may even be tasked, but what you do/will not know, is that this thing, whatever it is, goes right to the very top!

I'm sure of it now. They are **cleansing** *Szabo. I was warned some years ago by a trusted source that it was beginning. Well, it appears now that we have been infiltrated. If I'm right, they are removing those they do not control and they will not stop. I was top of their list but considered no threat perhaps? They may have left me alive to get to you? Whichever, you can trust nobody. Not now. To that end, I've taken some precautions. Prepared a little. I have a safe deposit box in Barclays Bank, Dundee. On the High Street. The key is in this envelope.'*

Kirsten turned the envelope upside down and a small silver key fell into the palm of her hand.

'Inside the box you will find secrets I could trust

to no one but you. But you must be careful! I tried my best to feign illness and cast doubt upon my mental capacity but I may have been followed. It's what I would have done. If they know about the bank, or bugged me, they may set a trap for you now. I am confident they know nothing of the contents within that box though. I placed a biometric lock on it, coded to the DNA of just you and me. Took a hair from your room. Clever, eh?'

Kirsten laughed a little inside. She would miss him so.

'If the lock is intact, so are my secrets. Sorry to put this on you. Good Luck.'

D.

She choked back her tears, folded the letter neatly, placed it and the key in the envelope and stuffed them inside the holdall. Ian expected her to talk but she remained quiet as she considered her next move.

'Well?' he said, impatiently.

'Mission priorities. In this case; the sniper, the bank, information retrieval, offensive action. In that order.'

'Okay.'

'That shooter came close to killing me, twice. Dunbar was no fool but if he *was* followed, the next logical step for them is to set an ambush. They will know I have to go for whatever he has left for me. I have no choice. And predictability gets you killed in this game.'

'So? You have a plan, right?'

'Yes. I'm tired of being a target. We're switching to counter-sniper tactics. Use what we have. What we know. You and I are going hunting, Ian. We'll hunt the sniper while he hunts us. First to blink, loses. You are going to the bank. You won't ask for the box, just walk in, nice and slow.'

'Me? Why me?'

'Because I will be busy and I am their primary. Your appearance alone will sew a little confusion and doubt at the right time. I'm banking on him hesitating. I will scope out the area beforehand, identify the most likely positions to set up. Predict the shot. Then, I'll take out the assassin before he can get to you, access the box and learn its secrets.'

Ian drew in a very deep breath. He swallowed hard. 'Why do I feel like a worm on a hook all of a sudden? I'll do it, of course I will, but… won't they send more than one now?'

'Maybe. But it will be a small outfit. They are conducting highly illegal business tantamount to treason. Their lives are on the line should they be discovered and they know it. The less who know what they are doing as far as they are concerned, the better. Stop at the next service station. We need to ditch this car and steal another. And I need to get cleaned up.'

They arrived at Dundee in the early hours of the morning, in an old and battered Audi A4. Ian drove by the bank just once before parking in a nearby back street. He caught up on some much-needed sleep as Kirsten disappeared to recce the area. She returned two hours later. It was still dark.

'Did… did you find it?' Ian asked, still half asleep.

'Yes. Two possibilities. Both give good elevation

and vision for targets entering or leaving the bank. Ease of access. Good exfil routes.'

'Oh, good. See you in the morning then.' And he drifted back off to sleep.

Kirsten fell asleep too. She awoke at first light. The streets were not busy. The bank opened at nine. She had taken an uncalculated risk in sleeping with no watch, which was a serious blunder. However, she had not been compromised and she prayed that kind of luck would last. She left the car.

At ten o'clock precisely, Ian climbed out and began the short walk to the bank. His heart was beating fast and his knees felt weak.

Kirsten had decided which of the two positions she would choose if the roles were reversed. She hoped she was right. The house in question was a large three-storey Georgian property which had been renovated and turned into a guest house. It had a rear staircase and exit which opened out onto a small, secluded resident's only car park. She spotted the Land Rover with blacked out windows as she approached and it raised her hopes. She opened the rear door to the property quietly and climbed the stairs to room six; the apartment which offered the best vantage point. Stopped at the door and strained to listen for any movement inside.

It was deathly quiet in that hallway for twelve minutes. Then, she heard a faint, hushed voice from within the apartment.

'There! It's him. But where is Erin?'

Her heart skipped a beat and she suddenly felt sick.

They called me Erin. They are from Grexley!

Her blood boiled at the thought of such betrayal.

It was up now so high that it would not be coming down until she had killed something. Her buttons were already pushed and nothing could stop her now.

On the other side of the door, the two assassins faced a dilemma. They would be deciding this instant on whether to kill her male companion whilst they had the chance. And the ramifications if they did. Professionals in her vocation decided such things easily, in the blink of an eye. If she needed another reason to act in haste, she had it.

She immediately took two steps back and drew her weapon. Then she kicked the door in with extreme force.

The Glock 18C machine pistol is a rare thing on the open market, or in dealerships. Not many are to be found outside of law enforcement or the Special Forces fraternity. Developed for the Austrian counter-terrorism unit in the 1980's, it fires over eleven hundred rounds a minute on fully automatic and has a thirty-three-round magazine. It is small, which means it is ideal for fire and manoeuvre in built-up areas. FIBUA. It is essentially a room clearer.

As the door opened, two targets presented themselves. They were positioned exactly as Kirsten had expected, in the centre of the room with the sniper staring down the barrel of an AR-15 with scope and suppressor, elevated and well back from the open window. A spotter sat on a nearby chair. Both were positioned expertly for the killshot.

Once again, instinct and training took over. And pure adrenalin.

Two Tangos. Sniper and spotter. Sniper is female. Spotter going for his gun!

Enraged, Kirsten unloaded the full magazine into them both. She ejected the empty mag without thought and replaced it with her spare. The sound was deafening. Too loud not to be heard.

She kicked over the sniper's bullet-ridden corpse and was horrified to discover that her wildest nightmare had been confirmed. It was Jay Jay. Her so-called best friend. The spotter was Neil; one of the guys who had completed the same SAS escape and evasion exercise.

She grabbed the rifle and an accompanying black haversack containing a separate weapon. Then she retreated quickly down the rear stairs and moved silently and swiftly out through the exit, without being seen. Stopped behind an industrial-sized bin and broke the rifle down into smaller parts, before packing them away, donning the heavy bag and returning to the car.

Ian arrived back half hour later. 'Oh my God! It's *madness* out there! There are police everywhere. They ushered everyone out of the bank. It's closed for the day, so what do we do now?'

'We stay calm. They are not looking for us, but some gangland hoodlum with an Uzi as far as they know. It will take them ages to get organised. We drive back the way we came. Stay the night somewhere and return in the morning.'

Ian placed the car in gear, reversed and drove away.

Chapter 14 - Operations

The colonel-in-chief of 5 British Military Intelligence Battalion, Royal Intelligence Corps was frustrated and mystified. Colonel Stewart Lawton was a fifty-six-year-old career soldier. He had many years of exemplary military service behind him and in all his time serving the crown, he had *never* received such a ludicrous, preposterous order as this. It was against all he believed, all he stood for, and it would undoubtedly create division and dissention in the ranks. He was not a happy man.

Nonetheless, Colonel Lawton was discipline personified. A man of impeccable character, he was without doubt an excellent soldier and though he disagreed wholeheartedly with the instruction he had been given, an order was still an order.

It came in the form of a surprise, unscheduled and unannounced visit to Catterick Garrison from the current Director of Intelligence Corps, Brigadier Charles Howarth MC, clandestine Szabo agent and fully-fledged hero. After exchanging pleasantries, touring the base and meeting the staff, a more private conversation was then held in Colonel Lawton's office, where the two men relaxed a little and broke out the scotch. It was only after he had consumed his second glass that the brigadier cut to the chase.

'Stewart, this was not a social call, as I'm sure you gathered. The real reason for the visit, the point of my being here, is this; I'm going to lay something on you that you will not like, I'm afraid. Something you just have to accept without question. It goes against the grain maybe, but I would not ask this of you if there were not excellent reasons behind it. Reasons which can never be aired, discussed or divulged. You understand what I am saying? This is sanctioned at the highest level and that is all you need to know.'

'Yes, sir. Of course.'

The brigadier filled his glass from the bottle again, helping himself as men of his lofty rank often do. 'Excellent. I am glad we are on the same page. I knew you would feel this way. You have a new lieutenant joining your staff.'

'We do? That's news to me. I know nothing of this,' said the colonel.

'I'm telling you now.'

'Oh, I see, sir.'

'She is somewhat of a rising star. Though I realise this may place you in a difficult position, you will allow her access to all areas and all investigations. Bar none. Particularly level one threats against this country, foreign and domestic. Anything you undertake in partnership with other agencies, you will share with her. She has top level clearance and the confidence of all at HQ. She will undertake duties assigned by you and you alone. Or your successor. You will indulge her, nurture her, and treat her as your aide-de-camp. Involve her in everything you do.'

'I will? That is highly irregular, if you don't mind me saying so? My current staff will not like it. And I am sorry, I have to admit that I feel the same way.'

'Yes. I understand. If I were in your shoes, I'd object too. But the decision has been made by those above you and frankly, I do not care. You have your orders.'

'Yes, sir.'

'You won't show your reluctance or mistrust to her or anyone else. You will give good face and have her back at all times. Defend her as if she were your own daughter. She is highly skilled and will provide you I'm certain with excellent support… Here is the real kick in the guts though; her *actual* role is, and will continue to be, as a highly specialised liaison officer with Special Forces Command. That is highly classified and for your ears only.'

'Sir.'

'Good. It means, unfortunately for you, that she will have license to come and go at will. She will disappear at a moment's notice and for undeterminable durations. You will not be warned, be told why or where to, nor for how long. Nature of the job, I'm afraid.'

'But that puts me in an unworkable position as her commander.'

Brigadier Howarth was sympathetic. 'Possibly. It is what we have to work with though. And selling it to you in any other way, would be doing you a disservice.'

Colonel Lawton looked into his scotch and then up at his senior officer. 'Anything else?'

'Yes. Should you deploy to an active war zone, she will not accompany you. We have spent a lot of money on her and to be frank, she is too valuable to serve in a frontline unit. Don't want an IED or stray bullet taking her out. She will be doing her fair share of fighting in her own way, don't you worry. More than any of us perhaps. But it will be at *our* discretion.'

'I have to say, sir, this will not sit well with the other ranks.'

'No, I dare say it will not. You can tell them she is my staff officer if you like, on secondment. That I forbade it.'

'Thank you. That will do.'

'In time, you will thank me for this, believe me. There is something special about this one. Wait until you meet her. She will enhance your staff no end. She's bright and forthcoming with her opinions. You may want to heed her advice from time to time.'

'Right. Such a glowing endorsement of a junior officer from you cannot be ignored. When does she arrive?'

'Monday. Remember, more perceptive eyes than mine are watching her and you. Her name is Charlotte Evans. Likes to be called Charlie though, as young girls do these days. Now, let's see if we can do some more damage to that bottle of yours, eh?'

It was two months since her first successful mission. She was beginning to become used to being called Charlie. She had selected the name herself, as always. And she had spent the past few weeks preparing for her new life as a lieutenant in the British Army. The delay in taking up her posting had been explained to her only briefly, when Dunbar had said to her one morning, 'You will find out for yourself, when you see your digs.'

The Saturday before she had to report to the barracks, she made her way to the address she had been given, her new home. It was all fully paid for out of the Operation Szabo slush fund nobody ever talked about.

Brompton-on-Swale is a small village just over four miles from Catterick Garrison in North Yorkshire. A peaceful hamlet comprised of new and old houses. The older cottages are picturesque marvels of the landscape. Steps back in time. And the most charming of them all, was now hers.

Charlie was overjoyed and awash with emotion at

having such a wonderful first home. It was exquisite. Everything she had ever dreamed of. And as an added bonus, it was cycling or running distance from the base. Perfect. She opened the old wooden door and took a long look around, falling in love with the place instantly. So much so, that she did not see the note on the kitchen table for almost an hour. It was from Dunbar.

Hope you like the place and will be very happy here. I chose it myself. Good luck in your new job. You'll find a picture hanging next to the door leading down to the cellar. Behind it is a retinal scanner. Make sure you are alone when you use it.

D.

She felt a surge of excitement flow through her entire body. She locked the front door for privacy and moved the picture. Placed her right eye to the scanner. Two laser-like beams of red light moved over every inch of her eye, twice. The old wooden stable door clicked loudly, opening only an inch. She reached forwards and pulled it to her. Behind it, was a floor to ceiling metal re-enforced blast-proof door and on the frame was a small biometric pad. She placed her thumb on the square and the whole door slid slowly to the left, disappearing behind the plaster board to reveal a set of dark and steep stairs.

So that's why they kept me at Herik; fixing this lot up.

She flicked the light switch and proceeded carefully down the old steps. She was immediately stunned and amazed by the sight that greeted her at the bottom. The entire cellar was pristine, bedecked floor to ceiling with racking. On every shelf sat oodles of equipment, from guns and ammunition to bags, explosives, timers, detonators, clothing and maps. On every wall too there were shadow boards, with weapons of all shapes and descriptions filling the darkness. Everything she would ever need to be an effective agent was right here in this room. It must have cost an absolute fortune and taken ages to set up.

In the middle of the cellar was a solitary table and chair. On the counter was a state-of-the-art computer, linked to Operation Szabo Command Headquarters and powerful enough to hack into most satellites or secure networks. She spent a long time checking out the equipment but then decided she should return upstairs and unload her stuff.

Just prior to leaving the vault she noticed a small glass case on the wall. It had a large red button under the glass and the wording simply read, 'Self Destruct.'

She wondered how long she would have to vacate the premises once the sequence was engaged. And prayed that she would never have to find out.

And so, Lieutenant Charlotte 'Charlie' Evans began her double-edged career. She was mostly an intelligence officer at Catterick, where she soon began to win people over with her professionalism and evident competence. She became a highly valued member of the team in no time. Her prowess on the range with any weapon won over most of the doubters, though she was never fully accepted due to the special treatment she enjoyed and the fact she could never speak of where she went, and what she did.

She loved village life and though she did not

socialise often, she did find time for a few short relationships with men she liked. They did not last however, as she would eventually disappear for long periods of time and insisted on keeping secrets upon return. Secrets which they could never accept she was not willing to divulge. Deal breaker.

She maintained contact with only Jay Jay and Dunbar from her time at Herik. They were the only people she corresponded with, called or visited outside of her new life. The only link she had with her past. The only ones she trusted when not on operations.

Szabo missions were frequent and unpredictable. She was often called on her mobile phone, the number registering on her display as, 'Auntie Cynth.' In reality, it was Szabo Command and the phone call was re-routed through numerous destinations across Europe in the blink of an eye, meaning it was a secure line, untraceable and safe. She would be given a time and a place, nothing more. There, she would meet her handler or mission co-ordinator and receive a full briefing. She would then travel to the target destination by whatever means, plan and complete the hit, before returning home and resuming army life.

In the first two years she built a solid reputation for cold efficiency. Straight forward assassinations were normally missions of relatively short duration. The trick was not to be compromised or captured. They took time to study and plan. The target had to be followed, all variables accounted for, an effective plan developed including logistics, infiltration and exfiltration, contingencies, weapons and tactics… However, often the whole assignment might only last a matter of days. Or weeks. And where the timeframe was dictated by an upcoming event such as a personal appearance, speech or conference, she could leave the country if needed, perform the hit, and be back in no time.

The lengthier missions involved intel-gathering before the hit. Often infiltration of a known group or faction. Fortunately, she had only received one such mission so far.

She had lost count by now of the victims she had dispatched. In the beginning, she kept a running total in her head. Saw their faces in her dreams, though she was not affected like some. Now though, they were no longer people. They were marks. Figure eight targets she needed to put down. Nothing more. She had taken out oil magnets, corrupt politicians, military dictators, gang leaders, spies, diplomats, presidential hopefuls, financiers, Mafia colonels, regular men and women delving into things best left alone…

She was a trained killer and she enjoyed her life. Both sides of it. Young, happy and carefree, she slept soundly at night, in the darkness, alone with her thoughts. She became a top-level assassin, living a life of danger and wild excitement. She knew she might have to leave that life at a moment's notice. Discovery and retribution were only a heartbeat away. One mistake. One fatal error. One miscalculation. That was all it took. It did not seem advisable therefore to become too attached to anything. Or anyone.

Chapter 15 – Present Day

The motel they found outside of Dundee was cheap and nasty. The type of place which constantly begs the question, 'How on earth do they stay in business?' At least the old beat-up Audi looked right at home in the car park though. The Discovery would have stood out like a sore thumb and probably have been missing some vital parts, like wheels, come the morning. The room was small and smelt of stale something. Maybe even a concoction of somethings. Ian spent fifteen minutes searching for what had died and then gave up trying. Some smells just refuse to leave. The entire place needed a good clean but no amount of scrubbing was going to suffice. Especially in the bathroom, where mould was growing upon mould in the shower grout, between the tiling.

Kirsten washed the cutlery and plates they would be using whilst Ian visited a nearby supermarket for supplies. He returned not long afterwards with a whole load of cleaning products, some ready meals, drinks and snacks. He dumped the bags on the floor, kicked off his shoes, jumped on the bed with a tube of Pringles and hit the remote, turning on the T.V.

He heard the shower start up and the bathroom door lock. Kirsten was in there a long, long time. It was afternoon now and Ian knew she had stated they could do no more until morning. Still, he was restless. Filled with nervous energy. The Pringles weren't doing it. They had the best part of an afternoon and an evening to kill together.

Eventually, he heard the water stop and Kirsten opening the cubicle door. He called out to her knowing she would easily hear him through the paper-thin walls.

'Hey, you alive in there? Do you fancy trying a restaurant tonight? I mean, is it safe? Got some meals if not, but we *are* in the middle of nowhere after all. Maybe we could find a bar and have a few drinks? It's gonna be pretty boring in here otherwise?'

The door was unbolted from inside and opened slowly. Out into the living area stepped the attractive young assassin. She was wearing only her bath towel. Her hair had been put up but loose strands were hanging down here and there dripping water, which fell tantalisingly onto her cleavage. The towel was tucked into itself and secured at her side, by her ample breasts. It was damp having been used to dry her and it clung tightly to her body, finishing high on her thighs, barely covering her shapely behind. The contrast of the white towel against her brown skin was mesmerising, intoxicating. Heaven.

Ian sat up straight, not knowing what to do and where to look. He could feel a stirring in his loins already, as she moved deliberately slowly, sexily, to stand in front of him.

Is she toying with me? No, surely not? I am old enough to be her father. And she is a beauty queen.

He had never seen such a vision of loveliness. Had never wanted a woman so badly in all of his life. He was like a teenager again, shaking with nerves and devoid of his usual confidence.

'We *could* go out and find a pub, if you'd like,' she replied, in a soft voice oozing sex appeal. 'But then, I think we should stay in and make our own entertainment, right here?'

His jaw just dropped at that. He was instantly

under her spell and completely helpless, found that he could neither speak nor move for a moment.

Slowly, her right hand reached for the towel and undid the fold holding it up. She opened the whole thing in tiny stages, as if deliberately putting on a peep show for her lover. Teasing him, tormenting, torturing the man she knew full well was fighting every sinew now, every primal urge raging though his mind and soul to ravish her.

Finally, her entire body was exposed and she let the towel fall to the floor.

That was like a bomb going off inside of him. He let out an involuntary gasp of delight at the sight of her. It literally took his breath away. She was perfection. Her dark skin was littered with various scars but they in no way detracted from her astonishing beauty. He could not believe his luck. What on earth could she possibly see in him?

He did not care. Not now. Not this instant. All thoughts of his wife, his life back home, his current problems and likely outcomes, everything, simply vanished. He was here in this moment and that was all he could focus on right now. All he wanted to focus on. He just wanted to seize this opportunity and make it last forever.

Ian stood up. Slowly, he inched closer to her as if she might bite, for some reason still uncertain and hesitant.

'I…'

She shook her head slightly and placed a solitary finger up to his lips. Even that simple action had him lost in a sea of ecstasy. How did she capture his heart and mind together so easily? Did she know the astonishing power she wielded?

Of course she did.

'No words. Let's just enjoy tonight,' she whispered softly into his ear.

Confidently, like the temptress she was trained to be, well-practised in the art of seduction, she took his hand in hers and moved it gently over her body, placed it on her breast, rubbing his fingers slowly over her nipple.

There was no ambiguity now. She wanted this as much as him. So why was his heart racing like a Formula One car and his head so light?

He could not resist staring down at her stunning body. It was like a magnet drawing him in, pulling his eyes away from hers, no matter how hard he resisted.

She countered this by moving her hand to his chin and gently drawing it upwards. She was in full control now and the next thing he knew, she had kissed him full on his lips.

It was surprisingly soft and tender. Moist. Loving almost. Sublime.

She drew back a little, inviting him to make the next move.

Sod the pub or restaurant!

And he kissed her again. Only this time, it was long and hard and passionate. Their tongues met. Hands roamed freely, exploring every accessible inch of their bodies. The pace became frenzied and his desire for her soon reached boiling point.

Then, just when he thought he could wait no longer, she pulled away and pushed him down onto the bed. He fell and she was straddling him before he knew it.

He relaxed then. Lay back and gave in to her

completely.

Ian was awoken by the sound of Kirsten brushing her teeth in the bathroom. It was morning and it was light outside. She returned to the room and began to dress. He just lay there and watched. He no longer cared that he was acting inappropriately. He couldn't help but stare at her, she was so gorgeous. Their lovemaking had lasted a long time. It was without doubt the greatest single night of his life. A fantasy realised which could never be taken away from him, one he would live over and over again in his mind, of that there was no doubt. He was still smiling ear to ear like a Cheshire cat.

The afternoon session had been enjoyable in the extreme. The following two nightly adventures though, had really blown his mind.

'What time is it?' Ian asked, breaking the silence.

'Just past nine. We slept in.'

'I suppose we did. But then, we were up rather late,' he replied, smiling slightly, unsure how to broach the subject.

She ceased putting in her earrings and stared at him. 'Look, may as well get this out in the open. Last night, was last night. It was nice, but it's finished. Don't go making a big deal of it, okay?'

He sat up straight in bed. 'Nice? Nice? Okay.'

'Yes. It was fun. Thanks. I had needs. You fulfilled those needs. Now move on.'

That was pretty much as good a conversation killer as he had ever heard. He rose out of bed and made his way to the bathroom. At the door, he stopped and turned to face her.

'Well, I just want to say, I had a good time too.

And if you ever have those needs again, please don't hesitate to ask. Always willing to do my bit for team morale.' He smiled cheekily. 'So, where are we going now? To the bank?'

'Soon. Shopping first. You are going to buy me some wigs, clothes and make-up.' She took a wad of cash from her holdall and threw it on the bed. 'Here. I'll wait in the car for you, just in case. I'll wear what you buy and go to the bank, so make it good.'

Great, he thought. *Back to normal.*

He turned around and closed the bathroom door.

At half past eleven a smartly dressed, red-haired lady in a fur coat and sunglasses strode confidently into Barclays bank, Dundee. She asked to see the manager and handed him the details of her safe deposit box. He checked her name was on the account and verified her identification. Satisfied all was in order, he led her to a private viewing room. Once there, he closed the door and left her alone with the box.

Kirsten opened it by placing her finger on the biometric lock and using the key Dunbar had left for her. She peered inside. The contents consisted of a Browning nine-millimetre pistol, two spare magazines, another key and a handwritten note. She pocketed the key, tucked the pistol inside her belt, the mags in her bag and read the note.

So, you got my letter then? Hope I died well. They must have thought I knew more than I did. It was only a matter of time though.

The key is to a locked garage on my brother's estate. He's my half-brother and not many know of his existence. He is both deaf and blind. Archie worked with your mother for a short time but he knows nothing as far as I know. In the garage you will find a few weapons. Also, some extra kit I managed to scrounge together for you. There are some bank details in there too. I set up an account when this all began. It is undetectable, in the Turks and Caicos Islands. I diverted some funds that way, loose change to them which will not be missed. There should be a few million in there by now. I'm sorry I can't help further. It's up to you to stop them. Whatever they are up to.

D.

Oh, the address is on the reverse of this note.

Kirsten closed and locked the box. She handed it back to the bank manager, thanked him and walked slowly out of the building.

They drove immediately to Archie's estate. It was approaching evening by the time they arrived. The whole place was huge. Archie turned out to be minor Scottish nobility and his estate was crowned by a fine country manor house. They rang the bell cautiously and an elderly lady answered the door. They showed her some identification, explained what had happened to Dunbar and why they were there. The lady was Archie's wife. She invited them in and informed them that her husband was old and frail, and taking a siesta. She showed them where the garage could be found and asked if they would like to go and take a look for themselves.

The 'few weapons' Dunbar had liberated turned out to be a complete arsenal. A massive haul of pistols, machine guns, sniper rifles… And the kit included night vision equipment, clothing, webbing and communication gear.

Kirsten's heart raced. 'We are back in this fight.'

Ian was happy too. And not just because of last night. At last, he was beginning to believe he might see an end to this horror show he was living. A resolution of some sort. A chance to clear his name and hopefully return to some kind of normality.

'Okay,' said Kirsten. 'Now, to really understand what is happening here, we need information direct from the source, from someone at the heart of what is going on.'

'Who? De Wigt?' Ian asked.

'Not yet. Too well guarded. Though, that day is coming.'

'Then who?'

'Roger Hanson. His Security Chief. The money man. We are going to kidnap him. Make him talk. If he arranged payment, he must be trusted. I think he will know a great deal and it's our best shot at getting to the truth.'

Ian was not so sure that was a good idea. 'Didn't Dunbar say he was some kind of a walking Terminator?'

Kirsten suddenly exuded extreme confidence. And happiness. She was in her element now.

'Yeah. So we need to plan carefully. Minimise the risks. Should be fun.'

Chapter 16 - Operations

At the Casa Rosada, or Pink House, in Buenos Aires, a lavish reception was being held in honour of a state visit by the Norwegian royal family. The palatial mansion is the seat of the Argentine national government and boasts the balconies from which Juan and 'Evita' Perón addressed the masses during the late nineteen forties and early fifties. The building and grounds are some of the finest in South America and an event of this magnitude was attended by the elite of Argentine society. The magnificent ball in itself was not headline news to many outside of Argentina though. What *had* caught the attention of Operation Szabo commanders, MI6, the CIA and many other intelligence agencies around the world however, was the anticipated attendance of General Jose Louis Ramirez, Chief of the Argentine Defence Staff. The hardliner was expected to use the occasion to meet with up to eight of his prospective allies. Szabo and MI6 in particular had been tracking Ramirez' associates and movements for many months now, in tandem with their counterparts in the CIA. He had been deemed a person of interest for many years, a heavy hitter likely to achieve high value target status.

Jose Louis Ramirez had been a rising star in the Argentine military for some time. His father was a hero pilot of the Falklands War who had also served in high political office afterwards. As his father's fame and prestige grew, the young Jose attended the finest Argentine schools before graduating from the prestigious Colegio Militar De La Nacion; the National Military College. He had been born and groomed for greatness and was considered now to be destined for the very top, possibly Argentina's next President. And he hated Great Britain and all her subjects with every fibre of his being. With unrivalled passion.

Argentina was in the midst of a financial and economic crisis. Inflation was virtually out of control, the economy in disarray, corruption in government rife, and elements of the police and military were operating independently with impunity. The civilian population were scared and angry, demanding change. Demonstrations were increasing in number, size and ferocity. The time was right, Ramirez and many in the armed services believed, for revolution.

In the twentieth century Argentina had endured no less than six military coups. The last of these occurred in 1976 and ultimately led to the full-scale military invasion of the Falklands Islands, or the Malvinas as the Argentineans called them. War with Great Britain followed. A war which Argentina lost heavily, affecting the whole country adversely for years. General Ramirez was now trying to do everything in his power to 'right this wrong.' Hungry for more authority and influence, he was energetically recruiting for the next military junta and actively vying for the top job. To succeed in his plans for domination, he needed the support of numerous top generals just like him; disaffected and disgruntled fighters and leaders who believed in him and his cause. He had arranged therefore for selected individuals to receive invitations to tonight's celebration, intending to use the opportunity to charm them in person and hopefully receive their pledge of endorsement.

Charlie was at work in Catterick two days previously when she received another text message from her 'Auntie Cynth.' It simply stated, *'Fox and Hound. 1400.'*

She sent a quick e-mail to the colonel informing him of her latest 'family emergency' and made her way home. She was met sometime later in the local pub by a man she neither recognised nor knew. He said hello, gave her the required password, finished his drink, handed her a sealed envelope and left.

Inside was another short note. She pocketed it and read it in her car on a deserted country lane shortly afterwards.

Buenos Aires. Wheels up 1900. Pick up 1800.

She had been taught to speak both Spanish and German whilst in training on Herik. She was fluent in both and looking forward to putting her Spanish accent to the test. She burned the note, drove home, took a shower and fixed herself something to eat.

At six o'clock precisely a black Jaguar X-Type pulled up outside her front door. Sitting at the wheel was a man she knew as Jasper. He had served as her Handler on two previous missions and given a good account of himself on both. She liked him because he was calm, professional and straight to the point. More importantly, she trusted him.

'Charlie. Get in. We have a Challenger 300 waiting at Leeds Bradford airport. I'll talk as I drive. You will receive a full briefing on the plane. All the gear you will need is on there too. We've picked out a nice evening dress for you this time.'

The young agent raised her eyebrows and then smiled. 'It will make a nice change from combat fatigues, that's for sure. What is it, honeytrap?'

Jasper kept his eyes on the road but shook his head. 'No. Well? You're going to a full state reception. Swanky do. As a guest of the American Ambassador no less. Girlfriend of one of his aids. Best bib and tucker. He is a widower. We've managed to persuade his real girlfriend to sit this one out. We thought you would be perfect as the local hooker?'

'Oi!'

'Ha ha… Okay, the local high-class escort then.'

'That's better.'

'Anyhoo, the Yanks are doing us a favour on this one. They have already got us in the front door. All you have to do is administer the poison.'

'Poison?' she asked, surprised.

'Yeah. Different, eh? It's new. From the Americans again. It's called BTX-15. Takes two days or more to kill the subject. Painful death, I'm told. But if you succeed, this one could actually prevent a war.'

'Really? Do tell?'

'That General Ramirez, your mark, he's up to no good. Wants to take over the country and blames the British for all the evils in the world. It's history repeating itself. He's a little Hitler. Give the people a common enemy and… You know the rest. He's going to start another war if he's not stopped. Going to try to take back the Malvinas. He's spent the last couple of years gearing up for it. Buying new fighters and missiles...'

Charlie took a deep breath, held it a second and then let it out. 'Ignoring the ninety-eight per cent of Falkland Islanders who want to remain British in the process. As well as the hundreds, thousands who will die if it comes to another fight. And we British don't usually shy away from mixing it up, if we have to.'

'Yes. Quite. Fisticuffs at dawn.'

'I'd say that places him high on our agenda.'

The Challenger touched down at Jorge Newbery airport, Buenos Aires and a limousine drove Charlie to her hotel. At seven thirty she received a call in her room to tell her that the ambassador's subordinate was waiting in his car. She checked herself over in the mirror one last time and was pleased with what she saw.

She was wearing an absolutely stunning off-the-shoulder Christian Dior evening dress in a subtle shade of gold, with matching gloves. A tiny belt hugged her waistline and accentuated her curves. Her hair was up but strategically placed strands were hanging down low to her neckline, which was itself bejewelled with diamonds on loan from De Beers no less. Szabo had both deep pockets and friends in high places. A pair of Loubutin high heels accentuated her long and tanned legs.

The American Ambassador's right-hand man was named Richard Johnson the Third. He was confident, tall, broad-shouldered and loud. Everything she had grown to expect of his countrymen. He seemed nice with it though and she could not quite decide if she liked him a little more than she ought.

They arrived at Casa Rosada and joined the long line of dignitaries waiting to shake hands with the Argentine President. They were greeted by numerous officials and VIP's before entering the main function room. For the next two hours Charlie talked, listened, flirted and danced the night away. She was the belle of the ball and turned a lot of heads, declined scores of invitations to dance. All the time she was scanning the room for the generals whose photos she had been shown on flash cards on the flight. Each one she identified, she radioed through a corresponding codeword to Jasper, who was listening on comms from a mobile rig. Soon, all the would-be conspirators were accounted for, but she had not yet located or seen the main prize; General Ramirez.

Suddenly, her primary target stepped out of a side room. Unbeknown to her, he had been in there all along, conducting several quiet meetings out of sight. He was almost immediately surrounded by well-wishers and appeared to be very popular. One by one the generals shook his hand and seemed to bow in deference, perhaps acquiescing to some previously divulged request. The hairs on the back of Charlie's neck rose. Something exceedingly dangerous was happening here, she was sure of it. Something on the world level which could end up killing a lot of people.

She slipped off the cap covering the tiny needle protruding from her ring. The hollow gold band was filled with just enough BTX-15 to kill a large man. Liquid death.

She made her excuses to the men gathered around her like flies and headed towards Ramirez and the bathroom beyond. Her chest was heaving, her heart racing. She was an experienced killer by now but this hit was to be conducted right under the noses of the cream of world society. Directly in front of the CIA, Argentine Special Service agents and royalty. And with the full knowledge of the Americans, it seemed.

She much preferred the smaller teams she was used to. It just did not feel right inside to involve so many others.

Despite her reservations, she knew she would

have limited opportunity to fulfil her mission. As she passed General Ramirez she slowed completely and flashed him her very best smile. A smile which would melt any heart and set any man's temperature rising.

He was only human and he took the bait.

'Excuse me, Senorita. May I have this dance?'

She glanced over towards Richard Johnson the Third. 'I'm not sure my date would like me dancing with someone so handsome. I'm with the man over there. He works for the American Ambassador.'

'Pah! Americans. I eat them for breakfast.'

He smiled and Charlie smiled too.

'Okay then. I will risk it if you will?' she said.

To the disappointment and consternation of many men there, he took her hand and led her onto the dance floor. They danced and made polite conversation for several minutes. He pulled her closer and predictably, his hands began to wander a little. She let it play out for a while but his left hand soon brushed the top of her right buttock. She slapped it away playfully and then acted shocked as he recoiled slightly, having felt a sharp and unnatural scratch.

'What's wrong?' she asked, her face a picture of innocence. 'Did my ring catch you? I'm sorry. You had better keep those hands up then?'

He was too embarrassed to risk causing a scene, though he knew something was off. They finished the dance in almost complete silence. Then, she let him kiss her hand and headed straight for the bathroom. She checked the stalls and the room but she was alone. She slowed her heart rate and contacted Jasper.

'Acorn to Pronto. Hope you got that. Package delivered. Over.'

She slipped off the ring, wrapped it in tissue and dropped it into the nearest toilet, hitting the flush. She pulled a duplicate from her bag and slid it on. The reply was almost immediate.

'Pronto received. Enjoy the rest of your evening. Out.'

She moved to the mirror and began freshening her make-up before re-joining her date. Seconds later however, faint shouts and cries could be heard coming from the ballroom.

'Acorn to Pronto, what's happening? Over.'

'Standby. We're picking up radio chatter. Checking CCTV feeds...'

A short delay of five seconds seemed like an eternity. A bead of sweat trickled down her forehead and she wiped it away.

'Bug out! Get out now!' cried Jasper in her ear. 'He's collapsed. The General. They will be locking the whole place down. Searching.'

The experienced agent's heart almost stopped.

Collapsed?! How?! The poison is supposed to take two days or more to work. That's what they said!

She took a few deep breaths, realising that she needed to remain calm so she could think straight. Prioritise. She could analyse events later, when it was safe to do so.

'Pronto, emergency protocol activated. I'm destroying evidence and anything that will incriminate me. One way comms from hereon. Out.'

She removed the receiver in her ear. Wrapping it in another wad of toilet paper, she threw the bundle into the same toilet and flushed it again. Then she checked her purse. Nothing untoward. Security had been as tight as expected on entry so she had been allowed no phone, no weapons, except the ring and the odourless and colourless poison she had just discarded.

The poison they had secured from the Americans.

Have they set me up? No, surely not? They are one of our closest allies. Why would they?

She checked her I.D. It was short term only. She was local; a high-class escort called Julianna Acosta. Hired by a lonely widower to make him look good in front of his boss and the entire world. The Argentines would believe that, she hoped.

However, closer scrutiny of her identification would reveal deep holes in her cover story. She would be fine for a limited time only because she looked Spanish, possibly Argentinian. And her accent was good. She would just have to bluff it out, see what would happen. She straightened her dress and strode confidently out into the corridor.

Straight into a palace guard and his sub machine gun.

'Hands in the air!' the soldier ordered in Spanish. 'What are you doing here?'

Charlie looked at him as if he were dense. She pointed to the senorita sign on the door like she was teaching a small child the alphabet.

'Oh. Very well. Quick, with the others in the main room. Move!'

He pointed his gun menacingly at her chest. She did her best impression of a very scared lady and rushed into the grand hall. She was herded into a group of detainees who occupied the centre of the room. More were joining them all the time, having been found in other areas of the palace. Around the edges of the room, surrounding them, were armed guards and police, with weapons drawn. She noticed none of the ambassadors, VIP's, royal guests, generals or dignitaries had been held. All had already departed, or were about to.

She caught sight of the U.S. Ambassador and his aid. They were making their way out but Johnson saw her and walked swiftly over. He asked the guard for two minutes and was granted one. He spoke in a hushed voice. And he appeared to be severely embarrassed by what he was about to say.

'I'm sorry. It's not down to me. I've been ordered to leave. Without you. I don't like it but my career is on the line here. I daren't disobey. Good luck to you.'

He turned to walk away.

'Wait! Is this you? Your lot?' she asked.

Silence.

'Just tell me why, please? We are supposed to be allies?'

She could tell he knew something. He just had that look about him; like he'd slept with her best friend but now regretted it. And he seemed reluctant to own up, even though he knew it was the right thing to do.

'Look, I had nothing to do with this, I swear. I knew zilch until just now, when I heard a soldier say they were looking for an English spy. If you are caught and linked to me, it will be an international scandal on a grand scale. Someone in the American Embassy aiding a foreign assassin on Argentine soil? So close to the ambassador and right on our doorstep? Against a supposed ally in the region? I'm putting two and two together, and maybe I'm making five, but I think the CIA would…'

The guard ordered him to move at that moment

and he did, in double quick time, as if his life depended on it. He looked back just once more before he was gone.

Charlie knew she was in deep, deep trouble now. She was alone. The evening had turned rapidly into what the British squaddies call, a 'Cake and Arse Party.' It had gone tits up real fast. The general was dead. The mission accomplished. But the Americans, or more accurately the CIA, had probably set her up. For whatever reason, they had left her to take the fall and beat a hasty retreat. Now, she had to deal with the aftermath. The British she knew would disavow her completely, deny all knowledge and culpability. That was the rules of the game and she had no complaints.

She also had no weapons. No phone. No backup to speak of. No viable exit strategy or contingency plan... Nobody had foreseen a fuckup of this magnitude. A double-cross. A hidden agenda.

She did not even know if Jasper had been compromised too. If he could hear what was happening or was languishing in some prison or police cell. Or worse. Had they already killed the one man who might be able to help her?

The only positive she could find was that the Argentine police did not appear to know who they were looking for. It had been a last-minute operation. The timeframe on target and in the kill zone had been very short. Perhaps, whoever blew the whistle had not actually seen her? Did not possess a description?

It was a slim hope which would not last long, but she was clutching at straws now and slim was quite appealing at this point. She would take anything on offer in fact.

The soldiers around her began searching their

captives. She had nothing incriminating in possession except for the minute microphone hidden in her dress, and she was confident they would not find that. So, why was she so scared?

She knew why.

I've just murdered a high-ranking member of the Argentine military in their own back yard. A golden child many here considered their great hope. In Argentina, that carries the death penalty!

Chapter 17 – Present Day

Archie Dunbar was not a well man. Cancer had ravaged him in recent months leaving him thin and frail. The octogenarian looked closer to a hundred now. He ventured downstairs for tea only because they had guests, whereas he would normally remain in his room. He could no longer walk unaided. Up until recently his disabilities had not curbed his independence in the house he had occupied all of his life. He knew every inch of the place and his mobility cane had enabled him to walk around freely. Now though, he needed his wife's help to do anything and was too feeble and weak to leave his bed most days. He communicated with her and others using tactile sign language and read using Braille. A specially adapted wheelchair which he lived in most of the time was fitted with a modified keypad and electronic voice box. Alice Dunbar would tap away on his arm with practised skill as his interpreter and he would respond moments later using a combination of his two devices.

Alice was his soulmate, partner, nurse and lifeline, his only connection to the world. She meant everything to him. She had explained why the visitors were there and what had really happened to his brother, was cautious and wary at first, advised that becoming involved would be too dangerous, that they should send the strangers away. But Archie was a rebel at heart and he wanted one last fling. One final act of defiance that he himself owned. To go out on his terms, feeling like he was still fighting and making a difference. He no longer feared death. He had accepted it was coming for him soon and made his peace with that fact. Had loved his only sibling dearly and wanted to know more of what he had been involved in at the end. Why he had been murdered. So, as they ate a delicious meal and he barely touched his own food, he asked numerous questions of his two guests.

Kirsten tried her best to respond truthfully. She told him all they knew in as much detail as she dared. All they *thought* they knew too; theories, guesses, knowledge gaps... Ian was content to let her do the talking. When she finished, Archie busily typed away and moments later the electronic voice sounded.

'I will miss Mikey. He was as tough as they come. But to me, he was always my kid brother. I never thought he would die before me. We have both served Szabo well in our own way. Faithfully. Sacrificed more than most. I want you… No, I need you to avenge his death for me. Avenge it for all those who have died because of this new threat. Expose them all. Kill them all!'

In his fury, he was typing so fast and hard that Kirsten thought he would break a finger on those weak and delicate hands. She stood up, walked to his side and knelt down, placed her hand on his in a surprisingly warm and generous gesture.

'We will do as you ask. That was my intention anyway. I will see it done. I swear it.'

The old man smiled a little and relaxed, as if a great pressure had been relieved. After a few seconds and now calmed a little, he typed once more.

'Take whatever you need from me. All of it if you like. I know what he was keeping in that garage of his because he told me. Said he needed it for a rainy day. Well, it is pouring now and it's all yours. We have no need and you are the closest thing to family he had. I know he would want this. There is a Jaguar F-Type under a cover behind it. It's yours too with our blessing. It's almost new but we hardly ever use it. Won't miss it at all. It's taxed, MOT'd and insured so nobody will trace it to you, unless you want to be found. There are several sets of plates in there too, just in case. Leave your car in its place and nobody will know a thing.'

'Thank you, but that's too generous of you. That's an expensive ride. Are you sure?' she asked.

He gave a small nod as he typed. 'Yes. You can't take money with you where I am going. And we have far more than we need anyway. Alice will be very well provided for. Mikey made sure of that.'

Kirsten patted his hand gently. 'Thanks again. You've been a real star. There's something else I'd like to ask if I may? I'm told you knew my mother?'

'That was a long time ago. And for far briefer than I would have liked. Like you, she was extraordinarily attractive. That was no accident your parents died in. I can tell you that, but not much else. There was too much going on at that time. We never paid too much attention to what agents were doing off their own back. There were rumours that she had upset some very dangerous people within the organisation. Asked way too many sensitive questions. And then… It was all too much of a co-incidence; her being sent away and both of them dying so soon afterwards. In the manner they did. It looked and felt like a hit and cover up, but nobody was interested in investigating. I do not have much more than that though. Just a feeling we all shared. After a short while, it was all forgotten. I'm sorry. I liked her.'

Kirsten's eyes lowered and she sighed in disappointment. She had hoped for more. They stayed the night in separate rooms and left early next morning, the boot of the Jag crammed full of weapons, ammunition, equipment and kit.

Daxton Hall in Buckinghamshire had been the ancestral home of the De Wigt family since Norman times. It lay in acres of open countryside just north of the quaint village of Great Missenden, where Roger Hanson lived happily with his wife and two daughters. The small commute down country lanes to the De Wigt estate meant he was readily at hand and on call at all times. To the villagers he was a pillar of the community, a family man and generous benefactor of several local causes. He was Mr. De Wigt's Security Chief and on the Board of Governor's at his girl's school. To those in the know however, he was a hired killer with a vast and varied C.V., ruthless and completely without morals, responsible directly or indirectly for thousands of deaths and untold suffering.

Hanson had no reason to suspect he was being targeted and acted accordingly. He knew nothing of the information given by Ryan Nylander and the fact that he had been linked to the attempt on Kirsten's life at the prison. Security was therefore light on his usual journey to work. He was picked up in a Range Rover SE with tinted windows by his regular driver, choosing to ride in the passenger seat as usual. Both men were well-armed given the often brutal nature of their work. A Heckler and Koch MP5K compact submachine gun was stowed in the driver's door bin. This was complemented by a Glock 17 pistol in the driver's shoulder holster. Hanson also carried his own sidearms; a H and K USP compact pistol in 9mm tucked in a shoulder holster, as well as a Smith and Wesson Model 442, chambered for .38 special which was hidden in an ankle strap as back up.

He had years of operational military experience behind him and many enemies so Hanson knew that the short journey contained numerous possible ambush points. These had been flagged as danger areas meaning the driver in particular would be on high alert. However, neither men had even considered the infinitely remote possibility of being engaged by a suppressed Remington 700 sniper rifle from a position on higher ground, at the hands of an expert.

Not far from the house, Hanson's journey took him into narrow country lanes. The road veered sharply to the left onto a long stretch with trees on one side and low rolling fields on the other. A small mound lay ahead which afforded perfect vision straight down the road. At around two hundred and fifty yards, it was the perfect ambush point.

The Remington 700 is perhaps one of the quietest sniper rifles around when fired with a suppressor. The 7.62 x 51mm round is high velocity and deadly accurate. Particularly when fired by experienced hands. The first well-aimed shot smashed clean through the windscreen, passing straight through the chest of the driver and the seats behind, killing him instantly.

Blood exploded upon Hanson before he even knew he was under attack. The vehicle careered violently into a ditch. The airbags deployed. Though shaken, he immediately began trying to scramble out of the car for he knew he was presenting a sitting target where he was. He opened the door and clambered out to hide behind the front wheel. Drew his USP. Trouble was, he had no idea where the sniper was hidden, nor if they were alone. He realised to his dismay that he had no choice but to locate his adversaries in order to take effective cover. He instinctively raised himself to scan the countryside, as he knew he was dead if he remained still.

Another bullet hit him high and ripped through his upper left shoulder, knocking him over and shattering a small portion of bone. He struggled to regain his feet and his composure. A third round pinged off the asphalt road, right next to his left foot. An aimed shot intended to warn rather than kill. He was in control just enough of his faculties to realise he was not going to be slaughtered. Though the pain was intense, it was not a life-threatening wound. The sniper had serious talent and could have easily taken him out so his best chance now was to entice a fight at close quarters, a contest he was more disposed to win. Or at least had an even chance. He stood up straight and held his weapon upside down, by the end of the trigger guard.

'Okay! Stop shooting. You obviously don't want to kill me, so come on in then,' he shouted loudly. 'I'm laying my weapon down.'

He placed the USP on the road, stepped back and waited, clutching his wounded shoulder.

Ian received instructions through his earpiece. He was concealed in a hedgerow several metres behind the ambush point, well away from any potential crossfire. He called out to Hanson the words he was instructed to say.

'*And* the secondary weapon!'

Roger Hanson feigned surprise and ignorance.

'Do it now!'

Still, he did not move.

Two seconds later, another high velocity round obliterated the second and third toes on his left foot. He screamed in agony and dropped to the ground. He writhed around but soon removed the small revolver from his ankle strap and threw it into the bushes. He was furious now but completely at their mercy.

Ian emerged slowly from cover upon command. He had been given rudimentary training in the workings of the Sig P229 pistol he was carrying and he pointed it directly at his helpless captive, like a seasoned pro.

'Lie flat down on your stomach. That's it. Feet together and hands stretched out, palms on the road.'

Hanson did his best to comply with the confident commands, despite the fact he was in excruciating pain and bleeding heavily. He lay there for a few minutes until a vehicle approached at speed and screeched to a halt. The driver exited, placed a hood over his head and zip-tied his hands behind his back, ignoring his screams of protest. He was stood up unceremoniously and dragged into the car.

They drove some distance in complete silence until they stopped at an abandoned barn Kirsten had found the night before. The car was pulled out of sight and Hanson was dragged inside, tied to a chair in the centre of a large open space. The hood was removed.

Standing before him was Kirsten. Once his eyes had adjusted to the changing light they unknowingly betrayed the mercenary, immediately informing his chief captor and interrogator that he recognised her as the woman he had paid to have killed.

Then, he caught sight of the table to her side, just out of reach. Sitting on top was an awl, a pair of carpenter's pincers, a ball pein hammer, a pair of pliers and a blow torch.

'And just what do you intend to do with them? I

am a trained soldier, remember? Torture will not work on me. I will not talk. Not now, or ever. As if there is a choice here. I am dead if I do. And if I don't, you will not let me live, now that I have seen you both and know you are here. You know it. And I know it.'

Kirsten circled him slowly several times without saying a word. It began to unnerve him a little when he could not see her and she did not speak. She could feel his anguish. Eventually, she stopped in front of him and replied.

'Yes. That is the one answer you seek more than any other, isn't it? Yes. I *am* going to kill you. Has to be. Simple as that. We are both out of options here. You tried to have me killed. That was naughty of you. Although you failed, I can't let that go. There is no forgiveness in our line of work. An enemy left standing is not good for the pension plan. You understand that, don't you?'

She paused and circled him again, letting it sink in. He was in agony and now looking very pale. Shock had begun to set in. However, in his current state, he was not likely to die and she was confident she had hours to play with.

'Out of professional courtesy, I'm going to forego my usual foreplay. The only questions you should be asking yourself right now, are how much pain can I endure before she puts a bullet in my head? And whether or not she has the guts or inclination to take out my wife and daughters too?'

Ian's face was a picture of horror and revulsion. But it was nothing compared to Hanson's. She had his full attention now alright. Though, he still remained silent.

Kirsten took the blow torch and lit it. She began

to heat up the awl. Within a few moments it was glowing cherry red. Then, without warning, she gripped Hanson's right hand and bent his index finger backwards. The mercenary began to suck in big lungfuls of air. He knew what was coming.

Kirsten looked him straight in the eye. 'Ready?' she asked, with a sinister half smile.

She pushed the red-hot awl under his fingernail. Hanson screamed. His flesh sizzled. After a moment, Kirsten began to wiggle the awl around. The screaming intensified. After a cursory inspection, she dropped the awl and picked up the pincers. Hanson had fainted. She slapped him around the head to bring him to.

'Wake up! We're not done yet.'

He shrieked again and yelled for mercy as his fingernail slid off with ease. The pain was beyond excruciating.

'One down, nine to go,' she said. 'After that, it's your toes. Then it's your teeth.'

'I can't!' he roared out, frantically. 'They will get to them anyway, so what does it serve me to talk? They are everywhere. You cannot win. You don't understand!'

'Who? Who are everywhere? Make me understand,' she cried.

'No, I can't! Aaaargghh!'

A gentle squeeze of his injured digit made him yell for England. Kirsten picked up the awl and lit the blowtorch again. This time it was driven underneath his middle finger with extreme force.

'Ooops. Sorry. Out of practice. I'll get the hang of it though.'

'Aaaarghhhh!' Another fingernail slid off.

'Eight to go,' she sang, happily.

Ian turned away to vomit. His face was green and he was struggling to stand, needed a seat. Nevertheless, Kirsten did not relent. Again, she lit the blowtorch and began to heat up the awl.

'Has to be nice and hot you know. I was taught by a Chinese...'

'Stop!'

Hanson cried out at the top of his voice, desperation echoing around the empty chamber. 'I'll tell you everything I know. Just stop hurting me. I'll talk… But you must promise me three things before I do. I want your solemn oath,' he said, panting heavily, a broken man.

Kirsten withdrew slightly and placed the instruments of torture back on the table.

'Speak.'

'Three promises. That's all I ask. Number one; you end it quickly. Between the eyes. No messing about'

'Okay. Easy enough. And two?' she asked.

'You leave my family alone. No reprisals of any sort when I am gone.'

'You have my word. Three?'

'You make sure they will be safe.'

'And just how am I supposed to do that?' she asked.

'By taking out the whole fucking lot of them. The entire network. Leaving nobody alive.'

Kirsten took out her pistol. 'I can do that. Those in command anyway. I will give you all three requests or die trying. Good enough? But *only* if you talk right now and hold nothing back.'

Chapter 18 - Operations

The incredible scenes at the Casa Rosada resembled a war zone. The action in the grounds was being played out on live television, streamed around the world by the many TV crews, cameramen and reporters who had gathered and jostled for the greatest vantage points on nearby streets. Helicopters flew low overhead. Troops were running everywhere. Emergency service vehicles, army transports and official cars began arriving and leaving in mass confusion, in amongst throngs and throngs of first responders, secret service, army and police personnel. It was like a major Hollywood blockbuster was being filmed and amazing to behold for the crowds that had formed on the Plaza de Mayo.

Inside, the situation was even more shambolic. Soldiers had begun searching every inch of the palace, every nook and cranny, every potential hiding place for terrorists, assassins, explosives or weapons. Guests who were not proven friends of the regime had automatically become suspects. They were now being escorted from everywhere into the main hall, barking dogs snapping at their heels. Identification papers were being checked, bags searched, clothing removed. Those with diplomatic immunity were released quickly, high profile dignitaries rounded up and taken to their cars under armed escort, before being whisked away.

Amid the bedlam, the corpse of General Jose Louis Ramirez was reverently stretchered out to a waiting ambulance, amid scenes of mass grief and hysteria. It was as if a member of a royal family had been killed, or the President himself. Still, the ambulance technicians deliberately took their time, perhaps enjoying the grand spectacle in which they were the centre of attention for once. There was no need to rush now. Ramirez had taken his last breath. Argentina would grieve his loss under the gaze of world media. Some exit. Some show.

Great Britain in contrast would now be breathing a huge sigh of relief. Another enemy vanquished. At least for now.

Charlie was in a crowd of thirty or more detainees. Mainly English-speaking individuals who had been herded together and were yet to be processed. It was a concern that she had been placed in this group. The soldiers around her were paying very close attention, confident it seemed that the killer was still among them. She knew she had to escape. And quickly. If she were caught or compromised here, there would surely be hell to pay, both for her and her country on the international stage. The ramifications would almost certainly lead to another war. A conflict in which Britain would be castigated and named as the aggressor this time, despite General Ramirez' actions and true intentions.

Finally, the soldiers began removing the detained guests one by one for questioning. When her time came, Charlie was escorted by two guards into a side room. A table had been placed in the centre and two high-ranking police officers were seated at it, waiting for her. The most senior of the two began talking. He spoke in good English, seemingly trying to catch her off-guard.

'So, you attended tonight as a guest of Mr. Johnson, from the American embassy. Is that correct?'

Charlie answered him in her best Spanish. 'I understand English perfectly Senor, but I am Argentinian. Why do you question me in a foreign tongue? Yes, that is right. I was Mr. Johnson's plus one. Why have you not released me along with him?'

He cast a quick glance up at the guard and Charlie immediately received a rough slap around her head. It was delivered to shut her up, rather than actually hurt her. She decided to play along and began snivelling. It worked, and he reverted to Spanish.

'Come now. No need for that. Just answer my questions, Senorita Acosta. Nothing more. We have your papers. It is good work. Very convincing… Who do you work for? Why did you murder the General? Who else is with you? I want to know everything!' he bawled.

'I do not know what you are talking about. I am here with Mr. Johnson, as his date. That is all. I do not understand what it is you want of me?'

The second officer then joined the interrogation. 'Yes, so you have said. What kind of an arrangement is that?'

She stopped crying and looked him in the eye, defiantly, as if he should know better than to ask such a sensitive question in public.

'The kind you probably keep from your wife.'

He smirked a little. 'You admit to being a prostitute then?'

'Yes. Why not? No point in denying it now, given the circumstances. He abandoned me quick enough to face you guys, didn't he? Though, I prefer the term, escort.'

'To be clear; he pays you for sex?'

'Not well enough. Girl's got to earn a living somehow.'

The second policeman seemed satisfied for the moment but his superior was having none of it. He looked up at the soldiers.

‘She has been searched thoroughly?’

‘Yes, sir. She has nothing on her.’

‘Well, I am not convinced by your act, or your papers. You will be taken to Huerta Grande police station where you will remain until morning. We will then resume our little talk when you have had a chance to think about the serious trouble you are in. You would be wise to co-operate with our enquiries or it will turn significantly worse for you later down the line.’

Charlie tried to react as she thought she should, as she’d been trained. Being too compliant in situations like this, could and would be viewed as suspicious.

‘What?! The morning?! You cannot be serious? You have nothing on me. Look at me. I’m no murderer. Look at these nails. I was paid good money to play somebody’s girlfriend for the evening, that’s all.’

‘We shall see, Miss Acosta. Though, *someone* at this party must be guilty, no?’

‘Yes. And I wouldn’t mind betting that you have probably already let them go,’ she said, accusingly.

‘What? What do you mean by that? Explain yourself!’

‘Nothing. It’s just that... the generals. The diplomats. One group have probable cause, as you guys put it. Motive? The other can literally get away with murder, and you can’t touch them.’

The two officers looked taken aback. Embarrassed somewhat, they decided to terminate the interrogation quickly.

'Enough. Take her away!'

She was placed in a pair of ratchet handcuffs by a good-looking young soldier in his twenties. She flirted a little, asked him to loosen them a touch as they were too tight, and was amazed when he complied. He undid them one click. She was then escorted to a waiting police van in the main courtyard, her head shielded from the assembled cameras by a well-used blanket. She calculated that the journey to the station would not take long. Though, the sheer number of suspects meant that many cells would be needed and that would dictate location, time and distance for some.

The young guard who had cuffed her sat with one other soldier in the rear of the van, watching her. Two more were in the front, one driving. All were armed with Browning Hi-Power pistols. On Herik Island all recruits had been trained relentlessly in how to escape captivity, including all methods of restraint. She had been made to dislocate her thumbs so often that it was now second nature, the pain barely noticeable. As soon as the van left the compound she set to work and her hand was free in no time, her thumb back in place. She waited several minutes before acting though, to place some distance between them and the palace. Then, she paused only for the right moment to strike, when she might catch both guards by surprise simultaneously.

Speed was as usual key. She planned to kill both guards quickly, take their weapons and shoot her way out of the van. That meant throwing herself from the moving vehicle blind, wherever they happened to be at that time. It was reckless and it was risky, two words not usually associated with her, but she reasoned she had no alternative given her available options. She would take her chances from thereon. Trust to fate.

The escorts took their eyes off her for only a moment.

It was enough.

The young, attractive male who sat opposite Charlie was kicked swiftly under his chin with explosive force. The strike was delivered so fast it was like a bolt of lightning and it knocked him clean off his seat. The second guard to the right of him was struck with the cuffs, across the left temple. He fell sideways under the weight of the blow. She turned back to good-looking one, grabbed his head and slammed it backwards, into the side to the van. A flurry of punches then crushed his windpipe.

The cuffed guard had recovered a little by now and was about to re-join the fight. A finger-strike to his left eye burst his eye ball, causing him to scream and cover his head in panic. This gave Charlie enough time to move behind the soldier and place him into a rear naked choke. She wrapped her arms around his neck and squeezed for all she was worth. Eased the life out of him.

She grabbed their weapons, placed one in her belt, checked and cocked the other. Then fired three rounds into the lock mechanism on the doors. Booted them open and hoped for the best.

She was in luck. They were travelling down a back street and traffic was minimal. She immediately hurled herself from the van, landed on the road with an intense surge of pain and rolled to a halt. Ignoring the agony as the van screeched to a stop, she darted into cover behind a parked car.

Within seconds, the two remaining guards exited the vehicle, weapons drawn, determined not to lose their captive. Charlie was behind the wheel arch of a car which provided excellent cover but she instinctively moved to the offensive, taking out the primary target; the officer who would be radioing through his position to control, asking for assistance.

Two rounds from her pistol hit him centre mass, close to or in his heart. His colleague opened fire immediately and a bullet hit the Szabo agent in her right shoulder. She whirled with the force of the blow and returned fire.

Double tap. Two rounds to the head. Unbelievable shooting, given the circumstances.

Charlie looked around her. Several locals were beginning to appear on the scene. She knew some would have mobile phones in possession so she decided she had to move. She was in serious trouble still and sure to be marked now as a high priority target. That meant every available resource would be directed to search and apprehend or kill her.

She decided to steal the police van. She had just reached the dead soldiers when another vehicle came careering down the road, headlights blazing. It shuddered and screeched to a halt just yards away from her in a whirlwind of noise, smoke and burning rubber. She raised her pistol and prepared for another scrap.

'Get in! Now!' yelled Jasper.

Charlie was immediately overwhelmed with extreme gratitude and relief. She ran to the car and threw herself inside, thankful for the help and daring to believe there was a real chance of escape now. The stolen car sped away at high speed before she had even closed the door.

'Pronto to Sunray. Vesuvius. I say again,

Vesuvius. I have her. Request exfil package. Over' Jasper stated calmly into his radio.

There was a short pause before a hesitant reply.

'Sunray to Pronto. Damage assessment. Over.'

This was new. Somebody needed convincing. Jasper looked at Charlie, betraying his surprise at the odd request for more information which was certainly not normal protocol.

'Minimal. They do not know who she is, or who she works for. We are intact,' he stated, forcefully.

'Received. In that case, exfil point, bravo. 0700.'

'Pronto received. Out.'

He looked her straight in the eyes again for a brief moment and then continued concentrating on the road. 'Are you okay? Did they hurt you?' he asked.

Charlie shook her head. She was fuming. 'I'm alright. Just a damaged shoulder, though it was a near thing. I don't think I would have seen the light of day for many years, if ever, if they had managed to cage me. Do you?'

Silence. As good as an admission in anyone's books.

'I'll say it then, if you won't. It was a clusterfuck. A balls-up. They know my face, for God's sake! I'll be on every camera in the known world, every watchlist going. This breakout was necessary and I'm extremely grateful to you, but it will only confirm my guilt. What happened, Jasper?!'

'Don't know for sure. Best guess? The Americans played us. Some of them anyway. CIA probably. Has to be them. Who else? The gun lobby is big over there, they control everything. The arms manufacturers. You can bet they want another war between us and the Argies. Good for business you see. I think it's that simple. They looked on this op as an opportunity. Saw dollar signs and served you up on a platter.'

'Yes. My thinking too. That's the very last time I work with people I do not know and trust. Thanks again. I owe you, and I won't forget it. How are we getting out?'

'Trust me. All in hand. We lie low once we reach a little village near Punta Indio. Steal a boat. Once offshore, they will locate us. HMS Audacious will do the rest.'

'A submarine? Really? You've had a sub on standby for me?'

'Ha ha… As if I have that pull. No, not me; Dunbar.'

Charlie laughed.

'Ha, ha... You gotta love that man.'

Three months later and she was almost healed. Her injured shoulder was beginning to hurt less and the daily physio sessions were not such torture. One look in the mirror and she did not recognise her own face. For good reason.

The plastic surgeons on Herik Island had performed miracles. She was still as attractive as ever, but she now seemed to have those perfect, film star looks where not a single thing was out of proportion. A tiny bump had been removed from the bridge of her nose. She had also had a little nostril reduction, a chin implant and a cheek lift. On the night of her last mission, she had long dark-brown hair, brown eyes and a deep tan. Now, she possessed natural blue eyes and a pale complexion courtesy of a wonderdrug stolen from the Chinese. The scars she had collected had healed nicely too. She was ready and eager to return to active duty.

The one thing that *did* upset her was having to say goodbye to her army career and cottage. The friends she had made. There was a chance that photos of her had been taken in Argentina which would be circulated worldwide. It was a risk her superiors were not willing to take. So, she had a new face, a new identity with paperwork and background to match, a new house and a new job. They had even moved her cellar for her. Well, the entire contents anyway. That was small consolation for having lost everything she loved but she accepted it was an occupational hazard. Part of the conditions of service.

She could and would start again. As many times as it took. She would rebuild her life and make a success of any cover she was given, though she knew in her heart that Argentina had been a badly run operation which came perilously close to disaster.

General Ramirez' successor turned out to be a more tolerant and moderate person. He healed many rifts and in the purges which immediately followed the assassination, those who remained militant were ousted and replaced. Argentina began to prosper again and plans to re-take the Malvinas were shelved in favour of a more diplomatic approach.

Suspicions of British involvement in the 'Ramirez Affair' were rife and would never go away. There was even a second-rate movie and a book or two. However, there was also a distinct absence of proof. And proof was essential. Toxicology reports from the post-mortem confirmed that BTX-15, or Batrachotoxin BTX Neurotoxin, was commonly found in poison dart frogs. Lethal derivatives were exclusively American in design and manufacture. Used solely by the U.S. on clandestine operations. With no history of British involvement whatsoever.

And the Americans could not admit to supplying British assassins. So, in the end, given the available evidence, the most plausible explanation for Ramirez' death was that it was the inevitable culmination of a rift between the generals, several of whom were vying with Ramirez for command in a supposed coup. They had vast contacts in the CIA and USA, motive and means to hire a killer.

Chapter 19 – Present Day

Roger Hanson was in unbearable pain. Every inch of his body was screaming for mercy, as if he'd just run through molten lava. His breathing was rapid and shallow, his skin pale, cold, wet and clammy. De Wigt's security chief looked as though he might pass out at any moment. Kirsten however, showed no sign of pity or remorse whatsoever. Just the cold, hard exterior of a consummate professional intent on completing a mission. She did eventually pack his wounds with torn rags she found on the barn floor, but only because she was fearful he may bleed to death before divulging the information she sought. The intelligence she needed above all else. The reason they had taken so many risks in kidnapping a trained killer. When she finished rendering rudimentary first aid, she leant in unnervingly close and whispered menacingly in his ear.

'Now, don't you go believing that my little show of kindness means anything, you hear? It is not a sign of weakness and I don't want you clinging to any false hope. You are still going to die for what you have done and it will be soon. You have one minute to speak to me now. One chance only to save your family. After that, and if I don't like what I hear I might add, I'm going to pay a visit to your little house in the village. Maybe to the school.'

The experienced soldier now turned hired security consultant knew beyond doubt that death was imminent. He wished he had a weapon and could take his own life. That would solve all of his problems. But his hands were bound. He had no such option and no way to speed up the process, to hasten his own demise. He was dying too slowly. A pathetic fly trapped in her web. The cold-hearted female assassin standing before him held every card there was, and he knew it. His shattered body and mind could stand no more agony than they had already been subjected to. He therefore had only one practical choice if he was to have any chance at all of saving his loved ones; to tell everything he knew. Spill his guts completely. And then trust in his own executioner to set them free from the likelihood of reprisals.

He sighed heavily with resignation and looked up with contempt into that beautiful face. Wished he had never set eyes on it. On her.

'How is your history?' he asked, his voice full of contempt.

'I get by,' Kirsten replied, short and sweet.

'Good. Because this tale goes way back…'

Over the next forty-five minutes, Hanson explained exactly who and what Kirsten and Ian were up against. The extent of the criminality they had stumbled upon. It was all too incredible, too huge and fantastic to believe. But somehow, they knew deep inside that they had broken this shell of a man before them and in his final moments on earth, he was speaking nothing but the truth.

They sat in stunned silence as he talked. Listened and soaked it all in.

In the reign of James VI, the Scottish king who became James I upon the union of the two crowns, shortly after the Gunpowder Plot had failed to destroy parliament, twelve of the most powerful nobles in the land held a secret meeting in the upstairs room of a Hatton Garden pub. They hailed from all four corners of the realm. Many had travelled a very long way to attend the unique gathering, but the incredibly high stakes made the journey worthwhile.

Unhappy and disillusioned with a Scottish monarch sitting on the throne of England, but not overly confident in the strength of their support and chances of overthrowing him by military means, the twelve richest men in the kingdom resolved to act. They formed a secret society. It would have no name. No identity which could be divulged and used to link them to acts of treason. It would be referred to over time using generic terms such as the club, the firm, the organisation, the house and many more. The privilege of membership was bestowed solely along hereditary lines, passed from father to first-born son. The penalty for disclosure of any kind was ruin and death. Not just for the member himself, but also for his entire family. Many members had come and gone over the hundreds of years since that first meeting. The organisation and its activities expanded beyond measure. But the twelve in the know, the leaders who possessed the sole knowledge of what was really going on, those who made the real decisions and formulated policy, enforced the rules, they were still comprised of ancestors of the original attendees. And they ran things with an iron fist.

The dozen in command and these days on the executive board, conversed daily and met twice weekly to plan and scheme. Their objectives were two-fold; money and power. The two were intertwined. Power was achieved through influence. And money was power.

It was all about pedigree for the twelve. Always had been. They hated 'new money', those 'plebs' who had taken advantage of the new age and risen to the top without breeding. The ruling elite, the establishment, the government they detested, infiltrated by public school vermin. Commoners. Each of the dozen was a direct descendant of an original. Proud of that fact because it marked them apart. All had been educated at Eton and Oxford, had titles and estates galore, bank accounts in numerous countries, wore designer clothes and drove fast cars, mixed in the highest circles, took whatever they desired...

From the very first meeting, those already in power ensured by hook or by crook that before long, the others had joined them. They looked after each other in every regard and became successful entrepreneurs, politicians, civil servants, tycoons, bankers… Some rose to serve in senior government. Many became captains of industry and police commissioners. One even became Prime Minister. And almost all had a vested interest in the manufacture, development and sale of technology, arms and munitions.

They kept their secrets hidden well but recruited and operated under numerous guises such as the English East India Company, the Lunar Society, Vickers, the Woolwich Arsenal and others. Their wealth and influence grew to be colossal and soon they began to operate across oceans on the world stage. They had the power they had always craved and they would never relinquish it. More and more capital was created by promoting, ensuring military conflict. The only thing that mattered to them now was money. It was like a drug. The dirty money was purified, washed, filtered. They operated with impunity because nobody knew they existed. Nobody was watching. Nobody suspected. Nobody.

The secret to their immeasurable wealth, power,

success and more importantly longevity, was discretion. Anonymity was everything, their greatest ally. People knew they were rich, of course they did. It is hard to hide such wealth so they did not try. But the unsuspecting and trusting masses had no idea at all just how enormously, filthy rich they became. Accounts can easily be hidden from sight if you know how. False identities and documentation can be provided. Now, from the boardrooms of the city to the corridors of Whitehall, from Hollywood and Washington to the United Nations, they had operators and associates everywhere. Police, private armies, spies and secret assassins, such as those working for Operation Szabo, were all at their disposal. And many who did their bidding, did not even know who they were really working for.

They were always watching, listening, waiting for the next opportunity to come. Were directly or indirectly involved in most of the world's conflicts and catastrophic events, unbeknown to us all. From the English Civil War to the British Raj, the American Civil War to World War One... they stoked the fires of conflict and profited as the embers burned, and countless millions perished.

And they *always* benefitted financially from the ensuing chaos.

They operated on the principle that the most valuable commodity on earth was information. The right people with the right information, at the right time, could do and achieve anything. And, of course, *anything* always entailed huge profits.

It was all so simple. The concept had not differed too much since the first meeting in Hatton Garden. Start a war or an arms race, preferably both. Play both sides against each other. Stand back, and watch the sparks fly.

As the combatants and those at home argue and squabble, spend and borrow, *you* grow stronger and stronger. More influential. More powerful. Selling everything from technology, weapons and state secrets, to political influence and promises, it does not matter who wins or loses, or the material and human cost. Only the numbers on the balance sheet at the end of each day count. Only the money matters in the final reckoning.

Today, according to Hanson, they owned umpteen thousands of companies worldwide, enjoyed a controlling interest in many more. They advised Prime Ministers, Chancellors and Presidents. They set interest rates, budgets, loan repayments and inflation rates. They devised foreign policy, chose electoral candidates and picked who won elections before they happened, controlled drug cartels, protection rackets and effectively ran parliaments and senates... They sold technology to the highest bidder, withheld vaccines and cures, organised coups and rebellions, ousted honest men and women from positions of power… They had infiltrated every section of society, every profitable criminal enterprise, every facet of government and policing, defence and security, commerce and technology...

'…That's who you are facing,' gasped Hanson, a tiny flicker of defiance in his eyes even now. 'You can't win against that. What can the pair of you do? They control everything. *They* decide your destiny, not you. Who do you think you have been working for? Do you honestly believe all those hits you did were sanctioned? That you fight for your country? Some would have been private vendettas. You can bet your soul on that. Kills which would enhance the firm and its profits, or benefit one individual. They have been feeding you a line all this time. You're a tool. A puppet. And they have wielded you as they see fit, to do their dirty work.'

Kirsten and Ian did not know how to react at first. They both felt physically sick. But eventually, Ian responded for them both.

'But that's insane. If we believe what you say, these megalomaniacs have been and are running the country. The world. Without being discovered. It couldn't happen, could it? How could they hide it all?'

He did not sound very convincing, even to himself. 'What if we expose them?' he added.

'Expose *what* exactly? You have no proof,' Hanson replied.

'Yes, but if you testified…?'

'No! Forget it!' interrupted the animated mercenary. 'Shoot me now and have done with it. If I said anything in public, every single member of my family on this planet would be erased, I know it. Not happening.'

'Twelve you say?' Kirsten asked, stroking her chin as she thought.

'Yes. I don't know them.'

'Twelve is an unusual number though. Like a jury, someone has to be calling the shots? Is it De Wigt? Does he lead them?'

Hanson shook his head. The pain was unbearable now. He was desperate to be put out of his misery. He gritted his teeth as he snapped a reply. 'That boy scout couldn't organise a piss up at Jack Daniel's gaff.'

'So, he is not involved?'

'Only because he turns a blind eye to what is going on, for a tidy profit.'

'Then who is running it all? Tell me, who do you actually work for?'

Silence.

Kirsten threatened again to leave and head for the village.

'Okay… Sir Charles Munford. He is the man at the top. De Wigt is shit scared of him. They all are. That's all I know, I swear. Now, you fulfil your end of the bargain. You end me right now.'

Kirsten lifted her suppressed pistol. Pointed it right between Hanson's eyes.

'Stop!' cried Ian. 'He could be useful…'

Phut. Phut.

She looked at Ian as if she had just been caught stealing his wallet. 'Sorry. You had a good point to be fair, but I didn't like the guy. And a promise is a promise.'

Chapter 20 - Operations

Rosie Williams had the entire world at her feet. She was young, fit, extremely attractive, popular and very, very rich. The kind of rich that made others sick with envy. She had just inherited her father's fortune, as well as a swanky London flat, a holiday home in Antigua, a luxury yacht, a property portfolio and a well-established fashion boutique in the heart of the city which was both profitable and thriving. If it wasn't for the pain in her shoulder which flared up from time to time, the alleged product of a 'skiing accident' in her youth, she would have thought life absolutely perfect.

Of course, Rosie Williams was not her real name. Her identity and her life were all one big lie. She was in fact a highly successful assassin working for an ultra-secret organisation with hundreds of kills on record, a fresh look and a completely new cover.

The boutique had been owned and run by Szabo agents for years under the fictitious patronship of a Spanish millionaire nobody had ever actually met. And they were highly unlikely to now. He had been 'retired' to give credence to the disinformation. To enhance the untruth. Operation Szabo had 'liberated' funds in his name and furnished Rosie with everything, from luxury flat and her own business, to a Bentley Continental GT, yacht etc. She even had a top team of designers working tirelessly and constantly to supply her with fresh lines for the shop, as well as a non-job managerial role which allowed for numerous trips abroad to fashion shows and houses, and months at a time at play in Antigua. A fantastic play-girl lifestyle which provided perfect cover for her real Szabo activities.

The business was just off Sloane Square, in-between Belgravia and Chelsea, in the heart of London. This enabled Rosie to rekindle her close relationship with Jay Jay. The two agents soon became firm friends again and both developed a keen and active social life.

Rosie undertook several missions over the next six months. She burgled, kidnapped, blackmailed, sabotaged and killed as ordered, never once failing to achieve what was asked of her. Her record of successful missions was soon second to none and she had grown quite the reputation amongst her peers and superiors, becoming to 'go to girl' for most difficult or sensitive assignments. Throughout the world in fact, her lethal skills were admired and respected. Though her true identity and employer remained closely guarded secrets.

One morning, another text from 'Auntie Cynth' preceded a meeting with her old friend and handler, Jasper. He briefed her on a new assignment she had been given and several days later she embarked for Switzerland. She landed at Zurich airport and reported to a mansion at Arbon, thoroughly prepared for her new role as the English governess to Mia and Nael Keller, the children of Julian Keller, who was Head of Raiffetsen Bank.

Julian Keller, unbeknown to his family, was laundering money for several cartels and terrorist organisations across the world. A complex arrangement he had inherited from his predecessor and continued against his better judgement for extreme financial gain. Amongst these armed factions were ISIS, Hamas, FARC and Hezbollah. The latter had suffered its fair share of internal disputes in recent times. A breakaway faction had emerged led by and comprised of hard-line fighters who were predominantly younger activists, now styling themselves as the 'Youth of Palestine Liberation Army', or YPLA. They were intent on attacking their enemies and their allies by any means possible and they were desperate for funds to buy weapons, explosives and training.

Hezbollah banked with Raiffetsen amongst others. Julian Keller administered the account. For security purposes, he was the only one in Europe with permanent access and the necessary codes to transfer their money. He signed off every transaction. The current Hezbollah leadership trusted him. The young fighters of the dissident group however, were now intent on *kidnapping* him and stealing the vast sum of money held in the account. Operation Szabo Intelligence Officers had learned of the plot and Rosie had been inserted undercover as a result.

Her mission had three strands. To protect Mr. Keller, or more importantly the information he possessed. To foil any kidnap attempt by any means necessary and eliminate the threat. And finally, to steal the codes, allowing Szabo to appropriate the funds.

Julian Keller could not be trusted to work with the British in an official capacity, or under duress, so a clandestine approach was favoured this time over kidnap and torture.

Mia Keller was six years of age. She had blonde hair and blue eyes. She was boisterous, lively, fun, playful and happy. Her elder brother, Nael, was eight. He was usually quiet and reserved. He was also polite and helpful. Both children were a credit to their parents and instantly likeable. Rosie had been hired to look after them and teach them English. Her impeccable references and work history, courtesy of Szabo, had bowled the Keller's over. They considered themselves very lucky to have found her and insertion happened naturally, without a single hitch.

The first three months passed by quickly for Rosie. She was accepted into the family home, became a close friend in no time at all and enjoyed living in the mansion, spending most of her free time in the pool and on the tennis court. The children adored her and she grew rapidly to worship them too. Mia especially had captured her heart. Rosie had never considered having children. Had not yet enjoyed what she would term a serious relationship. Her existence was way too hectic for that. But the joys she experienced caring for the two youngsters came as a real surprise. The bond between them all was instant and infectious. The kiss and hug that Mia gave her each night before disappearing to her bed, became the highlight of her day. She knew such feelings were frowned upon. That they could affect her judgement and performance in the heat of battle, but she could not help herself and trusted that her training would take over when it really mattered.

Adults were not complicated at all to deal with. It was simple with them. Big and small, right and wrong, good and bad, threat or not, live or die. Easy. Children though…?

All her efforts to find the codes had failed. In the time she had been in play, she had rifled through desks, cabinets and drawers, looked on phones and computers, in clothing and picture frames… but to no avail. Julian was clearly a more intelligent man than she had given him credit for.

There had been rumours of a terrorist cell in the vicinity but no independent corroboration. She maintained contact with Jasper daily through the usual comms devices, updating him regularly with situation reports and anything she thought required checking out.

It was Jasper who warned her one quiet Sunday afternoon of the impending attack.

There were two viable points of entry into the estate, the main one being the road which led to the front gate and drive. This was covered with surveillance from both directions, with outposts far enough away to give decent warning of any danger. Jasper was sat in one such location and watched with interest as four large Range Rovers hurtled down the usually quiet side road, towards the house. Instinctively feeling something was about to 'go off', he called it immediately.

'Vapor to Legend. Urgent message! Heads up. Probable contact coming in hot. Over.'

Rosie was in the downstairs games room with the children. 'Legend to Vapor. Verify. Over.'

'I say again. Contact! Unknown number of Tango's in four vehicles approaching your location fast. ETA three Mikes.'

'Legend Received. Request fire support or backup. Over.'

'Vapor received. We are ten Mikes out.'

Rosie looked at the stunned faces of the children who had seen and heard her talking into her top button. She picked them up in her arms without talking and ran the short distance to her room. Reached under her bed and retrieved a large suitcase, opened it and took out a FN Minimi Mk3 machine gun. She clipped a belt around her waist that contained a Sig P229 pistol with spare ammo, then slung a M4A1 Carbine over her shoulder.

The youngsters were really scared now. Mia was crying. She told them quickly to hide under the bed as they were in danger and placed the suitcase in front of them, so they could not be seen. Then she went searching for Julian and his wife.

Mr. Keller was in his study on the ground floor. His wife was in the living room and came to the door to see what was wrong, having heard her running.

'Quickly, come with me right now if you want to live! You are under attack and they have come for you,' Rosie said, speaking to the banker alone.

Keller was horrified and scared at the sight of his au pair armed to the teeth. She looked like an avenging angel and his face lost all colour.

'What?! My family?!'

'I will do what I can, but we have to move now!' Rosie yelled, assertively.

'Move where?' he replied.

'Upstairs. I have help coming but not soon enough. I may be able to hold them off for a while if I have a defensible position.'

'The children?'

'Hidden. Hopefully they will be safe. They want the codes. Where are they?'

Julian Keller was astonished at hearing his children's governess ask such questions. He realised immediately that he had been deceived and became reluctant to talk, despite the obvious danger he was facing.

'Look, you may be about to die, Mr. Keller! I am your only hope now. You can't let terrorists have those codes. They will use the money to kill thousands of innocent people.'

At that moment, she heard tyres screeching outside and a huge crash as the lead van burst through the gates to the property. She grabbed Keller's wrist and pulled him through the hallway, with his wife following behind. They raced up the stairs, taking them two at a time just as the vans skidded to a halt on the driveway.

Three teams made ready to enter the house, two at the front, one at the rear. The fourth team remained outside with the vehicles, covering the egress point.

Doors opening... Voices... Commands... They are surrounding the house.

Rosie ushered the anguished couple along the corridor and into a bedroom. She returned to the landing, lay down at the top of the stairs and deployed the bipod on the machine gun. Then she waited.

The doors to the mansion suddenly burst open and several windows smashed in unison. Stun grenades exploded everywhere with bone-shuddering blasts. Then another. And another.

Room clearing!

The smoke in the grand hallway of the mansion was dense, but the unmistakable forms of armed men rapidly came into view. Rosie immediately opened up with the Minimi. She had a two hundred round belt of ammunition on the gun and she was determined to use it. She swept the room from right to left and back again. Several bullets found their mark in amongst the flying debris and carnage she was creating. Three bodies fell to the floor. However, more were now entering the house, filing left and right in formation.

Trained men. Time to switch on.

She grabbed the Minimi and moved location,

deployed on the right side of the huge galleried landing, looking down.

Slowly, figures began to move again, cautiously. She heard shouting in Arabic.

'What the fuck was that?! Where did they go?'

A grenade landed at the top of the stairs where she had been lying only moments before. She ducked down, her back pressed against a large pillar. The blast made her ears ring. She took a deep breath and swung around. From behind the pillar now, she fired the Minimi again, this time from the shoulder.

Two more combatants below her perished. More moved for cover.

Click.

The Minimi had done its job but it was empty. She dropped it without a second thought and brought the M4A1 up. Another grenade landed next to her. Russian RGD-5. She picked it up with astonishing speed and hurled it back the way it came.

The black-clad hostiles below her dived for whatever cover they could find but it detonated and thousands of pieces of white-hot metal showered them. Screams and cries of wounded men followed. Another guy was down and not moving. His number two was crawling towards the exit in shit order. Rosie moved swiftly and put a round in his back.

The attack had stalled. They would regroup quickly though and come again. She ran along the corridor to the bedroom where Julian and his wife were huddled together.

'Go into the bathroom,' she ordered, as she pulled the mattress from the bed. 'Stay there. Lock yourself in. Get in the bath and cover yourself with this. And don't come out!'

Those who had surrounded the rear of the house now joined in the main assault, moving rapidly through the lower floor and clearing each room. She could hear the unmistakeable sound of flashbangs detonating, along with bursts of automatic fire, more shouts and commands.

Several men had by now entered the hallway and were making their way very cautiously up the stairs, firing into the walls and bannisters to keep the head down of whoever was firing at them. Suppressing fire.

Rosie was back out in the hallway. She pushed over a heavy table which had a large vase on top, crouched down low.

Breathe. In for four, hold for two. Out for four, hold for two....

Another grenade tumbled into the space ahead of her. She ducked, gritted her teeth and braced herself behind the table. She felt the shockwave of the blast move through her but somehow the force had been deflected by the thick table top. The rest she just had to deal with. Her ears were burning now and the ringing sensation was intense.

A body appeared in the hallway at that moment. A thick-set man wearing jeans, a military style jacket and black balaclava. He was wielding an FN90 submachine gun.

Recognising the immediate peril she was in, Rosie was up in a flash, responding to the new threat in the only way she knew. Aggression, backed by extreme force.

Bang. Bang.

Two in the chest. Another man down.

She heard more shouting, curses in Arabic. She fell back, retreating as they closed in on her position.

Soon, she found herself at the end of the corridor, sheltering in the doorway of another bedroom. More grenades came hurtling down the hallway. She dived onto the floor of the bedroom. Three loud bangs erupted, each a second apart. The floor, wall and doorframe absorbed most of the blast, all now severely holed.

Rosie rolled onto her back and unloaded the full magazine of her M4A1 into the bedroom wall. The rounds easily penetrated the damaged partition and peppered the men advancing through the hall.

More screaming and shouting. Her weapon gave a loud metallic click. She hit the magazine release with her trigger finger as her left hand took out a spare magazine from her belt and slid it home. Then she charged out onto the landing.

One gunman was dead. Another was wounded, writhing in agony on the floor.

Bang. Bang.

Rosie could see the door to the other bedroom was open. She realised quickly that more gunmen had decided to go hunting for the family. Anger coursed through her veins.

'Oh no you don't!'

She ran down the landing realising that speed was of the essence. Straight into a brute of a man as he stepped out of the open bedroom door. They bounced off each other and both reacted swiftly.

This guy was good. Trained. He knew what he was about. In an instant, he knocked the barrel of her gun away from his torso, just as Rosie squeezed the trigger and emptied the magazine into the opposite wall. The gunman was in too close to bring his own weapon to bear though, so he held onto Rosie and pulled her in, as his hand reached for the knife in his belt.

The Szabo agent dropped a headbutt onto the bridge of his nose. Blood splattered her face. Automatically, he relaxed his grip in that moment and Rosie slammed the muzzle of her weapon into his solar plexus, at the same time driving herself backwards to create space. It was just in the nick of time, as the burly thug threw a huge left hook, followed by a right that moved through the air rapidly towards the space she had just occupied. She slid onto her back and drew the Sig P229 from her belt.

Bang. Bang... Bang.

Two shots in the chest, a third to the head. Triple-tapped for good measure. The ultimate compliment.

Rosie was in the zone now and up swiftly. The final gunman was in the bathroom with Keller and his wife. He had his arm around Keller's neck and was using him as cover. His wife was cowering on the floor, pleading for their lives.

This terrorist was in overdrive, total and complete panic, hysterically trying desperately to seek a solution in which he could still achieve his mission. He was screaming frantically in Arabic.

'G… Get back! Moo… Move away! Who the *fuck* are you?!'

Rosie moved as if to signal parley. Her weapon was up and her left hand open. She spoke in a controlled voice. Soft and assured.

'Stay calm. Talk to me. Nobody else has to die here. We can sort this.'

The gunman shifted a little, revealing a little more of his head.

Bang.

He dropped onto the bathroom floor as befitted the dead weight he had just become, a perfect dark circle having just appeared through the centre of his left eye.

Then she heard another vehicle approach at speed. A firefight erupted outside and she realised with immense relief that help had finally arrived. She raced to the front bedroom, glanced through the smashed windows and saw Jasper and his colleagues engaging the four terrorists on the drive, hunting them down, killing them all.

She turned and searched frantically for more targets upstairs, just in case. There were none. She immediately ran downstairs to her room and was horrified at the sight which greeted her. It was a complete mess. There were multiple holes in the wall, spent cartridges, signs of explosions, smoke, flames, broken furniture… And blood. Lots and lots of blood.

It was pooling from underneath the bed, which was bullet-ridden and had taken the full force of at least two grenades. Tears streamed from her eyes and rolled down Rosie's cheeks as she realised the children had been caught in the blasts and assault. She barely registered Jasper's approach and he had to shake some life into her before she would respond to his urgent demands.

She informed him of the whereabouts of Mr. Keller and his wife and he raced away, leaving her alone for a moment in the room. She stared down at the remains of the children she adored. She was transfixed. The pain was like nothing she had ever known and she could not seem to tear herself away.

Seconds later, she heard two more shots. It jolted her out of her stupor and she raced to the hallway out of instinct, weapon drawn and eager to kill, the children forgotten now.

Jasper came walking calmly down the stairs however as she arrived. He holstered his weapon and smiled. She stared at him briefly before lowering her gun.

'Good job. Chopper's inbound. ETA two minutes. Let's go home,' he said.

She put her weapon away and wiped her face. 'What about Mr. Keller and his wife?' she asked.

Jasper led her out into the fresh air as the cleaners moved in.

'They won't be joining us.'

Julian Keller was a broken man when Jasper found him in the bathroom. He knew his children had just been slaughtered and did not need it confirming. Understood that it was all his fault. Could see it plainly in the British agent's eyes. He handed Jasper the crucifix he wore around his neck without being asked and explained that it had a microchip data file hidden inside.

The accounts were hacked soon afterwards and the vast sums of money were added to Operation Szabo's assets.

Not a single terrorist survived the assault on the Keller mansion. All had a single bullet hole in the centre of their forehead. The official story of the incident was released several days later. It made no mention of this fact but confirmed that the SAS had mounted a successful ambush on a terrorist cell and eliminated the threat of further attacks.

Nothing more.

Chapter 21 – Present Day

'He's right, you know,' said Ian, as they ate a takeaway breakfast in the Jaguar on a service station car park just off the M6 motorway. 'We only have the word of a killer. A criminal. We've no proof whatsoever of what they are doing. What they have done previously. Who is involved. How far this conspiracy travels. Nothing that will stand up in court. All we have are hundreds of unanswered questions, allegations we can't substantiate. I mean, for all we know, the Prime Minister, President and most the leaders in the free world are on their payroll. We are going to sound pretty silly trying to convince the world's leaders that they are being duped, controlled by a sinister force we know nothing about. Just think of it. Would *you* believe anything you have just heard, if you hadn't been involved directly and targeted? And you've just shot our only source by the way. Dead. So, where do we go from here?'

Kirsten finished chomping on her sausage and egg sandwich. She took a sip of her coffee before replying.

'It's a cliché but we deal with what we know, as usual. That's all we *can* do. We find the proof we need, expose them all and let the internet and popular opinion do the rest. Those in power will be too afraid *not* to act once I am finished. It will be everywhere. They will have no escape from the publicity and accusations and no other option. There are still enough good people in this world to ensure they do the right thing, believe me. That's why evil never triumphs in the end. It has its day, its time in the sun, sure it does. But it is always outnumbered.'

'Huh.'

'What?'

Ian stared at the beauty beside him. What a complex creature she could be at times. 'Never figured you for an optimist, that's all. After all you've seen and done, I pegged you as a little darker.'

'I'm not an optimist. Far from it. Bad shit happens to good people, that's just the way of life. I'm a realist. I chose all of this. So, I can't really start whinging about it now, just because I've been scorched a few times. Dealt a few bad hands. Look, I have seen the very worst in people, believe me. I know more than anyone just how far they will go, what they will do in the pursuit of wealth, power and status. How the lure of supremacy corrupts those who seek it. And what they would be prepared to do if their world was threatened by the likes of you and me.'

These scum were born privileged, with a silver spoon stuck firmly in their mouths. They've never known what it is like to have to fight and scrap just to survive. To be hunted, cornered. They have engineered a situation here which benefits only their kind, nobody else. Protects what they have and keeps others down just because of their lineage or social status. Condemns millions to suffering because they are poor. They have taken advantage of our naivety, our innocence. Well, the gloves are off now. They have messed with the wrong girl this time and I will show no mercy from this day forwards. They may be inserted into every government on earth, but that just means I don't have to look too hard to find them. All empires fall eventually and no tyrant lasts forever. History is full of revolts and revolutions, rebellions by the downtrodden overthrowing their oppressors. They had to begin somewhere. Once the general population is awakened to what we have learned and they bring their own brand of pressure to bear, you watch this space. How quickly it will all come crumbling down.'

'Oh, I hope so. I really do. But how are we going to make it happen?' Ian asked.

She took another sip of her drink. 'I've been thinking on that. We know now thanks to Hanson that Sir Charles Munford is the main man. And we also know the twelve are landed gentry. That they meet regularly.'

'Right. With you so far. How does that help?'

'Quite a lot, actually. We are going to need a really good camera. With a high-powered lens. That's your job; to secure one.'

'Can do, I suppose. Why?'

'We're going to follow Sir Charles. Observe the next meeting he attends and identify as many of them as we can. Then we establish who is likely to be the weakest link. The one who will talk when his buttons are pushed. There is always one.'

Ian put down his sandwich having suddenly lost his appetite. He did not like where this conversation was heading, but he had to ask.

'Then what?'

'Then, we are going to pay him a little visit.'

He wrapped up his food, saving it for later. 'Alright. No more blow torches though, please?'

Waddesdon Manor is a fine country house in the village of Waddesdon, Buckinghamshire. A rare example of a French Renaissance chateau situated in the heart of the English countryside. It was built by Baron Ferdinand de Rothschild in the late nineteenth century, to display his burgeoning art collection and as a place for extravagant entertaining. Among its many frequent guests these days were twelve distinguished Lords and Knights of the realm.

Kirsten and Ian were positioned in a small hide, concealed in the bushes at the base of a treeline on the brow of a slight rise overlooking the estate. They had followed Sir Charles Munford's car to the last meeting from a safe distance, careful not to be seen. They had then returned to set up an observation post in time for the next gathering. Kirsten was working the camera. With the seventy-to-three-hundred-millimetre telephoto zoom lens, she was easily able to photograph every guest and driver, from all conceivable angles. Ian then used an iPhone to search the internet and put a name to each face. Each time he identified a member of the twelve, he unearthed what information he could and advised his partner. She then deliberated, deciding which of the billionaires might provide information if provided with enough encouragement and motivation. Most, she knew, would not talk easily. And some were higher risk, surrounded by multiple layers of security. It was essential that they targeted the right person. Finally, Ian hit upon the perfect candidate.

'How about this one?' he hissed. 'Sir Nicholas Ingelby. He's from East Anglia. He's seventy-three, a widower, with one son and four failed marriages.'

'One son?'

'Yep. That's what it says.'

'His only son and heir. That may provide us with leverage. It's all about the first-born son, remember? Has to be a reason behind those four failed marriages too. He only arrived with a driver. No added security. Jackpot. He's our guy.'

Kirsten made a mental note of his car and

chauffeur. They returned swiftly to the Jag and she opened the boot to kit up. She took out a Mk18 CQBR, compact version of the M4A1 carbine, with suppressor and the Glock 18. She climbed into the driver's side and drove to a suitable vantage point covering the exit to the estate.

Sir Nicholas was being chauffeur driven in a Bentley Flying Spur. They let it pass and Kirsten followed at a safe distance. It was quite a journey to Sir Nicholas' estate on the outskirts of Norwich and darkness had fallen by the time the Bentley turned off the A11 dual carriageway, onto a B road. When they were out of sight of traffic and she was certain there were no witnesses, Kirsten floored the accelerator on the Jag and overtook the Bentley with ease. She veered violently to the left, careering into the car's path, making the driver hit the brakes hard and skid the luxury vehicle into the side verge.

Kirsten had already unclipped her safety belt and Ian had wound down his window, as instructed. She took the Mk18 from his lap, raised it and fired two rounds out of the open window. The bullets smashed through the glass of the windscreen and killed the driver instantly. She then discarded the Mk18, unlocked her door, drew her Glock and raced to the Bentley.

Sir Nicholas was in a state of panic and shock. Kirsten ragged him from the vehicle with haste and threw him roughly into the Jag. The back seats were covered in polythene sheeting and he slid along to hit the offside door with his head. She engaged the central locking and instructed Ian to keep his Sig P229 trained on their captive. Then she drove off at high speed, slowing down once they had re-joined the dual carriageway.

'Who are you?! And what do you want?' asked the peer of the realm once he had recovered a little, rubbing is sore head. 'Money? Name it. Because I can pay. Just say how much you want.'

Ian shot him a look of disgust. 'We don't want your blood money. You lot think that is the answer to everything, don't you?'

'Then, what is this? Who do you work for?'

Silence.

Kirsten spotted a nice quiet side road. She made a left, drove for a while and then pulled over on a verge in the middle of nowhere. She turned off the engine, killed the lights and climbed into the rear of the vehicle, alongside the terrified aristocrat.

'Look at me. In the eyes, so you can see inside my soul. Know what I am about. We are not playing games here. We want quick answers. Information. We have no time to mess about. You talk or you die. It is that simple. We know all about your secret organisation and what it does. How you have all amassed your wealth. We have been watching you. Observing. Photographing.'

'Who are you? MI5? MI6? Because...'

'Worse.'

'Szabo?! You can't be!'

Kirsten said nothing but she was clearly shocked by his knowledge.

'Put your guns away, girl. Don't you understand? You work for us.'

She shook her head and her weapon in denial. 'No!' she yelled. 'We serve the crown.'

Sir Nicholas sneered at her. 'That is a very quaint notion. You have no idea, do you? The way of the world we live in. Let me enlighten you; *everything* you say or do is controlled by me and my associates. We own you and your kind.'

'You and the likes of Sir Charles Munford I suppose?' she said.

His eyes started flickering from side to side briefly, as if he was thinking of escape. 'Yes. And others.'

'We know of them all. Every last one. And we are going to bring you and your cronies down, I swear it.'

'Pah! Impossible. Ridiculous. Let me go now and you may live long enough to regret your actions. I can keep a secret and find another driver. This never happened.'

Kirsten decided on a different strategy. She holstered the gun and pulled out her knife. Then she thrust it forcefully into his right thigh. The old man screamed out in pain as he nearly hit the roof. A look of complete disbelief and abject horror adorned his face.

'Aaarrghh! What have you done?! You are dead, both of you! Dead, you hear me?!'

Kirsten noticed that Ian had turned his face away, unable to watch such scenes again. She had never been the squeamish type though, and she applied more pressure.

'Maybe we are marked to die. But then, we all have to go sometime. You know now how I make my living so do you really think it scares me? I will tell you how this is going to play out from here. Listen carefully. I'm going to keep on stabbing you in non-vital parts of your anatomy, because I can. It is going to really, really hurt, because you are a big strong hero and will tell me nothing. No matter. It will therefore take a long time for you to die, but eventually you will bleed to death. That's just plain biology. I came prepared for it. Hence the plastic. Next, I will dump your body naked in a children's playground not far from where you live, just before I publish on the internet that you were killed by local vigilantes angry that you have abused their sons and not been prosecuted. Because you were protected by eleven of your friends who have bought the judiciary and police, and who I will name. All those poor young boys…'

Sir Nicholas was aghast. He was also turning red in fury. 'What?! You can't do that. It's not true! You haven't a single shred of proof!'

'I'm Szabo, remember? I can do what I like. What do I care for proof? Proof only gets in the way. We won't need it. All those failed marriages? It will be your legacy whether it is true or not, to go out as a filthy nonce. A dirty kiddyfiddler. The shame your family will have to endure. Just think on it. Not that your son will live to see it. For finally, I am going for him next. He will be my assignment as soon as I am done here. I'm going to ensure he dies a death far more agonising than yours.'

'No! Leave him out of this. He has done nothing.'

She wiped the blood from her knife on his jacket. 'Then give me something I can use.'

'No, I can't!'

The blade was plunged deep into his left thigh this time. High-pitched screams erupted immediately inside the car. But nobody was around to hear them. Finally, crying and breathing rapidly in short gasps, Sir Nicholas caved in.

'There's… There's a man... Lives in Guernsey... In a large cottage just north of Saint Peter Port... Name of Williams. He is the one you want. Now stop!'

'And what is so special about this man?' asked

Ian.

'He is the… accountant.'

'So? The accounts and financial transactions for a multi-national organisation will all be electronic. Everything will be password protected. Hidden behind layers of cyber security no doubt. One man can't do all that.'

'No, you don't understand. We can't leave evidence behind. Anything linking us to events. Nothing which can be traced, hacked, copied, intercepted…'

'No modern technology, is it? Are you seriously telling me it's all on hard copy? Paper and pens?' asked Kirsten, amazed.

'Yes. Believe it or not, that's *exactly* what I am saying. And Williams is the key. He's an autistic savant. Can't hold a conversation with you but he's an absolute wizard with numbers. Has a photographic memory of some sort. Similar anyway. Tell it to him once and he will recite it for you five months later. Five years later if asked. Has an old analogue phone and hundreds, thousands of legers.'

'The whole operation?' Ian asked.

Sir Nicholas shook his head intensely. 'Don't be ridiculous! We are far too large for that. Involved in everything. But there is always a front. A SPOC. A single point of contact. An individual, corporation or group who are being paid to act on our behalf. A fall guy if the shit hits the fan. A public face to do our bidding. Expendable if needs be. And behind them all in the shadows, are we twelve. Pulling the strings, making it all work. Our personal business is conducted using Williams and our own private bank in Guernsey which distributes funds.'

Kirsten thought for a few seconds. She stared

deep into his eyes. 'These legers, they will show payments to these fronts, as you call them? Demonstrate who is really behind everything, in control? Times and dates that can be cross-referenced with payments, world events, assassinations, stock market dealings, wars, invasions and the like?'

The aged noble did not reply. He was ashamed of himself for talking now and in too much pain.

'So how is your son involved in all of this? Tell me.'

'He knows nothing, except that he will inherit my fortune. He will only be informed of the true nature of our work upon my passing. That's policy. To avoid family feuds and takeover bids.'

'Then he will be safe, you have my word.'

Sir Nicholas let out a huge sigh of relief which gave rise to several minutes of further explanation and information.

'This is it!' said Ian excitedly, once the old peer had finished. 'If we can get to this Williams guy, it's all over. We can actually bring them down.'

'Perhaps. We have a shot anyway. What is security like?' enquired Kirsten. 'At the cottage?'

'We know his worth. This information will not help you much because you will not be able to get to him. He's too well protected. You would need an army.'

Kirsten smirked.

Ian smiled broadly. 'Or a single Szabo agent? You shouldn't underest...'

He was only half-way into his sentence when Kirsten calmly leant over and slit Sir Nicholas' throat.

Chapter 22 - Operations

Rosie was allowed only a few weeks respite before she had to embark upon her next mission. This time she was bound for Austria. Vienna, to be more precise. She was selected for the assignment for three very important reasons; she had an impeccable record and success rate, she spoke fluent German, and she was extremely attractive.

The National People's Alliance was a conservative, right-wing populist political party which had been vastly improving its performance in both local and government elections in Austria for the past four years. All under the auspices of a wealthy telecommunications tycoon named Gerhard Schmidt and his associates. The party had managed to seize the middle ground between the disaffected working class and the lower-middle classes. Such was their alarming rate of growth, pundits now had them pegged as holding the keys to forming a coalition government in the next election. Concerns had been raised however that their aspirations and intent were not limited to politics. Operation Szabo Intelligence Officers had learnt recently that Gerhard Schmidt had provided two million euros in funds to source weapons and explosives out of Libya. These munitions destined for unknown hands had now arrived in Austria and were being stored at an as yet unidentified location.

Schmidt was a known far right sympathiser. He had been very vocal on matters of immigration, border security and national sovereignty. Szabo commanders had therefore deemed establishing the location of the cache a top priority. It was unknown what likely targets the weapons were intended for, but many believed that it was only a matter of time before the arms were used for some nefarious purpose. The UK had a vested interest in securing a strong and stable Austria, an important ally in Europe. Terrorism of any nature, specifically by far-right activists in that country given the history, would present a real and present danger to world peace. With potentially far-reaching consequences.

It was therefore decided to insert an undercover operative and Rosie received yet another secret text from her 'favourite aunt.'

Mission parameters were simple. To locate and retrieve or destroy the armaments. To gather intelligence on group members and their activities, including finances, training and any planned terrorist action. And to disrupt the group by any means necessary, eradicate it if at all possible.

Emil Schneider was chosen as a probable target likely to fall for Rosie's ample charms. He was twenty-five years of age, good-looking with a private school education, and the PR advisor for the deputy chairman of the NPA (National People's Alliance), Lukas Aigner. Emil was considered popular and influential and tipped as a future member of parliament. He was also single. Recent surveillance had revealed his favourite restaurants and bars, as well as a penchant for drink and eye-catching women.

Rosie operated under the guise of a post-graduate economics student called Sabine Bauer. She wore her hair in a short, conservative bob and was clad in a figure-hugging designer trouser suit. If anyone asked, she was on sabbatical, taking a year out to decide what she wanted to do with her life, living with an elderly aunt. A

Szabo Handler named Christine.

The initial plan was to seduce Emil, gain his trust and infiltrate the meetings of the senior party leadership. With the ultimate aim of being introduced to Gerhard Schmidt.

On her first night in Vienna, she attended Vorgarten wine bar and was pleased to see Emil, his friends and co-workers sat drinking in a booth. She slipped off her jacket and took a seat at the bar, within sight and earshot. She ordered a large Aberlour sixteen-year-old scotch and looked around, as if waiting for someone who was late. Over the next thirty minutes or so she acted bored and frustrated. She gazed at her watch and phone numerous times and occasionally drummed her fingers on the counter. She cast several glances in Emil's direction, making eye contact and smiling graciously. Doing what came natural; flirting. She turned down two male advances from other strangers and waited. Eventually, she turned to find Emil standing next to her, ordering drinks.

'Forgive me, but whoever he is, he is a fool,' the young man stated, sure of himself.

'I'm sorry?' she replied, smiling slightly and feigning ignorance.

'The man you are waiting for. He must be an idiot, to leave such an attractive young lady alone.'

She pretended to be embarrassed by his flattery. 'That obvious, is it?' she asked.

'Yes. Your boyfriend, may I ask?'

She shook her head slightly, played with her hair a little. 'Lord no. First date, actually. Looks as though he received a better offer.'

'Ha! I seriously doubt that. Have you seen you?

His loss is our gain though. Care to join us?' He motioned towards their table. 'Come on, live a little.'

'Sure. Sounds like fun.'

They joined the others and over the next two or three hours they talked and talked. They could not take their eyes off each other and at the end of the evening, they swapped numbers and arranged to meet again. Things went from strength to strength. On their fourth date, Rosie wore a slim-fitting short dress, complemented by high heels, stockings and suspenders. The works. If it were a boxing match, it would have been stopped in the first round, considered an unfair contest.

One night of passionate lovemaking and the young Austrian was already head over heels in love. He just didn't know it yet.

Seven weeks later, the new couple were inseparable. They found that they shared the same political views; a strong dislike of globalism, socialism and the corrupt global financial elite, as well as a burning desire to revise a nation flagging under the strain of multiculturalism and mass immigration.

Eventually, Emil invited her to attend a party meeting together. It was held in a local sports stadium and was very well attended. A succession of speakers addressed the crowd. They were chants, songs and heckling. It was raucous but generally good-natured. A huge digital flag of Austria was displayed, fluttering in the breeze on a big screen behind the keynote speaker. The cheering rose to a crescendo and everyone present, including Rosie, sprang to their feet, clapped enthusiastically and roared their approval.

Two more local rallies were held in quick succession. They attended both and she was introduced to several group members, quickly winning them over with her wit, passion and knowledge. She made a mental note of names and functions for future reference. Towards the end of the fourth meeting, she was introduced to a man named Karl Burger. He had consumed a large quantity of champagne. She isolated him deliberately and it was not long before he began to talk of topics other than the usual politics and democracy. It was also not hard to goad him further.

He soon revealed that another group member, a man in his thirties named Hans Muller, was sitting on a cache of weapons which would be used soon to, 'make the world take notice.'

All her preparation and work to date had paid off. Rosie had struck gold. She couldn't believe her luck. She pressed him further.

'Tell me more,' she said, leaning in close and touching his sleeve. 'You are all very brave. What have you planned?'

'Ah, that's the clever part. As you know, the modern right has always had a hard time attaining office. People have grown soft and disinterested in politics and the concept of a nation, let alone nationalism. It has become a dirty word. A byword for a bygone age. Pathetic really. But that is where *we* come in. We have been raising our game in recent years. Pointing out how all this immigration and softly, softly governance is only setting us up for trouble in the long term. Free movement of people, open borders, jobs disappearing abroad, small businesses crushed by the mega corporations… the people are tired of all of it. They want change. Real change, not just talk.'

All they need now is the right motivation to take

action at the ballet box. We have been saying this for years, warning of the dangers, the injustices. Now, we are going to make our prophesy come true. We have acquired some Jihadi flags and get ups. We have made a fake video taking credit for the attacks and warning that more are to come. We will have a few of our men, each wearing a shemagh and speaking Arabic, attack the centre office of the Freedom Party, shoot up a Catholic high school and bomb the central train station. The Muslims will be blamed. Immigrants from the Middle East will be held responsible and targeted. The public will be outraged and demand action. We will have been proven correct and be ready to step in to form the next government when the people rise, with a firm plan of action to ensure this never happens again. We will receive more and more support as the attacks continue and walk home in a landslide for Austrian politics.'

From the way he was talking, his passion and excitement, Rosie suddenly felt an intense sense of dread, knew somehow that the first attack would be launched imminently. She looked over at her fake boyfriend and he smiled warmly. She understood there and then in that moment that he would be heavily involved in what was to come. Probably at the very heart of the action.

The following morning, she awoke early, threw on some sweats and walked the short distance to the address Szabo had supplied for Hans Muller. It turned out to be a small flat in the city centre, not suitable as a storage facility for a large cache of weapons, so she decided to follow him.

Hans was a busy man. He visited several addresses and businesses that day and her close observations skills were severely tested. She was just beginning to feel that it had been a complete waste of her time when Hans eventually met up with a large, well-built man she did not know. It was late afternoon and the man just had that look about him; the one which had the hairs on the back of her neck standing to attention. She had no backup with her and was ignoring all normal protocol but she tailed them to a large warehouse on the outskirts of the city nevertheless.

They exited their vehicle, unlocked a small door to the side of the building and walked casually inside, unaware they were being observed by one of Szabo's finest. Rosie decided to maintain surveillance from a distance at this point, rather than break cover. It proved to be the correct choice when twelve minutes later, more vehicles and men began to arrive. Emil and Lukas were joined by two large men Rosie recognised from the rallies she had attended. Finally, all the men entered the warehouse.

This is it. This is the day of the attack!

Rosie retrieved her Sig P229 from the glove box of the car and moved in for a closer look to make sure. She crept forward silently, edged her way around the structure and found herself at the foot of a large and dirty window. She knelt down, wiped the dirt from the glass and peered inside.

The place was huge, filled from top to bottom with crates, presumably containing munitions and ammunition. She could only guess at the contents of the hundreds of boxes but if she were correct, the group had enough ordnance in there to ignite a small war. They just needed the spark.

The six men inside were already gearing up, donning their disguises. Black combat uniforms, red shemaghs, tactical vests and boots. They dropped magazines into the pouches on the vests and fused hand grenades. Each man carried an AK rifle of various designations and a pistol in a leg holster. She saw PKM machines guns and several RPG 7's. Two large vans were also visible parked next to a loading bay entrance, the roller doors closed at present for concealment.

These guys were deadly serious, primed and fused, ready to rock and roll. If they were not stopped right now, it would be too late. She checked her weapon and prepared to move in.

All of a sudden though, something cold and hard pressed against the back of her head and a deep, hostile voice suddenly rasped, 'Stop where you are! Throw down your weapon or you die right here.'

Rosie was as brave as they come but this was a fight she could not win. Whoever they were, they had her trapped. She had to comply.

She raised her arms slowly and tossed the weapon, placed both hands on the rear of her head. From behind, her wrists were immediately manhandled roughly and zip-tied together, behind her back. She was pulled to her feet and two large hands ran slowly over every inch of her body, searching everywhere, lingering in certain areas, discovering her knife and ankle strap. Both weapons were discarded. Her captor then seized her neck and frogmarched her forwards into the warehouse, the gun remaining pointed at her head the entire time.

The assault group inside the building were alarmed when the door suddenly burst open and three of their associates appeared with a captive in tow.

'Sabine! What the hell are you doing here?!' asked a stunned Emil, as he pulled off his shemagh. He was aghast, concerned straight away for both himself and her.

'She's a spy, you fool!'

The voice came from the rear. It was calm and assured but also betrayed severe annoyance and frustration somehow.

Emil stared at her as if his whole world had just come crashing down. She shook her head at him in denial but was quickly clouted with the gun. A sharp jolt of pain ran through her head and neck but she tried to block it out.

'Tie her to the chair,' Lukas ordered. 'A spy? For who? We have to find out more; who she is, whether she is alone, what she knows…'

'Agreed,' sounded the unknown voice again.

Rosie turned slowly, expecting another thump for her troubles. Instead, she found herself staring into the emerald green eyes of Gerhard Schmidt, who was standing next to two military types, six feet plus, full of muscle and sinew.

'What have we here? I'm afraid you have poked your nose into business which does not concern you, Miss? But on whose behalf? We have been expecting some attention. Can't do the things we have done without upsetting someone. We have had a permanent security detail on this place just in case unwanted guests like you came calling. CCTV everywhere and motion sensors. These two gentlemen are my advisers. Former KSK. Our cameras picked you up whilst in the street.'

She was restrained and tied to the chair. As they worked, she could hear the leaders of the group talking, discussing their options.

'What about the attacks?' asked Emil.

'Not today. Not now. She is the priority now. She changes things a little. We could be overrun at any moment if she communicated with anyone, or walking into a trap,' Schmidt stated. He turned to the others. 'We are compromised. Abort. We will move to plan B. Get the kit out of here, now.'

Men scrambled to load the weapons and crates into the vans. The KSK minders had their pistols drawn and were watching the windows nervously. Herr Schmidt turned to face Rosie. He approached her with caution even though she was bound, staring at her as if she were from outer space, examining, probing her mind.

'Government agent? If so, which government? And where is her team? No. I don't think so somehow. This one looks like a loner to me. But who is she, I wonder?'

One of the men showed Schmidt the Sig pistol and her knife. 'She had no radio, or phone,' he said. 'Her car is parked a hundred metres away, down a side street. She's alone.'

'You see? Good,' Schmidt stated, and smiled at having been proven correct.

Rosie mumbled something from behind her gag. He leaned forward and lowered it so she could talk.

'It's… It's useless lying to you further, I know that now. It's quite obvious to you all that I am not who I said I was. Lying is a necessary evil in my profession and I'm sorry. The truth is I'm undercover. I work as a freelance journalist. Sell my stories to the highest bidder. My name is Erica Strondheim. I work alone and I do high risk stuff nobody else will touch. If you look me up on the internet, you will see I am telling the truth. I've been doing an expose on right wing factions within Europe.

The rebirth of fascism.'

Lukas looked at the financier and replied for them all. 'Bullshit. No journalist goes to such lengths just for a story. You've been shagging poor Emil for months. Too much dedication that is. Just doesn't happen. You've really done a number on him.'

'Yes, you're right. And I'm really, truly sorry for that as I said,' she pleaded. 'I was desperate. I am just trying to make a living. Make a name for myself in a competitive world. Please?'

'Enough,' stated one of the advisers. 'Fetch the hose. And a towel. We will soon hear the truth. Or she will die.'

Rosie knew what was coming; waterboarding. A truly awful torture banned by most nations but employed secretly by many more. She had not enjoyed the experience in training on Herik Island but at least it had prepared her and meant she knew what to expect, had been taught techniques which aided resistance and reduced its effectiveness.

The chair was suddenly and violently tipped backwards. She found herself staring at the ceiling for a brief moment. Water spouted from the hose and a wet towel was stretched tightly over her face so it was difficult to breathe. It was pulled downwards and the taut fabric gripped her nose and mouth. Water began to enter her through the material despite her efforts as she gasped violently for air. Within seconds, she was choking and gagging, wriggling and twisting to fight for any tiny morsel of oxygen she could find. Her breathing became ragged. Soon, her lungs were on fire, her entire body shaking in fear. Despite her training, the terror she experienced was palpable and she thought for certain she was going to die.

The wet cloth was removed moments before she was about to pass out. She turned her head and vomited, throwing up mostly water, which exploded from within her in cascades.

'Who are you? Who do you work for? What are you doing here?' Lukas demanded.

She delayed her replies for as long as possible, coughing, wheezing and spluttering. Every second she could hold out was a victory of sorts. Vital in aiding her recovery and survival. Her escape.

She stuck to her cover story and once again the chair was tilted backwards so the whole process could be repeated. She lost track of the number of times they tried to make her talk. But she did not break. Just refused to give in. Instead, she used the time to work on her bindings. She loosened them a little. Dislocated her thumbs and tried again. Still, she could not free herself. These guys were good. Damned good.

Time passed slowly. She could sense her strength beginning to fade. Every monumental effort to breathe began taking its toll on her shattered body. Sapping her energy. Soon, she would be physically unable to fight and that was unthinkable for her. Surrender was not an option, not in her creed, so that left only death.

And then came a tiny flicker of hope.

'We are out of time. We have to get moving,' Gerhard Schmidt suddenly stated. 'We can take no chances on being discovered. Use the burner to contact me, nothing else. Once I am gone, take her into the woods a distance and shoot her. Leave no evidence in here and be sure to bury her deep.'

And with that, Herr Schmidt and the two minders

turned and walked away. She heard a car start up and pull off. She could not help but smirk at being handed a chance to survive. It was just like the top brass to not want to get their hands dirty. God bless them.

'You heard the man. Take her outside to the van and don't take all night about it,' Lukas ordered his men.

'No, wait. I'll do it,' said Emil.

He took a pistol from another man and hit Rosie in the face with it. All faded to black for her. By the time she came to, it was dark. Rosie was jerked awake by the application of the brakes and heard them squeal. The two thugs in the back hauled her up. She could not see through her blindfold but could hear other cars and voices outside.

'Come on, move!' they ordered.

They walked her a while through some trees and she tried again to work her hand bindings free. She was close, but she was being watched and just could not free herself without making it too obvious. She was knelt down in a small clearing. Her blindfold was lowered and Emil stood over her. He handed his MP5 sub-machine gun to his comrade and drew a pistol. Chambered a round and pointed it straight at her head.

This is it. I'm going to die.

She closed her eyes and waited for the end to come.

'You bitch! You fucking bitch!' screamed Emil, tears in his eyes. 'I loved you.'

He squeezed the trigger.

Click.

Stoppage!

Rosie raised herself with astonishing speed and barged into Emil with her shoulder, bowling him over and sending the pistol flying. In the same movement, she wrenched her right hand from the restraint, ignoring the excruciating pain which followed. She kicked the second man squarely on his jaw. He fell backwards onto the ground with both weapons and she followed it up with another vicious kick to the head, rendering him unconscious. Then she grabbed a machine gun quickly, turned and fired a quick burst into Emil from close range.

She swivelled with demonic speed and put a bullet into the unconscious guy, before grabbing the other weapon and racing for cover behind a large oak. A stream of bullets hit the wood and ground around her as she huddled behind the tree trunk. She waited for the fire to die down and then sent a well-aimed two second burst back.

A third and fourth man appeared; the driver and another who had rode shotgun upfront in the van. They had hung back with the vehicle but both were now moving along the narrow path in-between the trees.

Short on ammunition, Rosie knew every shot would count. There were four combatants left alive that she could hear and see. She doubted any had remained with the cars. She knew they had to silence her and could not risk her escaping into the woods, so they would be coming en-masse, taking no chances

Most people would have run deep into the vegetation. But the thought never entered her mind. She darted from cover, moving from tree to tree, drawing fire, watching for muzzle flashes, using the darkness. She turned to see silhouetted figures on both sides of her position, trying to flank her. She fired short, sharp bursts, killed one with a head shot, one with two in the chest, hit another in the arm, heard him squeal in pain like a skewered pig.

Die with dignity, for Christ's sake!

The first gun emptied far faster than she would have liked. She threw it away and continued with the second. Lukas was close now. He had used the movement of his colleagues to close the distance between them. Clever.

However, he had not reckoned on the aggressive nature of his quarry. Rosie had not run as he had expected, like any outnumbered and outgunned adversary would normally react. And now she charged. Did the exact opposite of what any sane person would do.

He emerged swiftly from hiding to find a rampaging beast swamping him. Several bullets were fired into his face from a matter of feet whilst she was still running, before his weapon was up and his mind in gear.

More rounds then hit the trees around her. She turned and saw the injured man trying desperately to kill her from an impossible distance, firing his MP5K even though he could barely hold his weapon straight with his weaker left arm.

Another short blast from her weapon ended him too.

The hunters had been well and truly hunted. Amateurs taken down by a professional. A firefight hardly worth mentioning in her books. All in a day's work.

She herself had come close to meeting her maker though. There was no denying that fact but it had not affected her in any way. And from the moment her hands were freed, they were in serious trouble. Regardless of numbers. Regardless of weaponry. It all came down to ability and attitude.

If you gate-crash *her* party, best bring a cream cake, not a doughnut.

Slowly, she stood up and broke cover. The woods were eerily quiet now. Seconds later however, a solitary owl began to hoot. She gazed up and breathed in the cool night air, stared briefly at her handiwork; the corpses.

Not a bad day to die.

Rosie stripped some of the dead of weapons and ammunition and walked back to the van. The keys were still in the ignition.

Fortune favours the brave.

Gerhard Schmidt was picked up by police at the German border a couple of days later. He spent the next year being severely audited by an unknown watchdog that liquidated most of his many assets and emptied all of his bank accounts. He was charged with no crime. At the end of this time, broken and virtually penniless, Herr Schmidt officially retired due to 'ill health.'

He committed suicide two weeks later, a solitary bullet to his head from a Sig P229.

His family inherited the house and nothing more. The two German advisers disappeared without trace soon after crossing back into Germany. Nobody looked too hard for their bodies. The weapons were sold on the black market, somehow ending up being used by various organisations around the world, all of which were fighting for causes aligned with the interests of Great Britain or her allies.

Events which also turned a tidy profit for Operation Szabo.

Chapter 23 – Present Day

The fast ferry service from Weymouth to Guernsey runs on selected days only. The crossing takes a little under two and a half hours to complete. Kirsten and Ian caught the nine o'clock ferry on a crisp but sunny morning, paying cash at the very last minute. The boat was as usual rammed with locals returning home for the weekend from their employment on the mainland. The waters were relatively still making for a calm and pleasant crossing. As a consequence, they made good time and arrived at the New Jetty in St. Peter Port shortly before eleven thirty. Not long afterwards, they were driving a hired Audi A3 through the town and heading north, searching for the cottage which housed so many secrets. It had been described to them in detail in the deathbed confession of Sir Nicholas Ingelby. At this stage, their only plan was to locate the building, assess the on-site defences and security in preparation for further action, and formulate a strategy likely to bring down a leviathan.

Kirsten knew from experience that her every action, as well as all of her possible and probable intentions, would now be being surmised, dissected and analysed continually at the command headquarters of all the organisations whose agents now hunted them, including Operation Szabo. She had been anticipating trouble on their journey as a result, prepared for it in fact, but had been pleasantly surprised when no ambush or attack had materialised. It baffled her that the organisation she worked for would be so slow to act. She would never have been so sloppy. She could only conclude that the body of Sir Nicholas had not yet been discovered and the speed of her decisive actions had kept herself and Ian one step ahead of any chasing pack.

However, if they were somehow unaware of her plans, movements and intentions so far, they would surely know now.

The legacy of the war on terror following the terrorist attacks on America and around the world meant that all entry and exit points into and out of Great Britain, all ports, airports, train stations and ferry terminals, had been updated with state-of-the-art surveillance equipment. The high-tech cameras were often linked to facial recognition software at police and immigration control. Answers which used to take days or weeks to materialise were now at the tip of a finger, relatively instantaneous. The very moment they both set foot inside the ferry terminal at Weymouth therefore, their objective would be all too obvious to their enemies. And given the enormous stakes for those involved, Kirsten was in no doubt that an army of trained warriors would be coming for them.

It was a calculated risk she was prepared to take. She was not naïve enough to believe she could attack a static position with such a small force and prevent the defenders from raising the alarm. Word would spread regardless of the choices she made. And of the options open to her, the ferry was the easiest, fastest and best. The time which could be saved by using another mode of transport was negligible. The risks increased. This way, the target would only become apparent once they were almost there.

She gazed over at the mild-mannered civil servant she had quickly come to rely on. The most unlikely of partners. Ian Townsend; ex-prison governor turned assassin's assistant. Adviser, friend and part-time lover.

Well-meaning amateur.

She hadn't liked him at first. Thought him too much of a nerd. A little nervy, creepy even. Too eager to please and a bit too much of the Hugh Grant's about him. Too stereotypically English. Too good to be true. A backbone of sorts, but highly likely to become a liability…

That was all before she had really come to know him. How wrong she had been. He had proven to be somewhat of a surprise package and an inspired choice by those at the top of her organisation. They were probably kicking themselves now. The man they almost certainly chose as a patsy and expected to fold at the first sign of trouble, had dug his heels in hard, rolled up his sleeves, and fought alongside her like a Trojan.

You never know the strength inside you until it is needed.

Wonders never cease. If this was her last hurrah, so be it. But he didn't deserve what was about to happen to him.

'Ian, I have something to say. You've been real solid for me so far. You didn't have to do all you have done. I want you to know that I really appreciate all of it. Everything. But this is the end game we are entering now. I've thrown caution to the wind and the only thing left is to see it through. To whatever end. This thing we are about to begin, it's what the Yanks call a Hail Mary. An all or nothing play. Suicide run if you will. I'm risking everything and I can't guarantee the outcome. They know we are coming. We'll be trapped. They will react like a caged animal; fight tooth and nail, throw all they have at us like they are facing their doom, because they have to. Because they are. If we succeed in our mission, their whole world is going to implode around them and they know it. We're marked for termination now. Do or die.'

'So? What are you trying to say to me?' asked Ian, a little confused.

'Just that, this has been eating at me for days. I've just this moment come to a decision I maybe should have made ages ago. I can't see any scenario here which ends well for us. I've tried, but we have to face facts. I'm good, more than good even, but there is a real chance we will not survive this fight. The odds are greater than I have ever faced. Even if we do manage to breach the cottage somehow, they will react swiftly and in force. This is an island; there is one terminal, one way in and out. I need your help but I do not want to lead you to your death. It's not love but in my own way, I've come to care about you. As a friend. I'm not used to this. I don't have many as you probably know. None now actually. They're all dead. So, I'm going to drop you off here. You can walk away from all of this with your head held high. Slip out on the return ferry whilst they are looking for me. Go back to your wife, if she'll have you. Take your chances, or simply hide in some foreign land with the money. Up to you. If I succeed I will…'

'No! No way,' he stated emphatically, interrupting her. 'You hear me? Can't do it. You said yourself that you need me, so that's all there is to it. We've come this far. I'm going nowhere except with you. I couldn't live with myself if I cut and ran now, left you to face things alone. And if I'm going back at all, I want my name cleared. I want a public statement everyone can see. A full pardon in writing. The works. I don't want to be looking over my shoulder for the rest of my life, afraid to come home or walk the streets in daylight. That's no life. We have to expose them all. Every last one. It's the only way. Plus, they would only hunt me down anyway, if I legged it. I've seen and heard too much to be left alive. You know that.'

She slowed the car and pulled over into a layby. Moved the gear lever into neutral, let out the clutch and looked him in the eye.

'Are you absolutely certain? There are no second chances now. Things are going to have to get ugly. I'm a planner. One of the best. I don't usually act in haste and I don't leave things to chance, if I have an option. I'm a contingency girl. Love them. As far as I see it though, this is now a race against time. The sooner we can access this Williams guy, the quicker we can make him talk, the less of a force they can assemble on scene to send against us.'

Ian was pale. He could feel his stomach turning over and his hands were shaking all of a sudden. His words of a moment ago suddenly seemed a lot braver than him.

'Can't we just kidnap him? Take him somewhere else? *Make* time?'

'I'd like to, believe me. That would be plan A in different circumstances. But the evidence is not in electronic format. Not portable. It's in books, written by hand. They are heavy, so we will have to deal with them on site. We need to film the legers alongside an explanation, and that will take time. The ferry situation will delay them temporarily but they will most likely access other services; choppers, boats, anything to transport assets to our location and shut us down. We will be on target far longer than it will be safe to be. We will be faced by a superior force eventually. Surrounded.

They will come hard and they will assault our position in double quick time. You will have to play your part with Williams by spreading the word far and wide, whilst I try to hold them back for as long as I can.'

'Shit. Don't sugar-coat it, will you? We're really screwed, aren't we? I just hope our sacrifice is not in vain.'

'It won't be. And there *is* some good news if that's your thing. Remember, the last thing they want is publicity. They operate in secret. A full-scale attack would be extremely noisy, attract unwanted attention from the authorities. They know they are facing two individuals so for them there is no need for overkill. They will send small teams with suppressed weapons. No heavy stuff. At least in the beginning. And they will try to negotiate. That will buy us a little time. When they are through talking, I'll go to work.'

'Great. Whilst I babysit. Thanks?'

She smiled at his wounded pride and male ego. How stupid. How typically masculine for a member of the so-called stronger sex.

'Horses for courses, Ian. I'm trained for this shit. You are not. Don't thank me yet though. We've got to get inside that building before anything can happen.'

Kirsten undid her seatbelt, opened the door and checked nobody was around. She released the boot and rummaged around inside, returned several minutes later wearing a plate carrier and carrying an assortment of weapons. A M4 Mk18 CQBR with a holographic sight and suppressor, eight magazines for which were held in pouches in the front of the plate carrier. The trusty Sig P229 in her leg holster. And on her belt, two spare magazines for her pistol, a knife and four pouches holding HG85 hand grenades.

'Just in case we are made on the way in and receive a hot reception on target. You'd better load up yourself. Here, put this on.'

Kirsten handed Ian a matching plate carrier and a MP5 sub-machine gun. The carrier was olive green and it was heavier than Ian had anticipated. It held two eight-pound metal plates, one in the front and one in the back. Just enough to cover the vital organs of the torso. His carrier had a pouch for four spare magazines for the MP5 and a Glock 19 pistol was housed in a cross-draw position, higher up. A large pouch on the right-hand side contained a small medical kit.

He could barely stand as he exited the car. His legs already felt like he'd run a marathon. He pulled his coat over the plate carrier following Kirsten's example. They stowed their weapons in the passenger foot well and sat back down in the car, ready to drive.

Kirsten took Les Banques Road heading north out of St. Peter Port. She turned left onto Victorian Avenue and slowed to a crawl as she approached Les Osmonds Lane. The cottage on the hill had been visible from the main road. It stood out because it was situated on a slight rise and it was exactly as Sir Nicholas had described it, with white shuttered windows and a double garage.

'I'm thinking they will have seen us coming. They will have been warned and not too many cars come down this road. Okay, snap decision; we haven't time for a recce and we can't wait for nightfall. Best shot is a full-blown ram raid right here, right now,' Kirsten stated, calm as you like.

'Come again?'

'Make sure you are buckled up. We're going in. Hard and fast, all guns blazing. Shock tactics. You drive, I shoot. You mow down anything that moves. Get us to the front door as fast as you can before they have chance to set up their defences. I have breech charges if needed but most doors won't take a machine gun blast and a good kick. They won't expect us to be so rash.'

'No, I don't blame them. Hardly strategic brilliance. We don't know what they have in there.'

'Yeah, told you, Hail Mary. End of discussion. Get out and take the wheel.'

Ian climbed into the driver's seat. He put on the sunglasses Kirsten gave him and she donned hers. He checked the magazine and safety on his weapon like he had been shown and placed his MP5 across his lap. Then he put the car into gear.

Kirsten chambered a round in her Mk18 and flipped the selector to fully automatic with her thumb. She smashed the windscreen, used her feet and the butt of her gun to remove it. Then she wound down the windows.

'For Dunbar. And my parents.'

The cottage was large by any standards. Four bedrooms, two bathrooms, a large kitchen and two large function rooms on the ground floor. A cellar too. It had a large drive and parking area full of cars, along with the oversized garage. The driveway approaching the grounds was long and narrow, the gardens lawned and manicured, bordered with plants of all sizes, shapes and colours. Security was tight. Even more so, now that the off-duty mercenaries had been called in and instructed to prepare for a possible attack. With one likely point of vehicular entry, there were four men manning two observation posts on the front lawn, as well as another four conducting two roaming patrols. Inside, another six men guarded Williams by covering his location, the doors and windows.

Ian turned the corner onto the drive and the house loomed large ahead of him. He slammed his foot down hard on the accelerator and felt the car lift with power as it exploded into life. His head and shoulders hit the rear of his seat and dust and dirt filled his rear-view mirror. He was glad of the sunglasses now. The engine screamed and he found himself inexplicably roaring along with it, like some teenage thrill-seeker on a joy ride.

Almost immediately, the men in the gardens opened fire. Ian weaved as best he could in the confined area but heard and felt several rounds hitting the vehicle. Luckily, most were stopped by the engine block. Then, he jumped a little, startled by the sudden din of Kirsten opening up with her MK18. Despite the bumpy ride, she laid down rapid and accurate suppressing fire as they closed the distance to the door.

'Too hot!' Kirsten suddenly yelled. 'Dump her here. We're doing it the hard way.'

Ian slammed on the brakes. Kirsten's door was open before the car had screamed to a halt. She dived into the long grass which flanked both sides of the drive.

Ian heard her weapon spitting death and saw two men in the nearest position fall, whilst he was frantically trying to undo his seatbelt. He grabbed his own firearm and threw himself into the vegetation on the opposite side of the road.

'You okay?' the Szabo agent screamed at him.

'Yeah. Christ knows how.'

'Two in the O.P. on the right. Keep their heads down for me.'

'Will do,' he replied, feeling about as far out of his depth as it was possible to travel.

Nevertheless, Ian pointed the MP5 and squeezed the trigger. Bullets zipped around him like crazed wasps and he hit the dirt. He rolled out, changed his position and began firing again, exactly as he had been taught. He was almost out of ammunition when he heard Kirsten open up once more, from a completely different angle, this time from the left flank.

The defenders were taken completely by surprise and although some managed to fire their weapons in retaliation, Kirsten actually hit four of the six before disappearing back into cover.

Outstanding.

She followed this up by taking out the second observation post with a grenade. As she put rounds into all of the injured men, Ian moved forwards but began taking fire from the second-storey windows. He ducked behind the cover of a large stone pot on a plinth.

'Loading!' he shouted.

He did a quick re-load, pulling out the empty magazine, replacing it with a fresh one and racking the charging handle.

'Back in,' he yelled.

He darted out and fired two short bursts into the first-floor windows. As he did, Kirsten ran back out to crouch behind a parked van.

'From the boot, bring up the Green Meanie and ammo,' she ordered.

Ian did as instructed. He heard grenades and several bursts of machine gun fire but concentrated on the task he had been given. By the time he returned, Kirsten had relocated and taken out the downstairs window position. The guy in the upstairs window was still firing though and several bullets began pinging off the driveaway around them.

'He's a bit of a nuisance,' she stated, calmly. 'Needs to be taught some manners.'

She took the Green Meanie, or L96A1 sniper rifle, from him and crept under the vehicle. She fired off a single shot and the noise ceased abruptly. Then she took out her Sig P229 and sprinted for the damaged front window, vaulting through the wreckage in one effortless leap like an Olympic long jumper.

Ian heard four shots in rapid succession. She was unstoppable. He followed behind her as fast as he could with his MP5 up and ready, his heart racing and his palms wet with sweat, nervously trying to back her up as a partner should. He climbed awkwardly through the obliterated bay window and saw two more dead bodies lying on the floor, each with a small red hole in their foreheads.

Kirsten was already moving swiftly through the property. She stepped out into the hallway and another hostile form suddenly appeared on the stairs. Plaster and bricks exploded behind her as rounds hit the wall. She swiftly dropped to her knee and double-tapped her attacker in the stomach and chest, watched him fall to the bottom of the stairs and satisfied herself that he was done for.

She ran forward, booted the door to the dining room open and found it unoccupied. Another door ahead of her was closed. A concealed room. She took out a stun grenade, fired a few rounds into the hinge areas, booted the door off and threw it in.

Bang.

She entered crouching low. Smoke was everywhere filling her eyes and lungs but she could just make out three human forms. A smiling civilian was flanked by two taller men carrying weapons who were clearly temporarily disorientated by the blast. She put a bullet in each of the escorts. Head shots of course. Nice and efficient.

They fell like huge rag dolls. The civilian looked amused by it all, as if it were part of some thrilling game he was playing.

'Call of duty,' he said to her, smiling and pointing at the corpses.

'That's right, mate. You stay here for me,' she replied.

She cast her eyes around but could see no more targets. 'Ian! In here!' she called.

Ian popped his head around the door, tremendous astonishment and relief etched onto his face.

'Guard this one with your life. I need to check upstairs.'

Ian took hold of Williams and sat him down. 'It's okay sunshine, we won't hurt you. Stay with me a while.'

Williams wore a blank expression now as he weighed up the stranger before him. He said nothing and did as he was told. Three more shots rang out. Williams looked at Ian inquisitively and he simply said, 'That's Kirsten. She's doing what she does best. She'll be alright. She always is.'

And somehow, he knew she would be. The girl was indestructible it seemed. It was a textbook assault. If he hadn't seen it with his own eyes, he would not have believed it. And, true to form, she eventually returned.

'So, this is the jackpot. The almanac. I hope to God you are worth it. You work on trying to secure his help. I'll get some more equipment from the car, prepare a little party for our guests when they arrive. I don't think they will be long. Good work,' Kirsten stated, nonchalantly.

Ian scoffed at the gratitude on offer. 'Ha! Me? What did I do?' he asked with all sincerity.

She placed a reassuring hand on his shoulder and smiled.

'You stayed.'

Chapter 24 - Operations

Rosie was feeling spectacular. On top of the world. She was wearing her finest evening dress; a dark blue, sparkly Louis Vuitton gown with a low neckline, bare arms and tight boddice, designed to amplify a woman's femininity. As if she needed that. It had cost an absolute fortune, the equivalent no doubt to the national debt of some smaller countries, yet she had worn it only once on a mission so far. She was bejewelled in diamonds too, drenched in expensive perfume and had spent all afternoon at the beauty salon. She could not help but turn every head in the room and she was thoroughly enjoying her evening, sat at the best table of the finest restaurant in the most affluent area of London. The food had been prepared and cooked by the top chefs money could buy. It was delicious and of the highest quality, cooked to perfection. The 1928 Krug champagne was dry, warm and majestic, the company as rare and delightful as the invite had been unexpected.

All in all, everything was absolutely perfect. Privately, she wished the night would never end.

The conversation so far had been light and humorous. Deliberately so, for both parties shared a desire in equal measure; to be much more than they were to each other.

It was fun to pretend for a time that she was an ordinary person rather than a trained executioner, the taker of so many lives. She adored every aspect of her chosen career, was happy as could be, but a small part of her still envied the girls and women sat at other tables. Those lucky souls whose wealthy, carefree existence afforded them a kind of inner peace she was unlikely to ever know.

Time though, just would not stand still no matter how hard she desired it to. It was late. They had reminisced long enough, enjoyed swapping tales of their past loves, likes and interests. But now, the pretence had to end. The waiters cleared away the last of the plates and dishes and the atmosphere changed markedly. She knew it was the prelude to an adjustment in focus also. Nice as the charade had been, it was just that. Smoke and mirrors. Time for her to hear the *real* reason he had phoned out of the blue.

Dunbar cleared his throat in the way he usually did when he had something important to say. With several coughs that seemed to rise in volume and intensity before he eventually began to speak. She decided this time she would beat him to it and the fourth throaty bark he gave, was also his last.

'Alright, let's have it then,' she said, before he could utter a word. 'I've enjoyed tonight. I really have. Thank you. Moments like these are a rarity I treasure, especially with you. But you have that look about you now and you should just spit it out. Say whatever you've come here to say. The suspense is killing me. You clearly have something on your mind, an agenda of some description, so what is it?'

Dunbar looked a little sheepish all of a sudden. He appeared embarrassed and genuinely hurt she had seen right through his deception. Ashamed of himself.

'Sorry. I never meant to mislead you. You're right, but there was no point bringing it up sooner and I didn't want to ruin the evening. I had fun too. We don't see nearly enough of each other.' He rubbed the sweat from the palms of his hands onto his trousers and then leaned in to her, lowered his voice. 'We have a situation.'

Her eyes widened instantly and she was suddenly anxious to hear more. That was *not* a word Dunbar used readily. For him, 'situations' were nothing short of life-or-death events. Out of the ordinary problems of high significance or priority. She knew it had to be deadly serious for the old spymaster to come to London and visit her personally. For him to be seen out with her in public. For Dunbar, it was not seemly and bordering on reckless. A cry for help.

She cast a glance around the restaurant to ensure nobody was listening. Satisfied their conversation was as private as could be, she leaned forward slightly also and whispered firmly.

'Tell me. Where?'

'Ukraine.'

'That's a war zone. Tricky. Lots to consider. Okay, who?'

'Jasper.'

Sledgehammer. Right between the eyes. She gulped hard. Of all the people!

Whatever it was, whatever trouble he was in, whatever Dunbar said next to her, no matter what he wanted her to do and how dangerous it could be, she knew instantly right there and then that the answer was already, yes.

She would help him in any way she could. No was not an option. Not this time. Jasper had saved her life a hundred times over. She owed him big style. The Handler was one of the very best. A top-drawer human being and a superb agent. Someone she would walk through fire for, if asked. Experienced, competent, professional, brave and loyal...

'How?' she asked, her query tinged with emotion for a change. She just could not understand how someone of his quality had been compromised in a hot zone.

'I wish to God I knew. We dropped the ball on this one. *Somebody* did anyway. But something is not right. There are unexplained events which trouble me greatly. It was supposed to be a routine mission. Weapon exchange. A little ambush to boot. Appropriation of funds. That sort of thing. Nothing that should have ended the way it did.'

She inhaled deeply, thinking. She had that tingling feeling in her stomach now but he had given her absolutely nothing to work with so far.

'Details, Dunbar. Details!'

The old Scot looked towards the rear of the room for a second as if distracted. Then he nodded to her.

'Short version; the agent involved was Steve Arnold. Top guy. I recruited him myself. He was good. During the meet however, something went drastically wrong. Shots were fired and he was killed outright. Jasper tried to save him but was wounded in the attempt. The Russians arrived in force shortly afterwards and captured him. They were on scene way too fast for my liking. It was almost as if they knew. They bolted before our forces arrived and have been hard to track since. I've just this moment received word that he has been located.'

'When was the original contact?'

'This morning. Eleven hundred hours. Our time.'

'He has backup with him though? You've sent someone? Tell me you have despatched a team?!'

She could see in his eyes that the answer was no. 'Damn it, Dunbar! Why the hell not?!' she demanded, angrily.

'He's been disavowed. Our team was pulled immediately. By someone well above my pay grade. What could I do? I don't like it but we are denying everything. We have no comms up and as far as the Headshed know, we do not even know he is alive. We're supposed to be stood down. Blind. I'm keeping it from them and I may pay for that at a later date. Just you and I and a small team I trust are aware of the truth. As soon as they find out what I have just learned, you know they will launch missiles and flatten the entire area.'

Rosie chewed her bottom lip as she processed all she had been told. 'That buys us some time. He could already be dead I suppose. Tell me, what was the extent of his wounds?'

'Unknown. It is possible he was killed or has died of wounds, but I think we have to be certain.'

She agreed. If the Russians broke him, found out about Szabo somehow, his capture could do irreparable damage and place thousands of people at risk, cause the worst international crisis in history, maybe a full-scale war.

'Tell me straight. Is this a rescue mission, or a kill order?'

Dunbar shrugged. 'Am I a Scot or a Jock? One way or the other, he *cannot* be allowed to talk. You will be inserted by HALO jump. Link up with some old SF colleagues of mine on the ground. Mercs fighting for the Ukrainians. They have been in theatre for a while and know the terrain and opposition. You can leave right now,' he said, motioning towards a new waiter who had just appeared by the exit.

She grinned a little. 'This was all a set up. Pretty sure of yourself, weren't you?'

She stood up and gently wiped her lips with the napkin, placed it carefully on the table and invited the waiter to lead the way. 'Thank you for an enchanting evening. Don't leave it so long next time,' she said.

'Aye, you too, kid. Keep your head down.'

She landed just before dawn in the Donbas region of Ukraine. Buried her chute and tried her comms without delay.

'Echo One One. This is Sabre. Over.'

Nothing. She waited ten seconds and tried again.

'Echo One One. This is Sabre. Over.'

The radio crackled into life.

'Sabre from Echo One One. Welcome to the party. Location. Over.'

She checked her Navstar GPS device and read out her grid reference.

'Echo One One received. En route. Out.'

Several minutes later, she was crouched in a bush when she heard the recognition signal. Two ex SAS mercenaries revealed themselves and gave the correct challenge. She responded with the required password and followed them to their temporary headquarters. She was greeted there by a former SBS captain who was in command. He had been briefed by Dunbar and was waiting for her.

'You must be Sabre then? Time is short so I'll be brief. Your man is in a bad way I'm told. He was with some Ukrainian guides who managed to escape. They say he copped it in the stomach. Small arms fire possibly. They tried to reach him but the firefight was lost and it became too hot to stay around the area. They only just survived themselves. These guys don't spook easily so it must have been some show. Anyway, Dunbar asked the Yanks and their satellites picked up movement in this area immediately afterwards.'

He pointed towards a small village on the map just outside the city of Avdiivka.

'That's about six miles from here,' he added.

'And you think he's still there?' she asked.

The officer nodded. 'It's good odds. I'd take that action. If he survived, he's a valuable asset too wounded to move on foot. They will need transport. They will want to question him quickly so that means a vehicle. The Yanks have seen no traffic in that area which is swarming with RPG's and anti-tank missiles, just infantry.'

'Good. Do I have any support I can count on?' she asked.

The captain shook his head. 'Not much. Me and the two regiment lads love a shindig, so we're game. That's it though. The Ukrainians have been hit pretty hard here. They are really strapped holding on to what they have. Not really fair to ask them in the circumstances. We do have our choice of a lot of Gucci kit we brought with us though.'

Rosie smiled and her eyes seemed to light up at the prospect of action. 'Fine with me. The Brits it is. Won't be the first time we've had to go it alone. And six miles is a breeze. No time like the present. Let's go.'

The officer downed his brew without showing any sign of emotion. He folded his map, pocketed it and whistled to the SAS lads.

'Up and at 'em boys. Fun run. This young lady here requires our assistance.'

Despite the rugged terrain and active warzone,

they made relatively good time and reached the village just before nightfall. They moved swiftly from building to building clearing out Russian Forward Observers and isolated pockets of Spetsnaz until they finally neared the old cottage. It stood on its own at the end of an eerily quiet road. From a concealed position in the hedgerow of a house not far away, Rosie addressed the experienced mercenaries.

'Time to go to work. He's my guy so I'm calling things from here. Comms on open channel as designated at base. We surround the house from all sides. GPMG heavy machine gun to set up on first floor of this building. It overlooks their likely sentry points. I then go forward alone to recce. Don't worry, I've done it before. Wait for instructions. That means, wait for my command. If I buy it, scarper. Find a good firing position but do not open up unless ordered, or if it has gone to rat shit. You'll know if that happens. Understand?'

The soldiers all knew her reputation. By now, most in the SF community did, though that was all they knew. They were not happy however that she was taking all the risks instead of sharing. Regardless, they reluctantly agreed. The former SAS troopers were carrying sniper rifles along with sub machine guns. They had less distance to travel as Rosie was covering the rear, circling the building. Seemed like an unfair distribution of the workload.

Rosie donned her night vision goggles and moved off. She crawled stealthily through rubble, grass and undergrowth until she reached the relative cover of the garden wall. There, she stopped and surveyed the target building.

Two stories. Observation Post in the upstairs

bedroom window. Ditto downstairs living room. Guards front and rear exits. Two on roaming patrol in the front and rear gardens. Decent set-up. Has to be a high value target inside. Probably Jasper.

A firefight suddenly erupted in the distance, drawing her immediate attention.

We are too close to the front here. We have to get moving. Before they launch another attack.

'Echo One from Sabre. Over,' she transmitted, without delay.

'Send.'

'Fire mission. Targets to follow. On my mark. Echo One - Tango, roaming patrol, front garden left of building. Echo Two - Tango, roaming patrol, rear garden, right of building. Echo Three - Tango, front entrance, stationary. I have all Tango's at the rear entrance. Suppressing fire to follow on second floor windows and living room window front left only. All Echos acknowledge. Over.'

One by one the trained professionals signalled that they understood their assignments and were awaiting her command. She crawled to her chosen position overlooking the rear of the house without being detected and sighted her weapon on the guard. Then she immediately gave the order to open fire.

Four shots sounded in unison, as if fired by a single weapon. And four lifeless bodies fell to the ground.

The GPMG heavy machine gun opened up with a tremendous din and all hell broke loose. It was joined by bursts of rapid fire from all directions, hitting the building and the windows. Glass smashed everywhere, wood and bricks disintegrated, smoke covered the cottage and grounds.

The Russians in the windows were killed or dived for cover, out of sight. Rosie then sprinted as fast as she could to the rear door, leaping over dead bodies as she ran. She booted the door open and was confronted immediately by two startled soldiers who were running into the kitchen to man the windows. She took them both out with short bursts from her M4 carbine and continued into the hall.

Another soldier appeared on the stairway. She squeezed her trigger and hit him in the throat. He fell and tumbled down the steps in a crescendo of noise as his trigger finger jerked and rounds were sent everywhere. She ducked to avoid being hit and as he reached the last step, she put another round into his head.

She barged the living room door open with her shoulder. It was absolute carnage. The firing outside had ceased once she reached the house to prevent a blue-on-blue incident of friendly fire but the room had been almost obliterated by then. The high velocity rounds from the GPMG had torn through walls, furniture and men but somehow, miraculously, managed to avoid hitting Jasper, who was lying prostrate on a stretcher on the floor. Three dead Russians circled him, all having been standing and caught in the maelstrom of bullets. A fourth was badly wounded and desperately reaching for his gun. Rosie put two bullets into his back and he was toast.

She turned swiftly to face Jasper. His stomach was covered in bloody bandages and he looked done for. Still, he raised his hand weakly and she smiled at him.

'Hold on. Don't go anywhere without me. I'll be back.'

He coughed as he suppressed a chuckle and his

weak lungs reacted. His head dropped as she turned away.

She raced upstairs, cleared the building room by room using extreme violence, her machine gun, a bad attitude and some grenades. When she was satisfied she had eliminated every enemy soldier on site, she returned rapidly to her friend.

'Sabre to all Echo callsigns. Jackpot. I say again, Jackpot. Hold what you have. Remain on overwatch. Enemy in the vicinity. Out.'

She turned to Jasper and took his hand.

'Hello, stranger. What have you gotten yourself involved in this time, you dumb shit? Can't leave you alone for a second. Can you move? Things are a bit dicey here and we have to get going, if you're up for it?'

He simply turned his head away and winced in pain. His breathing was shallow and rapid. His face was grey and she could tell he was fading fast.

'It... It had to be you, didn't it? I knew someone would come and I'm glad it was you. Always had a thing for you. Out of my league though... It's nice to know… yours is the last face I will see. I... I didn't tell them a thing… Really I didn't. They know nothing. Tell Dunbar, I never… I need…'

Another firefight erupted outside and the radio sounded straight away. The captain's voice was calm but resonated with urgency.

'Echo One to Sabre. Time to go. Exfil now.'

'Sabre received.'

She kissed him on his forehead. 'Jasper, I have to do this. There's no other option. You know I have to, don't you? Forgive me?'

He smiled at her again and closed his eyes,

waiting.

'Between the eyes, please? Just like old times.'

Bang.

They re-joined the Ukrainian Army and mounted a fiercely contested fighting withdrawal against overwhelming forces, as the Russians launched a determined attempt to take the city. Jasper's body was lost during the fighting of course and his remains were never repatriated. But his secrets disappeared with him. Just another faceless hero consumed by war, in one guise or another. His name would never adorn any monument, either in Ukraine or Great Britain. It would never sound on a rollcall of the glorious dead, be mourned on Remembrance Day at the cenotaph, in church... No wreathes would ever be laid in his honour. His family would be fed with lies. Nothing but lies. The truth would be too dangerous to tell. Stories would be invented to emphasise his mundane existence and deflect attention away from his secret life. And death. They would no doubt mourn the passing of a guy of no consequence to any but his immediate family and friends.

To a select few however, he was another covert volunteer who made the ultimate sacrifice for queen and country. A genuine hero. A brother in arms. It hurt that nobody would ever learn of his true worth and valour. But then, that was the game.

Chapter 25 – Present Day

Anthony Williams was thirty-eight years of age. He was small and chubby and his medium length, brown hair was always a mess. His eyes were constantly darting around the room as he struggled to concentrate on any one thing, except when he was talking about a subject of interest, mostly maths or problems he had solved, when his intense stare would almost look right through you and his sudden enthusiasm could be a little full-on.

He was born in Leeds, the only son of a farmer and his wife who adored their little boy regardless of his so-called 'disabilities' and the social prejudices of the time. He attended a school for those with special needs up to the aged of fourteen, when his extraordinary ability with numbers and prodigious memory began to attract the attention of some very powerful people. As word spread, one of those who became obsessed with his obvious potential and exploitability was a northern baron who owned half of the county of Northumberland. The millionaire landowner and capitalist also happened to be one of the twelve. A meeting was convened and unbeknown to him or his parents, the young Williams was the main item on the agenda.

He was identified quickly as a prospective, ideal solution to the growing problem of electronic surveillance and interference. Put simply, he was the obvious answer to a whole host of prayers. Enemies had been made worldwide, technology had developed significantly and several law enforcement agencies were circling like vultures, too close for comfort. Williams instantly provided a solution; a way to avoid leaving an evidence trail wherever they went, as they schemed and profited from world events leaving behind data which was potentially accessible to government departments, criminal gangs, spies, and competitors. Most of which now employed the brightest minds from top universities, some of whom were idealists and not easily corrupted.

The resolution to several emerging threats was remarkably simple; the lower the technology used in this modern world, the harder it was to identify and trace. Thus, on the orders of Sir Charles Munford, Anthony Williams was abducted on a cold November evening. To leave no trace of the crime, his parent's farm was set ablaze with their lifeless corpses inside. Three death certificates were issued shortly afterwards courtesy of a bribed registrar and the teenage boy effectively became a ghost. As far as the world was concerned, Anthony had perished in the fire. The large cottage in Guernsey soon became his entire world. His prison. He had worked for his parent's murderers, the organisation, ever since.

To those who exploited his talents he was, 'Williams, The Accountant.' Valuable beyond measure, escorted everywhere in the cottage grounds at all times, worked tirelessly without holidays or pay. For he was ostensibly a child trapped in a man's body and knew not the wrongs inflicted upon him by others.

In many aspects he possessed the mind of a six-year-old. He could be shy at times, boisterous occasionally, immature and excitable in equal measure. Despite years in a working environment, he struggled to concentrate for any length of time and still could not hold a conversation on any other subject than numeracy. He came alive at the sight of puzzles though. Maths equations and arithmetic were his golden nectar. Literally child's play to him. His happy place. In this domain he was a human computer and there was none better or faster. No problem was too difficult to solve, no solution ever lost to his fantastic memory. It was as if he used a larger portion of his brain than other human beings when employed on one subject alone. Everything he had seen, read, solved or done from the age of fourteen was stored in his subconscious just waiting to be retrieved, and he could recite the entire contents on command if asked.

Kirsten had disappeared to fetch the stocks of weapons and ammunition they would need to defend the building. She stored them in strategic locations and was now setting up some defences, leaving Ian and Williams alone in the room.

The civil servant gazed around as an awkward silence set in. The partitioned area was crammed with filing cabinets, each drawer labelled with months and year, going back over two decades. It was a potential treasure trove and Ian knew he had to push fast and hard for information.

'Anthony, my name is Ian,' he began, in a soft and friendly tone.

'Ee.. an.'

'Yes, that's right. Well done. I am hoping to become your friend, if you will let me?'

'Friend.'

'Good. See? We're practically best buddies already.'

Anthony's eyes danced for a moment or two until he pointed at the two dead guards on the floor.

'Not friends.'

'No. No, they were bad people.'

'Bad. Very bad. Naughty, naughty men. They

shouted at me. And hit me.'

Ian instinctively placed his hand on Anthony's in a genuine display of compassion. However, the startled accountant jumped as if he had been struck and snatched it away.

Ian held up both of his hands to apologise. 'Whoa, I'm sorry. Okay? I shouldn't have done that. It was wrong of me. We are not there yet. I won't touch you again, alright?'

Anthony merely rocked himself back and forth as his eyes bounced. 'No touch. Nobody touch. No like.'

The softly, softly stuff was not going down well so Ian decided to change the subject, conscious of the immediate need for haste.

'You look like a very important person here. The main man. Tell me about what's in these drawers, Anthony. There are lots aren't there? Are they all yours?'

Anthony suddenly sparked with interest. The transformation in him was astounding. He sat upright, stopped rocking and looked Ian straight in the eyes, indicating he was now fully engaged and ready to focus.

'Mine. All mine. Game.'

'What? A game?' Ian asked, surprised. 'You want to play a game?'

Anthony now resembled a puppy waiting for a treat. If he'd have had a tail, it would have been wagging furiously. His eyes were wide and bright as he nodded vigorously and began clapping his hands.

'Okay, if that's what you want, let's play.'

Ian was ecstatic. Never in his wildest dreams did he think it would be this easy to gain the intelligence they required. He moved swiftly to the nearest filing cabinet and opened a drawer.

Before he had touched a file however, Anthony suddenly blurted out happily, ‘2015!’

‘Yes, that’s right. That’s the year. Oh, but that’s an easy one. Anyone could have answered that. You’re smarter than that, aren’t you? For bonus points, give me something that happened in that year? Anything.’

There was no hesitation at all. The reply he gave was swift, confident and very loud. ‘Saudi Arabia. March. Four million… China. August. Ten million…’

Ian was gobsmacked. This was pure gold and on tap. ‘Excellent! But to reach the next level, we need to set you more of a challenge. What was the money for, do you know?’

‘Currency.’

‘Yes, that is correct. Congratulations, you’re through to the next round.’

Anthony bounced up and down on his chair and smiled broadly as if he had just won the lottery. He seemed to be having the time of his life, showing no sign of being affected by the firefight or the bodies and blood around him. It was astonishing how he could blank out anything other than the questions he was asked, the problem he had to solve.

‘Now, what else happened in that year?’

‘Russia. September. Attack on Syria. Nine million.’

‘Outstanding,’ stated Ian. He moved to another cabinet. ‘You are the best. And do all these contain records like that? Who paid who and what it was for? Because that is where the big points lie in this game, in answering those kind of questions.’

Anthony nodded so fast it looked like his head might fall off.

'Brilliant. What about this one?' he asked, pointing at the furthest cabinet.

'2011. Iraq War. Forty million.'

'Well done. I think I have heard enough. That was the test and you passed. You are so good in fact, that we are putting you through to our world championships. How would you like to star in your very own show?'

Anthony was elated. He could barely contain himself. 'Television? I love television! Sometimes, if I am good and do as I am told, I get to watch an hour at night. Two at weekends.'

'Yes, you will be all over the T.V. and your face will be seen across the world by millions, I promise you.'

Ian took the jig he did and the beaming smile as his answer. He took out the iPhone 12 Promax Kirsten had sent him to purchase and turned it on.

'This small phone is nothing to worry about. I'm going to record you on this thing, alright? It's small but it's very, very powerful. It sends a signal right to the T.V. and something called the internet as well, which is similar.'

Anthony continued to jump happily, excited and eager to begin.

'Okay, Anthony, all you have to do is tell me about each file as I show you the cover. I will read the writing and film the papers, along with you. Then, you tell us who asked you to send the money and to where, or who. When we are finished going through them all, you win a trip to a burger joint of your choice and you can order anything you want off the menu. Understand?'

Anthony began clapping again. He looked like he was going to burst.

'I will explain to the audience first why we are

doing this. Making your movie. It won't make sense otherwise. Just give me five minutes to set up.'

'Five… Friend.'

Ian used the multi-streaming software he had installed to log on to a professional online video platform, happy in the knowledge that the content would be streamed live around the world on such popular social networking sites as Instagram, Facebook Live, Twitch TV, YouTube, TikTok and many more. He made a short introduction explaining who he was, what had happened to him and all they had unearthed about the organisation and the twelve. Then, he made a big deal of introducing the star of the show. The man who would prove everything he claimed was true. Filmed Anthony in full close up, much to his delight. Finally, he strode over to the first cabinet, filmed the labels, and took out a file.

'We will begin with 2002. Anthony, what happened in the year, 2002?'

Again, the response was immediate and loud.

'March. Anaconda. Two million. Deposit.'

Ian was confused. He sensed the audience would be too.

'Sorry? We need a little more than that. Anaconda? What was that?'

'Afghanistan. Al-Qaeda operation. Mr. De Wigt deposited two million pounds for arms sales from our companies.'

'Yes, that's right.' He filmed the papers and then removed another file. 'And in April?'

Anthony clapped excitedly once more. 'Easy. April 2002. Venezuela. Coup. Removed President Chavez. One million paid to reverse that and re-instate him. Paid by Sir Nicholas. Money for arms sales also followed. Two million.'

Again, Ian filmed the documents and the live stream continued.

Meanwhile, outside, Kirsten had been busy. She had arranged the cars in a block at the end of the drive, preventing vehicle access to the property, her ability to hotwire any motor in seconds proving to be a real asset once more. Windows and doors had been barricaded, weapons and ammunition distributed, firing positions located and strengthened. She had also laid a complex series of tripwires and mines, some deliberately visible and others undetectable, designed to ensure the main assault would come solely from the front of the property, and the drive itself. She was now lying down in the prone position on a table in the centre of the front right bedroom, staring down the telescopic sight attached to the L96A1 sniper rifle.

One hour and thirty minutes later, she spotted four large Range Rovers hurtling down the main road at breakneck speed.

'They're here!' she yelled. 'That show you two are putting on must be good viewing.'

Ian popped his head out of the door. 'We have their attention then?'

'I should say so, yes. Either that, or they are *really* desperate to kill me. Probably both.'

'Do you need me to do anything?' he asked.

Kirsten maintained her vigil as she replied, sweeping the horizon and beyond in case of other unwanted guests. 'Not yet. I'll let you know when the time comes. Keep going. Get as much as you can on film while we have the chance. The more we have, the more likely it is that somebody will believe us.'

'Roger that.'

Kirsten couldn't stop herself from laughing a little. 'Oi! Cut that out! We're not Yanks, you know.'

'Ha, ha, ha… Okay.'

Kirsten sighted her weapon on the lead vehicle as it turned onto Les Osmonds Lane. She breathed in and out twice and on the third breath, held it half way.

Bang.

The windscreen was holed and the driver hit squarely in the chest. Top shooter.

The car veered violently to the left, ran over the grass verge and ploughed into the field. Eventually, it came to a halt and three men exited rapidly. Two were killed outright by the expert sniper as they emerged and began searching for cover. The third was quick enough to dash behind the vehicle before Kirsten could get a bead on him.

The remaining cars pulled up in the vicinity whilst this was happening and successfully decamped their occupants. Soon afterwards, she began taking incoming fire. Weapons were blazing away at her from the direction of the field but the sound was muted as bullets hit the cottage.

Suppressors. Thought as much.

After a while, the man behind the lead car raised a hand and barked out an order to cease fire, exactly as she had predicted. The downstairs phone began to ring moments later.

Ian shouted up, 'Do you want me to answer it?'

Kirsten scoped for targets but the mercs were all

well concealed by now and it had become a waiting game. 'Sure, why not? Let's parley. Play for time, but keep filming.'

He lifted the handset off its cradle. 'Hello? Not sure where we are but how may I help you?'

'Who am I speaking to? Mr. Townsend?' asked a deep, upper-class sort of voice.

'If you like. Rather busy at present though. What do you want?' Ian asked, somewhat rudely.

'I should have thought that quite obvious. I want you to stop that damned recording right now. If you do, I will make you a very, very rich man. Richer than in your craziest dreams.'

'Oh, I don't know. I'm told I can be crazier than a box of frogs. And I can dream pretty big, you know.'

A sigh of exasperation was clearly audible on the line. 'Do not play games with me, Mr. Townsend. With us. You are way out of your depth here and your life is in my hands. The men accompanying me are veterans of combat, trained to the highest standards. There are many more on their way. You have one chance and one chance alone of surviving this day. I suggest you take it.'

Ian silently handed another file over to Anthony, who once again began to recite everything he could remember; names, dates, transaction details, authorisations… He showed no sign of tiredness or boredom and looked as though he could continue all day.

'Mr. Townsend? Are you still there? Answer me. The feed is still live.'

Silence.

'You are really testing my patience and rapidly running out of time, sir,' the voice warned, ominously.

'What? Yes. Yes, I'm still here. I can't say I'm

not tempted by your generous offer. But, if I surrender to you now, after all we have done, how do I know you will not just kill me anyway?'

'I have told you. We will heavily incentivise you. The financial rewards will be such that you will be able to live in luxury for the rest of your days. And we will have no need to act.'

'Hmmn… I've always fancied living in the Bahamas.'

'Stop this madness right now, you hear?! Do you have a death wish? It's *her* we want. I see no reason why you and I can't come to an agreement?'

Kirsten was listening to Ian speak, smiling to herself whilst sweeping the fields ahead with the scope. Suddenly, she saw a white hand protruding from behind the nearest Range Rover, pointing left.

Here they come. Flanking manoeuvres.

She took a deep breath and waited.

Bang... Bang.

Two shots. Two kills. High calibre marksmanship. The very best. The men had been very fast. She was faster. The rest had retreated quickly back into cover.

The phone line was still open. Ian heard an angry voice bellowing.

'Fuck! That fucking bitch needs to die and do it now! One million pounds to the man who kills her. You hear? My personal guarantee. She is just one person, for Christ's sake! Get in there and *end* her. What are you waiting for?!'

Ian hollered up to Kirsten. 'Sounds like you've well and truly pissed them off now. They're coming in force.'

He checked his MP5 as the phone line went dead. Almost immediately, there was one almighty shout of, 'Cover Fire!'

Bullets rained in on the window. It was intense and accurate so Kirsten hurled herself off the table. Wood splinters, glass, brick, and plaster flew in all directions. She grabbed her rifle, crawled out of the bedroom as the torrent of fire continued, sprinted for the next room. She arrived at the window just in time to see eight military types moving in all directions but converging on the house. She sighted the sniper rifle and dropped two of them.

That brought another hail of sustained gunfire onto her new position. Switching tactics, she discarded the L96A1 and took up her suppressed M4 Mk18 CQBR machine gun. Then she ran down the stairs and into the living room; the most likely point of entry.

Almost immediately she watched as one of the attackers leaned back, preparing to launch a grenade. A quick burst from the M4 scythed him down. There followed a large explosion as the grenade he was holding detonated harmlessly on the drive. Debris flew into the air and smoke covered the yard.

As always, Kirsten decided to adopt aggressive tactics where most would have hunkered down, defended what they had against superior forces. Attack, to her, was always the best form of defence. She had learnt that on the streets, in school and care homes, as well as on Herik and numerous missions. It was an axiom which had served her well in the past.

She peered out of the window. Two mercenaries were crouched behind the large van. She could just see some boots protruding from behind the front wheel and caught a glimpse of a head bobbing out.

Sloppy.

A grenade landed on the drive and rolled underneath the fuel tank of the vehicle. A huge ball of flame erupted almost immediately and the nearby car windows shattered, as a deafening blast shook the entire house. Metal fragments and body parts were thrown in all directions as the men were obliterated.

So much for wanting to keep things quiet then.

Seeing such destruction and fearing they were up against a heavily armed professional, the remaining three attackers decided to withdraw. Kirsten watched and let them go, content to conserve her remaining ammunition. She called out to Ian.

'Relax a little for now. They're regrouping. We may be in for a shit storm if they have anything heavy with them though. I've bloodied their nose and they will want to end things quickly now.'

Just then, the phone rang again. Kirsten moved swiftly into the hall.

'Here, give it to me.'

Ian passed her the handset and returned to Williams, showed him another file and continued recording every word he said. He was thoroughly enjoying himself still and had zoned out the distractions. He launched happily into another explanation which was aired around the world.

'Hello?'

'Ah! The thorn in my side no less. What name are you going by these days?'

'You can call me Kirsten. Who speaks?'

'Well, you have really done it now, my girl. That explosion will have been seen and heard for miles. This is your very last chance. You've sealed your fate already, and that of your little chum. But if you surrender this instant, I promise you both a quick and painless death. It's more than you deserve.'

'Maybe. Someday there will be a reckoning I suppose for all my deeds and actions. I've faced death before though. Many times. And you know what? It doesn't scare me. And neither do you. I may be a dead girl walking, worm food, but at least I've sealed your fate too, in the process.'

He's too calm. He has something large with him.

'Was that your aim? Mutual destruction? How pathetic. Don't flatter yourself, girl. You're the hired help, that's all. Plenty more where you came from. Despite your best efforts, we'll be just fine. My kind always are.'

Kirsten ran quickly up the stairs and into the nearest bedroom for a better vantage point as she talked.

'Your kind? Munford?'

'Hey! Show some respect for a peer of the realm. I've earned that title, so use it. It's Sir Charles to you. And it was rather unpleasant knowing you.'

A huge sense of impending doom consumed Kirsten. For a very brief moment she was terrified. Though, it was not for herself. She strained her neck to see past the cars and caught a fleeting glimpse of the man firing the RPG, at the very last moment.

'Incoming! Take cover!' she screamed out as loud as she could and then dived behind the bed.

Whoosh... Bang!

The rocket propelled grenade exploded and thick, acrid smoke and debris filled the entire house. Shrapnel was sent flying in all directions. A deafening ringing sounded in her ears, loud enough to drive most into hiding. Her senses were overloaded all of a sudden and she was struggling to make sense of what had happened.

Anyone less would have been completely incapacitated for minutes by that impact. But Kirsten was special. Very special. She was well trained and she was now mad. Hopping mad. She shrugged off the fear, hurt and incredible discomfort, reacted like a true professional.

The front dining room had taken the full force of the impact. It was completely destroyed. Absolute carnage. Wood, glass, bricks, broken furniture, smoke, plaster… Nobody could have survived that attack and Kirsten's anger rose even further. She was infuriated and in need of revenge.

However, the room behind had miraculously survived the blast almost entirely intact. Unbelievably, it was hardly touched by the explosion. The walls must have been reinforced somehow.

She let out a huge sigh of relief as Ian's head popped out from underneath the wreckage of the doorway and he gave her a thumbs up, to let her know they were both fine. She could not reach them through the wreckage so she decided to channel her anger into something positive, and once again move onto the offensive.

'Stay there! Finish the job. Record *everything* you can until the last possible moment.'

'We will. But where are you going?' Ian cried through the smoke.

'Hunting.'

Kirsten took her M4, the Sig P229 and two grenades. The rest she left with Ian. She turned around, ran and jumped through the living room window, out into the driveway.

A flurry of gunfire followed her every move. Rounds struck the cars, buildings, concrete all around her as she darted from cover to cover. The mercenaries she was assaulting had been converged on their leader, seeking instructions. The last thing they had expected was an attack on their position, from an entrenched enemy voluntarily leaving a defensible position. Consequently, they had to move now to disperse and take up decent positions.

And that meant exposing themselves.

Kirsten worked her way forwards firing aggressively at targets as they appeared. She took out one guy with a round to his neck. Wounded another in his leg. Moved rapidly, switching positions under continuous fire, keeping them guessing and ducking for cover, on the back foot. Winning the firefight.

Another head rose a little too high, trying to locate her. It dropped instantly with a nice, neat hole in its brow.

She was almost within grenade range now. But her M4 was empty. She took out her trusty Sig pistol and crept silently forward in the long grass. Waiting. Listening.

A faint rustle of vegetation to her left alerted her to movement. She raised her arms and legs and pounced like a leopard.

Bang.

The injured merc had been trying to crawl away to safety. He never made it.

Then, a tremendous thump in her left arm knocked her backwards. She heard the shot, allowed herself to fall to the ground, rolled immediately to her right and just avoided three follow-up rounds, which pinged into the dirt and grass she had just vacated.

She quickly calculated the angle of shot in her mind, recalled the sounds made by the last two bullets. Unhooked a grenade and tossed it.

The tremendous blast which followed threw up a vast amount of soil and vegetation along with the white-hot metal fragments of the casing. And, as the debris fell back to the ground, she came hurtling through it all at breakneck speed, her pistol in her right hand dealing out vengeance and death.

Two men in khaki uniforms had been peppered by shrapnel. They were both injured badly but rising to their feet, still able to re-join the fight. Kirsten ensured they did not by putting two rounds in each. She crouched down and crawled away.

Three more shots followed in quick succession but she had now left that area and was safe for the time being. Then there was silence. She stopped, tore off some of her sweater and tied it around her injured arm, wincing in pain.

A door opened and closed. Then another. An engine stuttered into life.

They're making a run for it!

Sir Charles Munford and the last of his fighters had decided to cut and run, to save their skins and take their chances with a police force and judiciary they owned.

Not on my watch!

Kirsten broke cover, though she knew it was foolish and could lead to her death at such close quarters.

As soon as she had, whilst the Range Rover was turning and trying to regain the road, Sir Charles fired a long burst from his machine gun out of the rear window.

She reached for her last grenade and hurled it as hard as she could, the very moment another round hit her like a freight train in her left leg, knocking her to the ground.

She heard the explosion and felt the heat as the car immediately burst into flames. Debris began falling all around her. She became dizzy. Her vision was impaired, hazy and blurred. She was losing way too much blood. Could feel it escaping from her broken body. Still, she hauled herself up and dragged her wounded and shattered frame forwards, step by agonising step.

The vehicle had been all but destroyed. In the front of the burning wreckage sat what was left of the driver. Which wasn't much. The rear seat was empty, the door missing. She limped around the car and yards away saw a pathetic, blood-stained, charred body crawling slowly for safety. She approached him as best she could and he somehow sensed her presence, turned over to face her, looking up pathetically into her gorgeous eyes.

'Please? Don't kill me. I'm worth a lot more to you alive.'

'No. Not to me you're not,' she replied, calmly.

Bang.

The sirens sounded in the distance before the gunshot had lost its echo. She turned and her failing eyesight spied several police cars racing to her location. They screamed to a halt not far away and several seconds later, she was aware of numerous loaded weapons all trained upon her.

She smiled. The game was up. She desperately needed medical attention now and she had nowhere to go.

No viable exit point. She placed her weapon on the ground and lay down, tried to put her hands on her head. Her left arm just would not move however and she eventually gave up trying.

A firearms officer approached her cautiously, ordered something she could not make out in her state of delirium and kicked her weapon away. He searched her for more and turned her over. The pain intensified and she had to bite her lip to prevent herself from screaming, drawing more blood. Finally, once they were satisfied she was not a threat, a paramedic was called in and allowed to begin working on her. It seemed to revive her a little and she re-joined the conscious world.

The officer in charge made his way over.

'I think they are all dead,' she said to him, before he could speak. 'I'm pretty sure I got them all. But there are two friendlies in the remains of that cottage. Don't hurt them. I'm not the one you want. They attacked us. I'm the good guy. They are…'

The high-ranking officer held up his hand to stop her.

'Save your breath, Miss. We'll take your statement soon enough. We've all seen the videos. I don't know how you took out so many but… you are a hero. The internet is on fire with what you've done. We have all been briefed. We will check on your friends for you. You might like to know that I was ordered by some very powerful people to stop the filming… But then, I do not serve the likes of them. I serve the British public. You and I both know don't we, that *some* orders are just crying out to be ignored?'

He winked at her and walked away to address his officers.

Kirsten was overcome with a huge feeling of joy and accomplishment. And gratitude.

'Thank you!' she shouted after the commander.

He turned to face her and called out, 'Don't thank me, Miss. You are going to be just about the most famous trio in British history I reckon. From what I've seen and heard, you three are going to be responsible for the fall of many a corrupt government. As well as some very rich, very powerful, truly despicable human beings. Good on you. I don't think anyone has impacted world history before on this scale.'

She lay down as he walked away and the medic began patching her up ready for transport to the hospital. While he was working on her, she looked up at the clear blue sky.

'One man did.'

Epilogue

The burger place in St Peter Port was empty. It was a school day, around mid-morning and the ferries were not running. Ian walked Anthony Williams up to the order point with a carefree feeling he thought had deserted him forever. The simple task of ordering food without worrying who was watching or listening, was something that was unthinkable yesterday. Then again, just surviving the day had seemed a tall order. It was so very good to be alive. He had a new perspective on life now. Was determined to enjoy every single second he could of it, and nothing would scare him anymore.

A pretty, young female employee with a pleasant smile asked what they would like. Anthony immediately looked to Ian, as a child seeks his parent's permission to speak.

'It's alright. You can order anything you want, remember? A promise is a promise. The whole menu if you'd like,' said Ian. 'It's no skin off my nose. After all, Kirsten's paying for it.'

'Kirsten. Lara Croft,' Anthony said, giggling to himself.

Ian laughed along with him, picturing the beautiful assassin in that fancy dress costume.

Yes please.

'Ha. Not quite. But you know what? I think she'd take that,' he said.

'Ian… she coming?'

He shook his head. Anthony was like a lost sheep now. He had no flock and he needed looking after. Ian had decided that was his responsibility.

'Not this time, pal. Maybe in a few weeks or so.

She has some healing to do before she'll be up to very much. But I'm here with you and we're going to be best friends you and I. We'll see Kirsten again soon. I bet she's making a terrible patient, all cooped up and not able to get about. Now, what you having, eh?'

Anthony turned, stared at the board for a few moments and then beamed. He bounced on his heels several times and lightly clapped his hands.

'Please, friend… Milkshake. Chocolate. Cheeseburger. Fries and ice cream. Please?'

The young girl behind the counter smiled graciously. 'Of course. Take a seat and I'll bring it over to you when it's ready.'

Out of the blue, Anthony suddenly grabbed Ian's hand and excitedly led him to a table.

Six weeks later, Kirsten was sunning herself on a lounger, soaking up some rays. She was resting and recovering on a spectacular sandy beach, on the Bahamian island of Musha Cay. Had just picked up a Jack Reacher novel and was twelve pages in, when a familiar voice called out to her.

'Thought I'd find you here. Hard at play, I see? Don't blame you, after all you've been through. Looking mighty fine in that bikini, may I say? Hospital food appears to have agreed with you.'

She sat up, smiling. Took off her sunglasses as Ian approached and looked him up and down. She wasn't impressed. He looked ridiculous. He was wearing the most garish Bermuda shirt with khaki shorts and brown sandals. Typical Englishman abroad. No fashion sense. His legs looked so white it was as if he had covered them in flour and treacle before stepping off the plane.

'You'd know all about the food, Townsend. Put on a few pounds since I last saw you, haven't you? Middle aged spread, is it?'

'Yep. That's my story and I'm sticking to it. Anything else is a slanderous rumour and a wicked remark. I have so many people wanting to buy me dinner and drinks all of a sudden. My diary is full for a change. I'm not bragging but I'm turning down rockstars and royalty. Well, bit of an exaggeration. It's rude to say no though, so I don't. Nice of you to notice. Thanks.'

'Ha, ha… Yes. Yes, you *are* bragging. And I'm trained to be observant. How was the journey?'

'Never mind that. Just look at all of this! It's all a bit extravagant, isn't it? Did you have to buy the *entire* island? Couldn't you have made do with a hotel or two?'

She looked around contentedly at the magnificent views. It was impressive she had to admit. Not a single person in sight.

'Yeah well, I like my privacy. Like you, I was besieged back at home. Couldn't take it anymore. Every man and his dog wanted an interview. I had people phoning me at all hours, pestering the nursing staff, lots of bunches of flowers, offers from agents… I even had six marriage proposals!'

'Anyone I know? I'll vet them, if you'd like? It's not surprising, the governments we've toppled, the stock market crash, the arrests... I was glad you contacted me. Was beginning to wonder how long it would take. What about those charges?'

'All dropped, eventually. In exchange for certain information and assurances,' she replied.

'Bloody cheek, after all you've done. Downright liberty. You should have been given a medal.'

'They wanted to. Several countries actually, not just Britain. I declined every offer, for all of us.'

Ian raised his eyebrows at that. Kirsten was the face of their alliance. Anthony and he had decided to stay away from the media if they could, let her take all the decisions.

'You did? Not sure how I feel about that. Why?'

'Think about it. The more attention we receive, the harder they will investigate the missing bank accounts. Better to keep a low profile. Eventually, they will move on. This island is registered in a false name, as all of my purchases are. Dummy corporations are us, from now on. No trail. Anthony has mislaid several documents and files for us. He has genuine talent in that area. Outstanding actually. There is no evidence linking us to the money, but why rub their noses in it?'

'Yes, fair point. I'm not bothered about accolades anyway, and I know Anthony isn't. I spoke to him before I left by the way. He wanted me to thank you again for the cottage. And the helper. He's thriving.'

She gave a huge sigh. It was the right decision to move him away from that prison in Guernsey, close to Ian. Still, she had worried that he would not settle.

'I'm really glad to hear it. He deserves a break. We all do. What about you? How are you faring now it's all over? You patched things up with your wife?'

Ian's eyes moved to his feet for a second or two. He was ashamed of how he had acted towards her and it showed.

'No. Some things just can't be forgiven or repaired. The pain goes too deep. I finally came clean. She has moved on and I don't blame her. We're getting a divorce. It's amicable though. I wronged her and she deserves to be happy. I hope she finds a man who truly deserves her. He'll have to be some guy. She wants the house and the dog but nothing more. I tried but she is very independent. We'll always be friends, I hope. I'll miss that dog.'

Ian sat down on the lounger next to hers. He looked out across the stunning blue. 'I think the rest here is going to do me good. I can feel it. I've been offered a position at the Home Office. It's a top job but I don't know if I'll take it yet. I'm sort of in limbo. What about you? What will you do, now that Szabo has been disbanded? You have earned your retirement but aren't you way too young for that?'

Kirsten eased herself back down on the lounger. She put on her sunglasses and picked up her book. 'At present, I'm going to relax some more, enjoy a good read, maybe do some swimming, and then take pleasure in a decent meal with a good friend. After that, I'll go where the mood takes me.'

'As good a plan as any. But seriously, what about long term?'

'Oh, we're being serious now, are we? You should have said. Okay, long term… I don't know. I think I will miss the buzz. The adrenalin fix. In fact, I know I will. It's all I've known since I was a child. The only thing that really makes me feel alive. Maybe I'll go freelance? Or offer my services to MI6? Or maybe, just maybe, Szabo wasn't really wound up after all?'

Ian remained silent, uncertain if she was joking or not.

'…If you want the truth, Ian, I thought I was in serious trouble at one point, when it all began. Thought I had lost my way. I'll admit that only to you on this island, in the middle of nowhere where there are no recording devices. I began questioning my focus. My sanity. My mental toughness.'

'You? Never. You're as tough as they come.'

'I'm being straight with you. It doesn't happen often so you should be flattered and just listen to me. The mind is a powerful tool, but we all have our demons. I made far too many snap decisions borne of emotion this time. Took way too many risks. Placed you and Anthony in danger because of an obsession I have, probably got Dunbar and others killed...'

Sometimes, in the heat of battle, I found that I just could not control myself. I was a loose cannon. That isn't what I'm about. I have to be better than that. I...'

Now though, when I stop and think of Anthony and all those countless millions we may have helped by our actions. The wars we may have prevented. The good we have done. The lives we might have saved… Well, there's a void within me. An emptiness inside. How am I going to fill it? I just don't know that I will be happy doing anything else?'

Thank you for reading this novel. I love hearing what people think so please review it and help spread the word.

M J Webb

Also by this author;

Fantasy genre – The Jake West Trilogy.

Jake West – 'The Keeper of the Stones'

Jake West – 'Warriors of the Heynai'

Jake West – 'The Estian

Alliance'

Available online now.

Printed in Great Britain
by Amazon

11673185R00192